# FRENZY

---

SHADOW BRED, BOOK 2

GRACE MCGINTY

# ALSO BY GRACE MCGINTY

## Hell's Redemption Series

The Redeemable/The Unrepentant/The Fallen

## The Azar Nazemi Trilogy

Smoke and Smolder/Burn and Blaze/Rage and Ruin

## Dark River Days Series

Newly Undead In Dark River/Happily Undead In Dark River/Pleasantly Undead in Dark River

## Black Mountain Mates

Hunting Isla

## Eden Academy Series

The Lost and the Hunted (Prequel)/Heart of the Hounded (Prequel)

Rebels and Runaways (Book 1)/Sweethearts and Savages (Book 2)

## Shadow Bred Series

Manix (Book 1)/Frenzy (Book 2)/ Feral (Book 3)

## Stand Alone Novels and Novellas

Bright Lights From A Hurricane

The Last Note

Castle of Carnal Desires

*For George*
*Best writing buddy, foot warmer, and fur baby any author*
*could ask for.*
*I miss you.*

# FRENZY

## PROLOGUE
COURTLAND

*Sixteen years ago*

I stood to the left of Juan Pablo, the last man remaining who my father really trusted. Although his hair was now streaked with gray and his shoulders were slightly stooped, I still remembered him as the tall, imposing man who had once put his gun to the forehead of a traitor and pulled the trigger. That had been the first dead body that I'd ever seen, but it wasn't the last. Not by a long shot.

He looked over his shoulder at me, bushy eyebrows drawn tightly together. "Are you sure about this?"

I nodded only once. There was no room for doubt in life. Procrastination was death by a different name. My father had said that to me many times. But he was dead, and this had little to do with procrastination and everything to do with blood.

His blood. His family.

A car rolled up from a distance, blowing up a dust cloud that was distorted by the wavy heat of the summer air. "Last chance, Little Prince. This is a lot of money."

I twisted my lips, glad that Juan Pablo couldn't see the anxiety that coursed through my veins. I was four-teen, and in this world, that made me a man. "It is what Father would have wanted."

Juan Pablo snorted, but he didn't disagree. My father had been a man with an almost chimeric nature. He'd been a ruthless and bloodthirsty criminal, who had cut down begging men with little to no remorse. But he'd been soft for one thing, and one thing only. For his family. Blood above all. Above money. Above power. *My children are my real legacy. All this is gone like the ashes of a funeral pyre. But you and the girl? You are forever.*

The girl. He'd never called her by her name, nor did he mention his wife—like losing them was too painful to bear. He'd gone to get them back and died in the process, but I didn't blame him for leaving me alone in this world filled with sharks. I would have done the same thing.

I was *doing* the same thing. And that's why I knew my father would have wanted this.

The car slowed to a stop, and two figures got out. One man was in a bad brown suit that hung from his soft, bulging body all wrong. The other was a boy, no older than me. Actually, as he got closer, he was possibly slightly younger than me. The man stopped in front of Juan Pablo, barely sparing me a glance. He didn't realize that the money paying for the merchandise was mine.

My eyes fell to the bundle in the boy's arms. It was wrapped tightly, but was so tiny I didn't think it could possibly be the right one.

The boy stepped closer, his blue eyes cutting into my face like knives. He looked between the bundle in his arms and me. Swallowing hard, he handed it over.

"I named her Rosa. I hope you don't mind." His voice was so soft that it was almost lost in the guttural arguing of Juan Pablo and the brown-suited man.

I shook my head. "Rosa is fine." I took the bundle from the boy and held it close to my chest. From beneath the blankets, a tiny sleeping baby face peeked out. Fifty thousand American dollars had bought her safety, and never in my life had I been more sure about a choice.

The boy continued to stare down at the baby, even after it was in my arms. I held it awkwardly, but kept my body taut. Confidence was a state of the mind and of the body; my father had said that too.

Finally, the boy lifted those blue eyes back to my

face. They speared into my soul like he could see my every intention, see the blood on my hands already. It was obviously just my imagination, because in the next moment he whispered, "Promise you will be good to her. That you won't..." I had no idea what he was going to say, because he snapped his jaw shut and shook his head.

I tensed my jaw. "She'll be happy. I am going to make sure of it."

The boy nodded. "Good."

I couldn't help but ask, "Why? Do you know her family?" I was desperate for news of The Girl, but didn't want to sound too eager. I didn't want people to know I had any emotion at all, let alone an interest in a mother and daughter who were supposed to be dead.

But the boy just shook his head sadly. "No."

He reached out and touched the baby's face, and I had the strongest urge to draw him to me, to kill this fucking suit and take them both. I must have growled, because Juan Pablo sent me a warning look, and I drew the attention of the suit.

"Pryce, get back in the car," the suit grunted, and the boy—Pryce, I guess—hesitated, but eventually moved away. My eyes watched him unblinkingly as he made his way back to the nondescript sedan, climbing into the back seat and shutting himself away from me forever.

I had to grit my teeth and dig my heels into the red dirt to stop myself from following him.

Finally, Juan Pablo handed the man a stack of cash, and the guy grinned, flashing tobacco-stained teeth. "Good doing business with you."

He turned back to the car and walked toward it. I couldn't help myself as I yelled, "Where are you taking the boy?"

The suit looked back over his shoulder. "None of your fucking business, kid." His sneer dragged at the jowls of his face.

I fought the shift. "I will buy him from you. A hundred K."

Juan Pablo looked at me like I'd lost my mind, but he didn't contradict me. The suit just threw back his head and laughed.

"He's worth way more than you have, Dirt Dweller. Keep your brat and be happy." With that, he climbed into the car and gunned the engine, peeling away in a spray of rocks and dirt. I spun my body so they connected with my back and not the baby.

I grunted as one particularly large stone collided with my shoulder, and decided I hated that smarmy fuck and would one day water this dirt with his blood.

When they were no more than a speck on the horizon, Juan Pablo looked down at me with both of his eyebrows raised. "What was that?"

I just shrugged, unsure of how to describe the draw

of the boy to the beast in my soul. Anyway, I didn't need to justify myself to anyone, even Juan Pablo.

We picked our way over the fallen down fence that marked the front of the derelict gas station from the rear. Parked around back was the brand new SUV that I'd bought with my inheritance. It was bulletproof and bombproof. I had learned from my father's death. I climbed in, and Juan Pablo slid into the driver's seat. I didn't have one of those baby seat things, so I continued to hold Rosa.

It was an hour's drive to the compound, and despite being tiny, the weight of her body in my arms was beginning to make my biceps ache by the time we pulled through the compound's gates. Men with AKs stood on every corner, keeping watch. My father's death had caused a feeding frenzy as other cartels tried to step into his territory, but Juan Pablo had held them back for me, and would continue to do so until I could take full control on my eighteenth birthday.

As soon as the car stopped, Dominic appeared. He wrenched open my door and had his face in my lap, staring at the baby.

"You got it."

I nodded. "Her."

He pulled back, screwing up his nose. "Smells like shit."

My nose twitched, and I realized he was right. "Probably is shit."

Dominic was my best friend, but he was also fucking weird. Actually, people thought he was great and that I was the weird one. They just didn't know we were both fucked up beyond repair. I trusted no one the way I trusted Dominic. We were halves of the same whole.

Dominic leaned down and sniffed the baby again, before looking up at me, confused. "Her blankets smell weird."

He had a great nose. Probably had something to do with him being a wolf shifter. "What do you mean?"

"She smells like one hundred percent tiger shifter, but the blankets? They smell a little bit like you. Like Manix."

I froze, flashes of the boy with the blue eyes playing on repeat in my mind. "Are you sure?"

Dominic nodded solemnly. "You know I wouldn't fuck around about something like that."

Holy shit. It made sense now, why I had wanted to keep Pryce with me. Father had said that we were the only Manix remaining in the world, but he was wrong.

Pryce was Manix. He was like me, possibly one of the last three remaining Manix in the world. Me, The Girl, and the boy with haunted blue eyes who I'd let go.

**1**

---

DOMINIC

While I'd always pretended to understand Court's obsession, I'd never seen the point of burning everything we had built in the quest to fulfil a promise that no father should ever have elicited from a twelve-year-old kid.

But Courtland was my best friend, so when he found 'The Girl' and wanted to sink our entire fortune into rescuing her, I'd had his back.

Now we'd done it, rescued his sister Naja, but in the process, we'd drawn the eyes of the Convocation—the ruling Council of Supernaturals. Each supernatural race had a leader in the Convocation, and we fell under the purview of Alexander, the motherfucking Dragon King. As thankful as they were that we'd helped save the last remaining female Manix Omega, they weren't going to let us sit on our asses down here in the desert, running fucking drugs and drawing the gaze of humans.

I threw back the last of my tequila. Fuck it all. I glanced over at Courtland as he stood at the window of his office, his suit perfectly pressed even though he'd just hopped off a flight from Montana.

"What's the plan?" I asked the back of his head, and he lifted a single shoulder but didn't turn.

"Pack it up. Try being a civilian for a while. This whole thing"—he waved a hand at his walled kingdom—"it's served its purpose now. Perhaps hand it over to Juan Luca; he's the next logical successor." He stopped and turned, his eerie black eyes staring into mine. "Unless you want it, Dom? The Convocation doesn't know about your involvement, or that you're a shifter. You deserve all this more than most."

I snorted and got up to pour myself more tequila. "Fuck off, asshole. My place is with you, always has been. And if that means wearing Hawaiian fucking shirts and speedos in Cabo, so be it."

As I predicted, Courtland shuddered. Hell, I'd pay good money to see Courtland in a flower-printed shirt. Juan Luca was human, and the Convocation didn't give a shit what humans did—whether they killed or maimed or irrevocably destroyed themselves—just as long as one of us wasn't at the helm.

"Juan Luca has been good to us all these years.

Trustworthy. He'll continue his father's legacy." Juan Pablo had died nearly a decade ago of cancer, a testament to how tough the man really was. Because in this business? You didn't live long enough to die of natural causes.

I slumped back into the couch and tried not to think about all the money we were flushing down the toilet to become fucking average Joes. But in the back of my brain, I might also have been relieved not to play this game anymore. Always watching my back. The drugs and bitches and the constant double-crosses.

Courtland finally turned to look at me completely. "What do you want, Dom? We've been chasing my dreams for so long, I don't even know what it is you wanted to do with your life."

Now it was my turn to shrug, because I didn't know either. I'd been sold to Courtland's father as a child. I didn't remember my parents or Pack. Courtland was my Pack, my whole world. His missions had become my missions. His needs became my needs. He was ingrained in the very fabric of my being.

I loved him. Too much. He was my Pack, and he was so much more. Not that he knew that.

I cleared my throat and gave him my manic grin. "Fucked if I know. I've always been about the mission, you know? And a life of fucking pretty woman and spending bucketloads of money hasn't hurt. You don't need goals when you have pretty red lips wrapped around your cock, right?"

He snorted, shaking his head. "They aren't dreams. That isn't even a lifestyle." He cleared his throat. "I think I'd like a quieter life. Take Abuela and the kids somewhere where Uzis aren't as common as teddy bears, you know?"

I nodded. Courtland was my Alpha, of that I was certain, and if Courtland was my Alpha, then that ragtag bunch of brats was my Pack. I loved each one of them, even if they fucking drove me crazy. "We'd have to leave Mexico. Abuela won't like that."

Courtland's grandmother was as steadfast as an old tree, rooted deep into the rocky dirt of the town she'd lived in her whole life. I knew she wouldn't leave. Courtland knew it too, even though he was pretending he didn't know he'd have to leave her.

I'd noticed a difference in him since he'd arrived back from Maxton, the stronghold of the Manix. Fuck me, for so long we'd thought he and Naja, and that damn kid from when he'd been fourteen, were the last of the Manix, but we'd been so damn wrong. There were literally hundreds of them hiding up in the wilds of Montana. Being in that town had awoken something in Courtland, and the restlessness of his energy was beginning to rile my wolf.

As if he could read my face, he stepped closer until

I felt his breath on my cheek when he whispered, "Do you remember the boy? Pryce?"

Fuck. I knew it. I knew this was coming as soon as he said he was done. Courtland had shaped his entire life around being a savior, so I knew he'd have this void when he was done saving Naja. And that boy, this Pryce, had plagued Courtland for nearly as long as Naja. I should have known that we wouldn't just up and leave with that decade-old mystery burning a guilt-ridden hole in his soul.

"Yeah, Court. I remember the boy." If I thought hard enough, I could almost remember the faint notes of his scent too.

"Do you want to burn some shit down on our way out of here?" he asked softly, his face so close to mine I thought for a moment he might kiss me. But we didn't do that shit.

Instead, I leaned away and took a gulp of my tequila, and hoped his superhuman fucking senses couldn't hear the race of my heart. "Hell fucking yeah. Let's fuck some shit up."

He gave me a rare smile, the one that meant we were either going to get rich or get beat to shit. I hadn't seen it in years, and now my heart was racing for all sorts of other reasons. While Iago's organization was scrabbling to replace their numbers and their head honcho, I knew now was the perfect time to strike at a different enemy, one that would definitely get our asses kicked if the Convocation found out.

The fucking suit who had delivered all of Rosa's siblings? We'd later learned he was some sort of government lackey. Discovered that they had some underground lab in the desert somewhere that held a whole bunch of people. Some like the kid, Pryce. Some humans. Who the fuck knew who else?

"You know he's probably not there anymore, right? He's probably dead."

Courtland sucked in a deep breath, his nostrils flaring. "I know. But there are others there that are alive. I don't know, Dom. It feels unfinished."

And unfinished business drove Courtland crazy. I reached out and slapped his bicep. "Don't have to woo me to madness, Alpha. I'm with you all the way."

Courtland straightened and shook his head at me, amusement chasing away the normal coldness of his eyes. He kept that mask up for everyone—everyone except his family and me. "I don't know what I did to deserve you, Dom, but I thank your Moon Goddess every single day that you're my Beta."

I flipped him my middle finger, because I didn't know how to respond to something as insane as *feelings*. "No you don't, fucker. You don't believe in her."

He just smiled at me enigmatically, but didn't contradict me. He pulled his cell phone out and started mashing numbers, doing whatever it was he did to work his magic.

"I'll prep the muscle," I said softly, throwing back the last of my tequila. He did the brain work and I did the brawn. Because I was much more comfortable with a gun in my hand than delving around inside my head.

## 2

BONNIE

"Listen, Bonnie. Your predecessor ran the Sanctum with half the money and less help. You're a smart girl. You'll figure it out."

I gritted my teeth to stop myself from snarling. You didn't snarl at the Alpha General. "Yes, Sir."

The Alpha General gave me a patronizing look and sent me on my way with a flick of his fingers. I gave him a tight smile, hotfooting it out of there before I said something I regretted.

Radic was waiting for me outside the door, a pained look on his face. "Didn't go well?" he whispered, because we all had spectacular hearing. For instance, I could hear the Legion Generals inside the office talking about how it was a shame that a Beta female of my age hadn't found a Pack yet. Hell, at this point they'd even take just a mate, as long as I was doing my bit to increase the population of the Manix. Yet those bastards didn't want to give me a cent, or another set of hands, to solve the problems we had with the growing number of half-Manix kids being dumped on the doorstep. They wanted to pretend it wasn't an issue, but we'd had two this year alone. As the number of Manix females decreased, the more the Manix men roamed, and not just the Alphas. The Betas too. And the babies almost always ended up on the boundaries of Maxton—sometimes at the age of two, sometimes not until they presented their Manix traits in their teens. There were fifteen kids in the Sanctum now, and no one would take responsibility for them.

I fucking hated men sometimes.

Radic pushed my hair back from my face. "I'll bring ice cream tonight and we'll talk about it," he said softly, his eyes flicking between me and the closed door of the Alpha General's office.

I nodded, straightening my shoulders. I knew Radic could hear what they were saying as well as I did. He was my age, but because he was a Beta male, there was no pressure on him to reproduce, to join a Pack. There were too few Omegas to go around anyway, so another bachelor was just that.

He kissed my cheek. "I'll get you what you need, Baby Girl."

I gave my best friend, and part-time lover, a half

smile. That was another thing of which the Legion wouldn't approve. Radic and I had been friends since... well, forever. In our teens, we'd naturally fallen into bed together after a night of way too much peach schnapps, and he'd never really climbed back out. But he wanted a Pack, and I didn't. Well, not one that wanted me anyway.

I sometimes wondered if that was why he was still a bachelor—because he couldn't find a Pack that wanted us both. Heaven knew that Radic was an excellent choice. A job as high up as you could go as a Beta in the Legion. And so fucking handsome.

Me? I was too curvy for a Manix, my lips too full, my eyes too wide. My mouth was too opinionated. My subservience was nearly non-existent. The only person who appreciated me was Rad, and I was holding him back.

I sighed heavily. "Thanks, Rad." Kissing his cheek once more, I turned and strode out of the Legion building. I should have known better than to ask for more resources for the bastard children of our people, because even the Alpha General had fathered a kid accidentally with a human. I wouldn't be surprised if they all hadn't 'accidentally' knocked up a human once or twice. Quite frankly, Alphas were the fucking worst. Always putting their biological desires above the good of everyone else.

I remembered that I needed to stop by the commissary to pick up the special order of nut-free food, because Taylor had a peanut allergy. He was just one of the kids I cared for over at the Sanctum, the place the Manix put their cast-offs until they were old enough to be of use to the town.

But I loved every single one of those kids, no matter how short a time they were with me. Some, like Duncan, had been with me from toddlerhood. He was as much my child as anyone born from my body. No one had claimed him, and he'd grown up in the Sanctum. Taylor had only come in this year—a moody teenager who didn't understand why he was being abandoned by his mother, and why his body was basically his enemy. He grew too fast, and couldn't control his emotions. Everything was just too much. If he'd had a father around, maybe he would have adjusted. But all he'd had was an unaware human, who'd been left with a vague idea that if she had a child that didn't seem quite right, it should be dropped off here.

Funny that the Alphas never failed to mention that until after they'd finished getting their rocks off.

When I pushed open the door to the commissary, all my packages were already on the counter, ready for me to collect. Trevor, an aging Beta, stood smiling behind the counter. "Saw you coming down the street through the front window. Looks like you've worked up quite a respectable head of steam, and I'm a smart man. Don't want to get in the way of a Beta on a mission."

I worked up a smile for the hunched old man. He'd run the commissary for the better part of a century, as weathered as the countertop that my packages sat on. I grabbed the invoice that sat on top of one of the boxes. Two hundred bucks. Fuck. I pulled out my purse, and swallowed hard.

"Can I pay the other half when the new month rolls over, Trevor? The food budget is looking tight." God, it burned to say that, but I had to tell myself that it wasn't a failing of my own making. It was a failing of a fucked up system.

Trevor waved a hand. "Consider the other half a donation."

Trevor had been donating 'the other half' of my invoices for months now. I knew the commissary was one of the busier businesses in town, but Trevor would want to retire eventually, and he couldn't do that if he was giving me handouts.

On the other hand, I wasn't actually in a position to say no. So I gave him one more tight smile. "I'll pay it on the first of next month, Trevor. You've donated enough to me."

Trevor shook his head. "Not to you, Bonnie. To the Sanctum. And I know that is where all your pay goes too, so it looks like we both donate beyond our means."

Gah, I needed to get out of here before I did something stupid, like burst into frustrated tears. "I'll see you on the first of the month."

He nodded his gray head. "See you next month."

I juggled the multitude of boxes and bags back through the door and over to my car. I was one of the few in town with a car, a perk of the job. Mashing the packages between my torso and the side of the van, I opened the passenger door and threw them in. I really wanted a donut or a cookie or some shit, but if my kids couldn't have treats because money was tight, neither could I.

Maybe I'd make cookies with the little ones. Nut-free so Taylor didn't go into anaphylactic shock.

I slid into the driver's seat and rested my head on the steering wheel. I would figure it out, of course. And the Alpha General was right—I had help. Three times the kids, compared to when the last Den Mother retired nearly six years ago, but at least I had Darius to help me. And his Alphas, on occasion. None of whom had gone out and produced any illegitimate children, despite their urges.

When Darius had first offered to help, I'd been overjoyed. His Alphas managed to fix all the little problems that had been pushed to the wayside so I could just cope with fixing the institutional problems plaguing the Sanctum, like the discrimination and bullying amongst the children.

The previous Den Mother had had a dog-eat-dog

view of survival, and had decided that letting them figure out the pecking order with little to no interference had been good for their character.

To say I disagreed would be an understatement. I wanted them to feel loved, supported. Then maybe we wouldn't end up with so many parentless by-blows because they'd struggled to find their place in our world.

The only problem with Darius and his Pack helping out had actually been Rad. My amazing best friend had decided that they were trying to steal me away. They'd always been quite vocal about not wanting any others in their Pack, but female Omegas had been a myth until recently. A female Beta could help satisfy some of those urges.

Rad had thought they were going to steal me, and he'd challenged the goddamn Alphas. I had to make it really clear—to both the Wiley-Fletcher-Reid Pack and to Radic—that I had no interest in being a consolation prize. A band-aid solution to a biological problem.

Once that had been all figured out, it had worked beautifully, really. Everyone got support, the kids had good role models, and I got a break once every couple of days.

I drove to the huge mansion that doubled as the Sanctum. I had to give the Legion points for that. We weren't cramped, and it was right beside the school, so that was one less hurdle. There was an empty house on the other side that had once housed dorms for the older kids, before I'd insisted they were still children and needed love and support too. Sure, they were moody and kinda mean at times, but they still needed to know that there were people who cared whether they lived or died in a town that already saw them as less.

I parked in my spot and took a deep breath. I had to leave my frustrations at the door, because like bees and wild animals, children could sense your emotions. They'd know if I was frustrated or angry, and then they'd be riled for the rest of the day.

As soon as I put my hand on the door, the call went up.

"Bonnie's back!" someone shouted from the back of the house, and I could hear the tiny pounding of feet from all directions.

"Bonnie!" A tiny body slammed into my knees, and I grinned down at Duncan. Darius appeared in the doorway, a pout on his face.

"Sheesh, you'd think I was chopped liver. We were in the middle of a thrilling game of hide-and-seek, but that stops when Bonnie arrives," he teased, shifting a toddler to his other hip. Only the little ones were here now, the rest at school next door for another hour.

I grinned and raised an eyebrow. "What can I say? I'm the only one who knows where the chocolate is hidden."

Another tiny body plowed into me, and I laughed. "Come on, we'll have some hot chocolate and watch a movie, Chicklettes." I did a rough head count as they ran, or toddled, from the room. Except the toddler in Darius's arms. He was more than happy to be snuggled into the chest of the sweet Omega.

Once the kids were out of earshot, he raised an eyebrow. "How'd it go?"

I huffed. "You know how it went."

A low growl from Darius's throat had the toddler wiggling in his arms to get down. Darius kissed the top of his curly head. "Sorry, Harry." He put him on the ground and Harry took off down the hall after his friends.

Darius lifted half the bags from my arms, following me through the house. "Did you tell them how much you're subsidizing this place?"

"And you," I said softly.

"Hell, Old Trev too. And Luna at the bakery. Terra over at the school sends the kids home with new clothes all the time. We are all paying for these kids, except the people who should be."

I looked over my shoulder at him. "Preaching to the choir, Darius. Radic said he'd pull some strings, and hell, maybe he can get the old bastards to just sign some paperwork without reading it."

Darius sighed heavily. "Sometimes I wish Gatlin would just overthrow the Alpha General and take over.

I know he wouldn't let this shit stand." Gatlin was a half-blood Manix too—the illegitimate offspring of the Alpha General. If anyone would be sympathetic to the plight of the Sanctum, it would be him.

I hushed Darius, in case there were any ears around to hear his near traitorous words, but secretly I agreed with him.

Something had to change soon, or we were looking down the black hole of extinction.

"I can shoot as well as Dom," Rosa whined, and my Beta snorted.

I shook my head. "No, you can't."

Rosa huffed. "Well, he taught me, so maybe he's just a shitty teacher."

Dominic continued checking out his semi-automatic and flipped her the finger absently. I shook my head at them both. "Irrespective of the fact, you aren't coming on this raid."

"This is just as much my fight as it is yours, Courtland. They *sold* me."

I resisted the urge to pinch the bridge of my nose, instead giving her my signature blank stare. "And I saved you. I'm not undoing all that good work by letting you walk into a highly dangerous situation, completely inexperienced. My answer is no, Rosa. I need you to stay here and pack up your siblings for a quick escape."

All the fight left her, and she nodded tightly. The week before, I had sat them all down and told them that it was time to go. The children—though most of them were teens now, with only Marguerita still in her preteens—had taken it in their stride. Rosa had looked relieved, despite her arguments now. But Abuela had refused to leave, and it had cast a pall over the decision. To most of them, Abuela had been the only parent they'd known, and it was because she loved them that she insisted they come with me, rather than staying in the compound with her and the rest of my men.

My wards would come with me, wherever I went. Dominic too. I had a few men in my crew, the ones I really trusted, who would do this job with me and move up to the US. The kids would have good opportunities there, proper schooling and safe lives. Once we were settled, my men could come back down here, or I would help them disappear into the US or Canada. It was up to them. I was done being the Lord of this Castle.

Antonio poked his head through the door. "We are ready, Prince."

"Coming." I softened my face as I looked at Rosa. "I do not need another warrior, Rosa. I need you to be safe. All of you."

She blew out a long breath. "Okay, Court. Go rescue some experiments. I'll get everyone ready to go."

I touched her cheek. She was the younger sibling I'd never gotten to have; they all were. Dominic felt the same. We'd created a family from nothing, from the worst circumstances, and while my father had believed blood was everything, I'd learned that blood had little to do with it. I looked at Dominic, who ruffled Rosa's dark hair on the way out the door, even though she snarled at him.

In the foyer were my men. Twelve men I trusted more than any. They were all supernaturals, though their breeds varied dramatically. Loren was a witch. Federico and his brother Alvaro were both wolf shifters, but they sat below Dominic in ranking. Still powerful, though. Antonio was something else; given his proclivity for death, I thought maybe some variation of Djinn.

All outcasts, all criminals. Brothers in arms, not in blood.

"Let's roll out," I said softly, and they jumped at my words. I ruled them with an iron fist, all except Dominic. The rest feared and respected me in equal measures, and I'd shed blood and lost pieces of my soul to ensure that I could control them. If they got away from me, as a unit, they could raze the world in the way only dangerous men with no morality could.

They were my muscle, and I was their soul. May the Goddess have mercy on our enemies.

We didn't go over the plan again, because it was deceptively simple. We would go in, fangs bared. We would kill anyone who resisted.

Once we'd cleared the building, we'd have twelve minutes until reinforcements came. We'd save as many as we could, and that would just have to appease my guilt. We were traveling in three vans so we'd have space to transport survivors. It was the best I could do in the short amount of time available to me.

The compound was three hours from my home. Such evilness on my doorstep. Well, maybe I was the evil on their doorstep; it really depended on your perspective. We were silent on the drive, since Dominic was in the car behind us, and he was the only one who was comfortable enough with me to chat. I wasn't a talker, Dom was just persistent.

Finally, I could see the chainlink fencing glinting in the moonlight. I indicated to Loren to pull over. We would go the rest of the way on foot. Only the drivers would be left.

I climbed out of the van, removing my tactical gear. My body came with its own tactical gear. I could feel the eyes of my men on me as I shifted from man to Manix. My body got larger, broader, until I was giant-sized. Hard plates spread across my flesh, impenetrable to most bullets. Fangs and claws slid out, and fluffy ears sprouted from my head.

I could hear Dominic laughing behind me. "The ears get me every fucking time, man." I bared my fangs at him, but he just gave me a shit-eating grin. Only Dominic could get away with that level of disrespect; no one else would even try. Not even my longest-serving men. I put my gun holster back on, now stretched to its widest setting.

Shooting a gun was always an interesting experience with claws, but sometimes, shooting someone from ten feet away was easier than tearing out their throat. Cleaner, anyway.

Everyone peeled away in their pairs, each knowing their entrance and their role. Dominic stepped up to my side. He'd stay in his human form for as long as possible, because he might be a wolf, but he was also a damn fine marksman.

Everyone had a partner. I paid them as a pair. If your pair died in battle, his family got both his half and your half. If you intentionally killed your pair on the job, I feasted on your liver. It only took one real world example of this for everyone to adopt the partner rule. Your pair would take care of your family if you died, and they'd have your back.

It was always good to have someone watching your back in this business.

While everyone else was going through side

entrances and the loading dock, I was walking through the front doors. I half-shifted, which made me harder to see, my fur naturally camouflaging me against the hot sand. Dominic stepped behind my back and he'd stay there until the time for stealth was gone. I melted into the shadows; there were plenty of them, because they didn't want anyone to know this place existed. There weren't any big spotlights or signs to avoid. It was as unobtrusive as it could be, while still being nearly impenetrable.

Impenetrable to humans, anyway. I was no human.

I could see a guard up ahead, prowling the perimeter, and I felt Dominic peel from my back, then heard the telltale gurgle of someone having their throat slit. I continued toward the front door, smashing my fist through the plate glass. Oh, was that meant to be bulletproof? I wasn't a bullet.

I was Manix.

I smiled at the wild eyes of the guard as he went for his gun, but he was too slow. They all would be. I tore out his throat before he even managed to draw his gun, and he flopped to the ground with a nearly noiseless sound.

A scent drifted through the open door, wrapping itself around my body like a vine. An Omega. A Manix Omega. My whole body froze as the scent permeated my every sense, my Beast intent on discovering the direction of its prey.

Another guard came out of the door, jarring me from my Alpha fugue. A knife flew by my head and lodged in the guard's eyeball.

Dominic.

"Even I can smell that, Alpha. Let's go." He appeared in front of me. "Control yourself," he growled. "If you die because your Manix smells a pretty Omega, I'm going to be fucking pissed."

I gave him a feral grin and let my Beast loose. He'd scented his prize, and now it was time to hunt.

**4**

─────────

PRYCE

I could hear the dull thud of bodies hitting the floor. It was probably disturbing that I knew the sound so well, but I'd been in this facility for more than half my life. I'd seen more dead bodies than I cared to remember. The sound of a body hitting the floor was never soundless, especially when your hearing was better than most. Being Manix had its upsides, even if it was the reason I was here.

I moved to the infants in the corner of the room. I hadn't named them. They rarely lasted longer than twelve weeks in here, and I'd learned the hard way that naming them just resulted in more suffering. But they always lasted longer than their mothers, who inevitably died during childbirth. It had only been three or so years since they'd started putting the offspring in here with me. It usually increased their lifespan slightly, but never enough.

I swaddled them tighter, hoping they would sleep through whatever was happening outside these perspex rooms. None of the lights had gone on, but I could see the small, flashing blue light that meant the wards had been tripped and someone had breached the perimeter of the building.

Good. I hope they burned this place to the ground. So much suffering had happened in these walls that they were soaked with the screams of the innocent.

I breathed deeply, and the scent made me still. Another Manix was here. An Alpha. My Omega whined at the scent of a savior, but I pushed it back down. It could be a savior, or just another captor. I'd learned long ago that there was no hope without consequence.

The alarms finally blared to life, waking the rest of my fellow inmates. There weren't many of us left anymore. We'd died off slowly, one after another, and as government administrations changed, the passion to see what made us tick, to breed us into soldiers, had waned. No one wanted to spend millions on an experiment that had failed consistently for nearly twenty years. The old-timers—the ones who'd been here when I arrived—had long since died out, their will to live failing before their bodies did.

I shifted to my other form, hovering in the back

corner near the cribs. Baby One's breathing sounded rattly, which was concerning, but there was nothing I could do for her. They'd been trying to crossbreed me with other supernaturals, but it always ended the same. If you crossed me with a full-blood shifter, the children inevitably died. Too many souls occupied their tiny bodies, and when their Beasts fully manifested inside them, one snuffed out the other. Half-bloods apparently had better success, especially with other half-breed supernaturals.

"Pryce, what's happening?" Katya yelled from the room next to me. She was young, barely out of her teens. I didn't know what kind of creature she was, but I had no doubt they'd try mixing our DNA together eventually and she would die too. Unless someone saved us tonight.

"I don't know."

Finally, the lights all flamed to life, filling every inch of the facility with light. The shadows disappeared, and a man outside my glass box was revealed. I couldn't help the gasp that fell from my lips. A Manix stood in front of my cage, his body large and powerful, guns strapped across his chest. We stared at each other for what seemed like an indeterminable amount of hours, but was probably only seconds.

Another man, with shaggy brown hair and full lips appeared beside him. "Facility is clear."

The Manix nodded, but never took his eyes off me.

"Free them and call for the vans. No one gets left behind."

I tensed, swallowing hard. "What do you intend to do with them?" My voice sounded stronger than I felt.

"Set them free."

I blinked at him, because what the fuck even was freedom? I heard the metallic noise of the locks releasing and then my door slid open. The scent of the Alpha hit me like a wave, making me feel confused and needy, but also hard as a rock. Fuck. Now was not the time for some Omega bullshit.

The Manix stepped inside, his size a foot taller than mine, and his shoulders nearly twice as wide in this form. I took a step backwards toward the cribs, and he slowed his progress. Then, as I watched, he shifted back to a man.

I knew his face, even though I had only met him briefly when we were both way too young. "It's you."

He nodded, but the guilt that crept into his eyes kept me tense. I was silent as he walked closer, this time not shifting away. "I am sorry. I should have come sooner."

I wanted to laugh. He didn't have to come at all, but I was so glad he did. Any anger that I held inside me—and that anger filled a deep and bitter well—wasn't directed at a near stranger who'd been a child when we met. Who had no obligation to rescue me, but here he was anyway.

I couldn't say all this though, not with my heart pounding. So I just said, "It's fine," like he was late picking me up from work, and not like I'd spent sixteen years in a fucking prison.

"We have to go," he murmured again, and now he was so close his scent was everywhere. I cast a look back over my shoulder at my progeny. They'd been created in a test tube, but they were mine. They might not survive, but they wouldn't die alone.

"They have to come." I shifted back to human too, and in this form, I was still several inches shorter. He nodded, holding out an arm.

"We'd never leave them behind, but we must hurry."

I picked up Baby One, and handed it to him slowly. The irony wasn't lost on me. "We should stop meeting like this," I said softly, and he huffed out a laugh, before rearing back in surprise, like he wasn't used to the sound.

One huge hand supported the baby's tiny body with ease, and with the other hand, he pulled a gun. "Wait," I hissed, and he stopped immediately. "I don't know your name."

You couldn't run away with a man whose name you didn't know. I was trusting him with my life, with all our lives, and I couldn't hand that over to a stranger. Not again.

"I'm Courtland. You're Pryce."

I blinked again in shock. "You remembered?"

He gave me a look that was loaded with meaning. "Of course."

That meant something, though I didn't want to examine what while I was this close to freedom. I picked up the second baby and cradled it to my chest before Courtland swept from the room and I hurried to keep up.

The man who'd spoken to Courtland before flanked me, inhaling deeply. "Hello, Omega."

I tensed, but while the look in his eye was wolfish, it wasn't threatening. "I'm Pryce."

"I know," he said with a quick grin, his eyes darting around the room, never resting in one place. "Dominic."

Courtland remembered. This guy knew my name. I had a feeling something else was going on here, but I didn't know what. It didn't matter right now because I was about to be free.

We stepped through a shattered glass door, and a black van appeared in front of us. Dominic slid open the door, and I climbed in voluntarily. Courtland maneuvered the other baby out of my arms.

"Seatbelt."

I quirked an eyebrow at him, but did as I was told. Part of it was the Omega wanting to please an Alpha, and part of it was just Courtland's natural authority. When I was safely anchored in the car, he handed me both babies and climbed in after me. He didn't put his own seatbelt on though.

The van skidded away from the facility that had been my prison for more than half of my life.

Panic began to set in, no matter what my brain was saying. I didn't know how to live in a regular society. I didn't know how to cook, or have any identification.

Dominic growled low from the driver's seat, and Courtland reached out a huge hand and wrapped it around my thigh. "It will be okay, Omega. I'll make sure of it."

There was Alpha power in his voice and I believed him with every fiber of my body.

Baby One made a rattling noise in her chest again, and Courtland's eyes flew to her. "Why is it making that noise?"

I pushed down the anguish that welled in my chest. "They're dying."

Something scary flashed across Courtland's face, but he inclined his head once. "Why?"

I shrugged, because I didn't know. Not really. "They never survive past three months. Whatever the scientists do during the conception stage, it never works."

I could see he wanted to press, wanted to ask questions, and I felt myself shut down. I couldn't handle those questions or the memories that accompanied them.

But Courtland didn't voice his curiosity, he just met

Dominic's eyes in the mirror. "Call ahead. We leave tonight. We'll go to Maxton."

Dominic nodded, grabbing his phone from his pocket and putting it to his ear. "Hey kid, get your siblings ready. We are coming in hot and shooting through straight away." He paused. "It means we're leaving as soon as I pull into the courtyard, so get your bags together and get the hell in the car." Whoever was on the other end must have been mouthing off more, because he threw the phone onto the passenger seat. "You sure we have to bring her?"

Courtland nodded.

"Bring who?"

This time, a small smile curled his lips. "Rosa."

Bonnie was sleeping on my chest, and it was the most relaxed I'd seen her in a week. I stroked her pretty honey-colored hair back from her cheek and watched as she pursed her lips at the slight tickle.

Damn. I fucking loved her. I'd loved her for so many years; it was hard to remember a time that she didn't own my heart completely. I hated seeing her so damn stressed, though I wouldn't dream of suggesting she hand off some of the responsibility to anyone else. Bonnie was a beautiful soul, but she was fucking fierce when it came to the Sanctum.

I'd secretly been squirreling away resources for the Sanctum, but I knew eventually the people from Stores would realize. I wasn't overly worried. Finlo Grey's parents had always been a bit soft, and also a little anti-

Legion—well, as anti-Legion as you could be while still being a cog in the proverbial machine. If they caught me, I didn't think they'd turn me into the Alpha General. Though I'd been wrong before.

I shifted slowly from beneath Bonnie's sleeping body, doing my best not to wake her. I kissed her full lips softly because I couldn't help myself, and then dragged on my sweats. I needed to head back to my apartment to get changed for work. I tried not to wake up here too often when she was working at the Sanctum; there were a lot of teenagers hanging around, and I wanted them to learn about respecting women. Sneaking out of a woman's bedroom before sunrise was hardly the best example to set.

But she'd needed me more these last few days, even if she wouldn't admit it. I was helpless to resist her, especially when she would never come out and ask for help. She was too fiercely independent. She saw needing help as failure, even though that was ridiculous. The strongest people needed help sometimes.

It was just a result of our childhood; I knew that. Bonnie had been unlike any other Manix kid. We were supernaturals, usually tall and lean like the warrior race we once were. Not Bonnie though. Bonnie had been shorter, rounder. She'd been a shy, small, chubby kid, and I'd gotten in more fights than any other Beta sticking up for my beautiful friend.

Even to this day, I couldn't understand how they

didn't see the absolute beauty that shone from her. Were they all fucking blind? She'd grown into a woman who stole my fucking breath away, and I was so glad she was mine. But I would have done anything for her to escape the small poisoned barbs that had shaped her into a woman who found it hard to trust, who underestimated her worth to me and to a potential Pack.

I was Beta, through and through. My Beast craved a Pack. But not nearly as much as it craved Bonnie. The Manix and the man would happily sacrifice everything for her happiness.

"Is it that time already?" Her sleepy voice was low and scratchy, and it made me hard as a rock. She was naked beneath the sheets, and it outlined the curves of her hips, the mounds of her breasts. Dammit. I bit my lip and grabbed my cock, giving it a tight squeeze to warn it to behave. I wanted to crawl back in there and have her wrap her gloriously thick thighs around my head until she either came or I passed out.

But the boss had an eight a.m. meeting, so there was no time. I wondered if I could call in sick?

Manix rarely got sick though. Fuck. I leaned forward and kissed her cheeks, and then her lips. She tasted like heaven.

"Yeah, I have to go." I kissed her once more and then stood, staring down at her, all rumpled and sexy in bed. "Love you, Bon. You know that, right?"

She gave me the softest, sweetest smile. "Love you too."

I let out a long sigh and dragged myself toward the door. "Is Darius doing a night shift tonight?"

She nodded sleepily, her eyes already closing. "Yep."

"Come over. We'll do pizza and I'll give you one of those full body massages you like."

One eye popped open. "The ones with the warm coconut oil that we use as..." She trailed off, waggling her eyebrows. I grinned back at her and winked. She gave a happy hum and snuggled further into the blankets. "You're on. Now get out of here before I drag you back in here to do something with that impressive morning wood you're trying to hide."

I laughed, blowing her a kiss as I tiptoed out of the house. The sun was just starting to pinken the sky as I jogged back to my apartment. I did everything by muscle memory: showering, getting dressed in my suit, doing my hair. The whole time, my mind was on Bonnie and the Sanctum and what the hell I could do to ease her load.

There were no easy solutions. There weren't even any safe solutions. She wouldn't quit. The Alpha General wouldn't spare more funds. We could reach out to the rest of the community, I guess, but that would create more work for her. Plus, she'd hate people thinking that she was fucking it up.

I jumped on my ATV and drove the short distance to the Legion building. We went everywhere by ATV in Maxton, with a few exceptions. Bonnie's van was one, as well as people who needed a vehicle for work purposes. Honestly, the less we had to do with the human bureaucracies, the better for us.

I wasn't the first person here; the Legion were the biggest employers in Maxton after all. There were people here getting deliveries early, plus the Legion Force—our army and security arm—which meant that the lights were nearly always burning in the Legion building.

I went through the routine of setting up the office for the day, sifting through emails and paper requests, sorting through who wanted to vent and who had actual issues, and moving them into the schedule as needed.

The Alpha General strolled into the office five minutes before his first appointment for the day and grunted in my direction. Well, that was close enough to a greeting. No sooner had he shut the door than his first appointment arrived. Settling everyone in, I let myself get lost in the minutiae of my work.

The other Legion Generals turned up through different times of the day to take meetings and generally shoot the shit, like they were prone to doing. They made the hard decisions but as a general rule, none of them actually worked very hard.

I approved several requests for aid—none of them were large amounts, and I knew the Alpha General would have rejected them just because he believed in survival of the fittest. Might work for anthropology, but not for leading an entire race of people.

Just before lunch, my phone rang once more. I thought about ignoring it and pretending the desk was unmanned, but that was unprofessional. I loved my job, most of the time. It was frustrating but I could do some real good for my people from behind this desk, even if I was only a Beta.

"Hello, Alpha General's office."

"Uh, Rad? It's Tom. I'm working down by the ward entrance, and three huge vans just rolled in. They don't look like regular Maxton people."

I blinked. "But they got through the ward?"

"Uh yeah, just drove straight through."

My mind whirled. Since the female Omega had been found by the Huxley-Grey Pack, we'd had our wards tightened so extensively that you wouldn't be able to cross them if you so much as thought about junk-punching your Manix husband.

But three carloads of strangers just drove straight through them?

"How long ago was this, Tom?"

He paused at the other end of the phone. "Oh, I dunno, Rad. Maybe five or ten minutes? I didn't know if I was overreacting or—"

The door flung open, and in front of me was a huge Alpha Manix. A stranger that I had never met.

"Don't worry about it, Tom."

I looked at the men with the Alpha, my nose twitching as I took in all their scents. There was an Omega Manix, and he was fucking beautiful. Warm skin, bright blue eyes, dark hair that was too long.

Actually, they all looked like the polar opposites of anything in town. Tall and dark to our fair and blond. It was hard not to throw up my guard. There was a shifter beside the Omega Manix, though I couldn't pick what flavor. He was covered in tattoos from the neck down, covering even his fingers, giving him an aura of danger. That was contrasted with the way his eyes crinkled at the corners like he was laughing at me, and the small dimple on one cheek. He was like a happy pitbull or something.

My eyes were dragged back to the huge Alpha. His face was kind of familiar, but where did I know it from....

"You're Naja's brother!" Naja was the new female Omega who lived up with the Huxley-Grey Pack. Her arrival had been the most dramatic thing to happen in this town in a decade.

The Alpha was in a beautifully tailored three-piece suit, though he'd obviously lost his jacket at some point, and he'd rolled the sleeves of his dress shirt up his forearms. Holy hell, he was delicious. That hard-on that I'd been nursing all day from Bonnie sprang back to life, and I cleared my throat.

"Uh, how can I help you guys?"

The Alpha looked at me with fathomless, dark eyes. "I would like to speak to your Pack decision makers."

I hesitated, but picked up the phone. I needn't have bothered though, because in the next breath, the Alpha General was there, eyeing the Alpha in the doorway as well as the seven or so men behind him. Each one looked dangerous, and if I judged the bulges beneath their jackets correctly, armed.

"Call the Force, Radic," the Alpha General barked, and I did as I was told, picking up the phone and speed dialing the Force. I murmured softly for them to get their asses over here, while still keeping one ear on the conversation.

The big Alpha ran his eyes appraisingly over the Alpha General. "I would like to request aid for this Omega Manix and his young from your healer. He is part of my Pack, so I would request that my family be able to stay close while the babes are treated." The Omega started, looking at the Alpha in surprise, but didn't contradict him.

The Alpha General ran his eyes over their ragtag Pack, stilling on the babies swaddled in the Omega's arms, his face twisting in disgust. The babies did smell... wrong somehow, but they were still innocents.

We respected the life of the young here, but much more so if they were full-blooded Manix, apparently.

The lead weight in my stomach doubled in size as the Alpha General glared in their direction. "The Omega can stay. The rest of your *group*"—he sneered the word— "aren't welcome to stay in Maxton. This is a Manix only community."

I knew what he meant though. I could feel the power coming off this Alpha in waves. The Alpha General *knew* this stranger was stronger than he was. He was a threat and the Alpha General wanted him gone. I wanted to shout at the Alpha General that he was going about this all wrong, but he would be too stubborn to listen anyway.

The big Alpha's eyes turned as hard as black ice. "Unfortunately, that will not work for me." His voice was so cold that it sent a chill down my spine. "I don't believe I've introduced myself. My name is Courtland De León, and I am challenging you for control of the Manix."

Holy fuck.

## 6

COURTLAND

I silently cursed my impulsiveness, though Dominic would laugh at the idea that I possessed such a quality. But I did; sometimes my anger overtook my good sense and I did stupid things like challenge an aging Alpha to the right to rule an entire fucking town. An entire species. But there was something about the twist of his face, the condescending tone he used to speak to me, that made me see red.

Dominic whistled, so maybe he wouldn't be laughing so hard at the idea I was impulsive. But I'd learned that once you put something like this out there, you couldn't take it back. All you could do was commit to it or bluff your way out of it.

The older Manix stumbled back a step like I'd physically struck him. "You can't."

Now it was my turn to sneer. "I can." I looked at the handsome Beta behind the desk. "Are your leaders democratically elected, or is it done by Alpha battle, like old?"

The Beta looked between us, his face a little pale. "It hasn't been, I mean, I think an Alpha battle? The strongest Alphas are the Legion Generals." His voice was strong and sure, despite his obvious shock at my statement.

I let my eyes flick over him quickly. Sandy blond hair that contrasted with his straight, dark brows. Bright blue eyes and almost pretty pink lips. My Alpha roared to life, and he wanted to devour this Beta inch by inch. I pushed down the urge, concentrating on the problem at hand.

Dominic stepped closer to my back. "Boots coming up the front steps."

I nodded, trusting that my Beta would handle it. I waited until the troops were slightly closer before raising my voice. "Are you too weak to accept my challenge, or do you not respect your own laws, Alpha?"

I could smell the gun oil, and sensed the tenseness of my men around me. There were seven with me and the Omega, and the rest were guarding the cars with my family in it. They were on a shoot-first order. The Manix were meant to be warriors, but the Alpha General was proof that they were out of shape, and probably unseasoned.

Iago, my uncle, had plucked my sister from these lands, from this security force, as easily as taking candy from an infant. I knew my men were more than enough to hold them off while I discussed finding a healer and a place to stay for my Pack.

And they *were* my Pack, even if the little Omega didn't know it yet. *Mine!* The Beast roared inside my mind.

Yes. Ours.

"I requested aid for these two Manix infants and you rejected my request." Well, basically true. "I think you are an unfit Alpha for this race, and I challenge you for control," I repeated again, just so there was no doubt amongst the troops massing at my back.

The Alpha General shook his head. "No. If you think you can waltz into my town and make ultimatums, you're fucking insane. No. I reject your challenge."

I threw back my head and laughed. "Old man, you don't get to reject a challenge. That isn't how the laws of nature work, and according to the Beta, not how your society works." I met the Beta's eyes. "I promise, I mean this town no ill intent. I just want treatment for the young, somewhere safe for my Pack. Maybe get to know my kin." And there it was, that softness I wasn't known for but that had somehow wormed its way inside my heart anyway. I'd chosen Maxton because I wanted to be closer to Naja and the last of my blood.

I'd worked so hard, for so long, to free my sister, that when it was over, I was lost. Dominic would say I had a savior complex. The asshole would probably be right.

I didn't take my eyes off the Beta, who was obviously some kind of assistant. I didn't know why it was important that he knew I meant the town—and him—no harm, but it felt vital.

Finally, he nodded. "The laws of Maxton, of the Manix, have always been that the strongest lead." He cleared his throat. "But you're a stranger, an outsider, and there's going to be resistance, Mr De Léon."

The corners of my lips turned up. "Call me Courtland."

I wanted to tell him he could call me Sir, and I would stroke that pretty golden hair while he knelt beside my feet. Probably too far though, for now.

"You traitorous little fuck," the Alpha General growled, leaping toward the Beta. I was across the room with my hand around the Alpha's throat in an instant. Sweeping out his legs, I slammed him backward, his head hitting the polished wood floor with a thud.

"No," I growled low, and I heard someone whimper as my power flooded the room. "You do not touch him. Do you submit?"

The Alpha General spat in my face, the warm saliva sliding down my cheek. "Never."

I bared my teeth. "Fine, your death is your choice."

I tightened my grip, and then there was a hand around my wrist. I looked up, briefly glancing at my Pack, their guns all raised at the doors of the office.

"Wait," the Beta said softly, loosening his grip around my wrist as I met his eyes. He was so close I could taste his scent on my tongue. "There's a protocol for this. You have to do it right, or you'll be fighting challenges forever."

I gave him a feral grin. "I like fighting, and I don't need forever. I just need until they are well."

The Beta looked down at me with something like disappointment. "So the getting to know your kin thing was bullshit?"

Ah, he had me there. I released the old Alpha's throat, standing back up so I could look down at the Beta. "Your name?"

"Radic."

Radic. I tasted his name on my tongue—it felt good. "You will arrange it?"

He nodded, but looked down hesitantly at the Alpha General. Then he straightened his shoulders. "Yes. But it might be best if I do it from my home office."

I gritted my teeth at the idea that he could be in danger. "Is there some place for us to stay?"

He paused for a long moment, his eyes searching my face, and then the men behind me. Finally, he nodded again. "I know a place."

He grabbed up his stuff and stepped around the desk. The aging Alpha climbed to his feet. "You're fired, you fucking lizard," he growled, and Radic tensed his jaw.

"Sir, I honestly think you have bigger problems right now." With that, he strode through the two groups of armed men like they were nothing. I grinned at his back before looking over at Dominic, who was staring at Radic's ass. I knew that Dominic liked men and women. I believed the sexuality of supernaturals was more fluid by necessity, so it had never fazed me, outside of giving me aching balls. Because as much as I loved my Beta, emotional attachments in the business we'd been in was a weakness.

A little voice in the back of my head reminded me we weren't in that business anymore. My dick gave a throb of agreement. Fuck. Now was not the time. I looked over at the Omega who would soon be mine, and saw him watching me intently with eyes that noticed too much.

I gave him a tight smile, and stepped closer to him. My hand was on my gun, but I wouldn't need it against any of the soldiers in this room. I could kill them all easily, or make them bow to my will.

"Are the babies getting heavy? Would you like me to hold one?"

They were twins, but the smaller of the two was pale. I didn't like it. I would ask Radic to direct us to a doctor before our lodgings. Pryce had told us not to name them, and the pain in his eyes had torn at my insides. He handed me the slightly brighter baby, who had his father's bright blue eyes.

I made eye contact with every single one of the soldiers who bracketed the hall on the way back to our vehicle. Most of them dropped their eyes, though some looked at me with hostility. More concerning though, were the ones that looked at me with something like hope. What was going on in this town that they would look at a stranger like that?

Once we reached the SUV, I noted that all my men had their weapons drawn, as well as Rosa. "Put the gun down, Rosa. It's fine."

Rosa threw me a look that could only be perfected by teenage girls. It was part *you're an idiot* and part *don't tell me what to do.*

"Umm, they're pointing guns at us, Court."

"He challenged the Alpha General. It would be against our laws for them to shoot him or any of you," Radic said. I had a feeling he wasn't really talking to Rosa, but the rest of the town that had now gathered around. He looked over his shoulder at me. "Let's go."

I raised an eyebrow at his tone, and Dominic actually laughed. Radic flushed pink but didn't backtrack, and I could appreciate that.

I waved at the passenger door. "Sit up front. You

can navigate." I paused as the tiny bundle in my arms moved. "But first, the medical office, if we could."

Radic's eyes dropped to my arms, his face softening. "Absolutely."

**7**

---

BONNIE

I stepped out of the shower and realized I had fifteen missed calls. Five from Radic, and another ten from Darius and his Pack. I'd barely shimmied into a dress when Darius came barreling into the house.

"Bonnie!"

I rushed from the bedroom and into the entrance foyer. "Darius, what's wrong?"

"There's been a challenge to the Alpha General's position!"

My gasp echoed around the foyer. "Who?"

Corvin, Darius's Alpha, came up behind his Omega. "A stranger. The brother of Naja from the Huxley-Grey Pack."

A stranger. What the hell?

With that, my phone rang again. Radic. I grabbed

my phone out of my dress pocket and answered it. "Rad! Are you okay?"

"I'm fine, Bon. It's all okay."

I let out a relieved whoosh of breath. "It's true though?"

He made an affirmative sound. "Mm, yes. I need a favor. Is the Wiley-Fletcher-Reid Pack there?"

Because everyone had insane hearing, Corvin answered. "Yeah, we came straight here, just in case it was a less peaceful challenge."

My heart felt too full of gratitude for this Pack who'd taken my crusade and made it their own. I gave Corvin a grateful look, as Radic made another relieved noise. "That's good, because Bonnie, I need a favor, but you don't have to do it. I don't want you to do anything that makes you feel uncomfortable."

I frowned. "What is it?"

"I need you to come down to the Doc's office. The, uh, challenger for Alpha General has some kids with him—mostly teenagers, but a couple of babies. Doc wanted to know if you could please come down and give him a hand."

I'd done a rudimentary nursing degree because Doc was the only medical treatment in the area, and I figured it pretty much went hand-in-hand with my role at the Sanctum. Besides, if I was going to be a spinster, at least I'd be an invaluable one.

"Is it safe?" I asked, though I knew better. Radic

would never endanger me, even if his life depended on it.

He said as much in his next breath. "You know I would never ask you to do this if I thought you'd come to any harm, Bonnie."

I rolled my eyes at myself because I did know that. "I'll be there in a minute. I'll see if Darius can stay with the kids." I turned to Darius and Corvin, raising my eyebrows hopefully, and they both nodded.

"Thanks, baby. I'll see you in a minute. Love you, Bon."

"You too. See you soon."

I hung up and gathered everything I thought I'd need. I grabbed two of the infant seats, just in case, and Corvin installed them in my van. I checked all the kids, who were still immersed in the cartoon I'd put on before having a shower.

Finally, Darius shooed me out the door. "I've got this, Bonnie. Take care of yourself."

Corvin met me at the driver's door. "We'll set ourselves up here for as long as you need. Call us if you need anything, Bonnie. Anything. We're all quite fond of you, and you're one of Darius's closest friends."

I gave him a quick hug. "Thanks. I honestly don't know what I did before you guys." I climbed into the driver's seat, giving Corvin a quick wave as he shut the door. My mind whirled as I made the drive down the dirt roads to town. I tried to wrack my brain for gossip about the new female Omega and her family. Naja had been pulled from obscurity in a town near the base of the mountains. She'd been on the run, and then someone had breached our wards and stolen her. Rumors about that had been rife in town for weeks now, about how the Convocation had stepped in and rescued her with the help of some long-lost brother. He'd come to the cubs' presentation but hadn't spoken to anyone.

But that was it. I knew nothing about him, and if I had to guess, neither did anyone else. I'd met Naja though, and she was lovely. Gatlin, the Alpha from the Huxley-Grey Pack, was the son of the current Alpha General, but was nothing like his father. He often donated stuff to the Sanctum, like cribs and highchairs that he'd built himself. Plus, their Omega and Beta always cooked Christmas dinner for the kids and dropped it off. They were good people.

There was no one on the streets in Maxton right now, and it was an odd sight. What the hell had happened to send people running back home like this? I pulled up to the front of the Doc's office and climbed out. No one was on the sidewalk, or waiting in line at the commissary. So weird.

I pushed the door open to the Doc's office, and seven men turned around. Holy shit. My feet stilled as my eyes automatically bounced to the Alpha in the room. I gasped and took a step back. His power was like a hand around your throat, where you were scared but a little excited all at once. His eyes were as black as pitch, and he had a few days of growth along his jaw, giving him a villainous look. He held my eyes like a snare, until Radic appeared between us. He wrapped me in his arms, and I hugged him back.

Pulling away, he gave me a meaningful look with his eyes. I think it was reassuring. "Bonnie, may I introduce you to the De Léon Pack. This is their Alpha, Courtland. His Beta, Dominic. Uh, the rest of these guys are their friends, I think."

I looked at the Beta, but my nose told me he wasn't Manix. Some kind of shifter though. I tilted my head, and he tilted his right back at me, his eyes laughing as much as the skull tattoo that wrapped around his throat. "Wolf, little Beta. I'm a wolf shifter."

I flushed bright red. "I'm Bonnie."

He grinned, and it made a dimple appear in one cheek. "I know, Radic just said so."

A low rumbling sound from Courtland had me whipping my eyes toward him and resisting the urge to submit. "You smell of Alpha. Are you mated?"

Woah, hold the fuck up. "Uh, I don't see how that's your business, Mister Tall, Dark and Scary as Fuck."

Radic looked at me like I'd lost my mind, but he didn't really understand that I'd been dealing with Alphas who saw me as a commodity for way too fucking long. But instead of getting angry, Courtland just laughed.

"You're right. Apologies, Bonnie."

The way he said my name was like foreplay, and I felt the heat rushing to my cheeks, and also somewhere significantly lower. Radic turned toward me, hiding his face from the other men in the room and raising an eyebrow at me. Yeah, he could scent my arousal, which meant they all could.

Fuck being a female sometimes.

I cleared my throat. "I, uh, better give Doc a hand. Excuse me."

I rushed into the treatment room, and straight into the back of another huge man. No, a huge Manix. I bounced off his back and he spun to grab me, wrapping his fingers around my upper arms. I looked up into deep blue eyes, and my heart thudded against my ribs. "Omega," I whispered softly, and his lips curled in a smile.

He was so fucking beautiful. "Beta," he said, in a voice that was nearly too soft.

"Well, if we are done with the introductions..." Doc said dryly from the other side of the room. I pulled away from the Omega—even though I really wanted to rub myself all over him—and stepped toward Doc.

I cleared my throat. trying to calm my racing heart. "You called for me, Doc?"

The old Manix gave me an amused look. "Yes." He

moved aside, and lying unwrapped on the examination bed were two of the tiniest babies I'd ever seen. One look at them told me they were woefully underweight. I glared at the Omega over my shoulder. Who could let their young get to this state?

Doc gave him a sympathetic look, and speared me with a more chastising expression. "Bonnie Flexland, I taught you better than to jump to conclusions."

"Sorry, Doc."

You see, that was the other reason I was almost considered ineligible, why I had always been on the outside looking in. I was a full-blooded Manix, but I'd been rejected by my parents from birth. They'd been teenagers, and freaked out about accidentally conceiving without a Pack. Later, they'd gone on to join a Pack and raise a whole family. They still lived in town, though we had little to do with each other. Doc had raised me. It was why I'd felt so passionately about the Sanctum.

But that stain, the drama of my birth? It had stayed with me forever. That rejection had colored my perceptions, colored other people's perceptions of me. I'd always been a factory reject, and the Alphas who had approached me to join their Pack had merely seen me as a vessel. A way to carry on their family genes, or a way to appease their Omegas. Never for me. Except if I came with Radic too.

I leaned down and looked at the babies. There was

definitely something wrong, but other than the lack of weight, there weren't any physical signs. They were not as active as you'd want babies to be either. I inhaled their scent and frowned.

"They are half-shifter? Why would that make them sick?" Naja, Courtland's sister was part tigress and she was fine.

Doc shrugged. "Pryce thinks it's their Beasts battling for control. They don't have the strength to withstand the toll that takes on the body."

I mean, philosophically that made sense. I'd never read any studies about this kind of thing though. I wasn't sure any had been done. "What's the treatment?"

Doc scratched his chin. "I'm not sure, but I think perhaps having an Alpha will help the Manix side of them to overcome the other beast. What was their mother, Pryce?"

The Omega looked so incredibly sad, it broke my heart. "She was a cougar shifter." His voice was rough and it was too much for me. I walked over, my body language gentle, and wrapped my arms around this big, sad Omega. My Beast howled to make him better, to soothe his pain and to help him heal. I wanted to wrap him in my arms and give him boob snuggles. Radic always said my boob snuggles could cure a broken arm, they were that healing.

He was stiff for a moment, his hands out from his

body like he didn't know what to do. Eventually, he wrapped his arms around my back and dipped his nose into my hair, inhaling deeply. I felt his body relax slightly.

When I was sure he was feeling better, I stepped away and gave him a soft smile. "I'm sorry for your loss."

He shook his head. "We barely knew each other; she was just a voice down the hall. These two were created in a lab."

I pulled back in shock. "What?"

**8**

---

DOMINIC

Courtland was still talking to the hot as fuck Beta, Radic, when I overheard the Omega about to spill all our secrets. I slipped into the examination room and touched his shoulder. "That's a story for another day, Omega," I said softly.

He was so fucking wounded, this Omega, and I didn't know what to triage first. His heart? His confidence? Driving up here, he'd been like a newborn or something. He'd never seen a cellphone before, never driven a car. Never had a gas station hot dog. His entire life had been pain and suffering behind bombproof glass, and I hated it.

"Sorry Dominic." His face fell, and the pretty Beta female, Bonnie, gave me a stern look. Mmm, I wondered if I could get her to spank me?

I stroked Pryce's back, easing him into the touch.

That was the other thing; he'd been so touch-starved that for Pack animals like the Manix, he may as well have been beaten. He didn't flinch away anymore, and I took that as a tiny victory. "Don't be sorry, Pryce. We just don't want to lay it all out so soon, do we?" I didn't really care if he told Bonnie. I wanted her in my bed sooner or later. Besides, with a secret like this, everyone would find out eventually.

What was it about this town? Every person I'd spoken to, with the exception of the Alpha General and the grizzled old doctor, had made me hard as a rock and made my wolf pant with need.

I looked over at the older Manix, my usual cocky smirk on my face. But when I took in the cubs, my smile fell. "What's the treatment?"

The doctor sighed. "I suggest having your Alpha spend as much time with them as he can, in both his shifted and unshifted form. Being surrounded by a Pack, or at least several Manix, should soothe that part of their nature. Being around other two-natured shifters such as yourself might help also. Are there many shifters in your group?"

I eyed him carefully. Was he fishing for intel or actually wanting to treat the babies? I took a punt that we could trust him. "Yes, most of us are. None are Alpha though."

He waved a hand, picking up what looked like an address book. "Doesn't matter. Spend as much time as you can with them in your shifted forms. I suggest your Alpha and the Omega be their primary carers. Actually…" He looked at Bonnie. "It would help if you were there too, Bonnie, because you can monitor their condition. If they struggle to feed, we will need to put in a gavage tube." He paused, looking at me and Pryce. "That's a feeding tube. Just until they are strong enough to feed on their own."

"Doc, I can't…" she began, then looked down at the babies. "What about the Sanctum?"

He raised a graying eyebrow. "Darius will look after them for the time being, and you know it. But don't do it if you feel uncomfortable, girl. I am not going to force you into anything." There was a hint of history there, and I desperately wanted to ask what. But I kept my mouth shut; there'd be enough time to delve into her history later.

She straightened her shoulders and set her jaw. "No, it's fine. Darius can look after the Sanctum. These little ones need me for now." She looked over at me and Pryce. "But Radic comes with me."

I grinned at her. "Sounds delightful."

Three hours since we first set foot into Maxton, we were on our way to what would be our temporary home. The Doc had given us—well, Bonnie —a box full of medical equipment and relayed a whole bunch of medical advice to her. She seemed to understand it all, so I was glad she was coming with us because it meant nothing to me. May as well have been a different language.

When we'd come out of the examination room, only Courtland had remained. He'd sent the crew and all the kids with Radic to our new digs. He looked between me and Pryce, but I noticed his eyes linger quickly on Bonnie. Oh, our enigmatic Alpha liked the pretty Beta too, hmm?

"Is everything okay?"

I shrugged, and Pryce sighed softly. "As well as we can hope."

The Doc nodded sagely. "I am going to call an old medical acquaintance, see if he has a better course of action. I was calling him to see if he could take a look at your sister's tests anyway, and maybe help us with our female Omega problem."

I frowned. "What, you're going to genetically engineer them?"

He gave me a look that no one in our former life would have dared give me. It was the *are you a fucking idiot?* look. I kind of found it refreshing. "Do I look like Doctor Frankenstein to you, son? I'm going to study how her genetics differ from those of someone who is generationally from this area. It's science, not science fiction."

Well, consider me schooled. Even Courtland

looked amused. The Doc cast one more look between Bonnie and the Alpha, like Courtland's presence made the good doctor less sure about sending this sweet little Beta off into a den of wolves. But she made his decision for him, climbing into the driver's seat of the mom van she drove. She'd managed to strap both babies into car seats while I'd been chatting to the Doc. Hell, I think she'd even strapped in Pryce.

"Bring them back in a week. Bonnie will keep a weight chart and if they haven't grown any, we will consider other options," Doc told me softly, then dropped his voice lower. "Hurt a hair on her head, I will kill you in your sleep and make it look like natural causes."

Now it was my turn to laugh. "I promise, we'll make sure she's well looked after during her stay."

The Doc turned on his heel, muttering under his breath, and I climbed into the back of the van. Courtland slid into the front, and I was surprised he didn't protest her driving. Court was a control freak, but apparently we really were on our best behaviour.

After a moment or two of silence, he finally said, "Tell us about yourself. What is the Sanctum?"

Bonnie was silent for a moment longer, like she was concentrating on driving, and then she sighed. "It's a home for the illegitimate, half-breed Manix children whose fathers wanted to knock up humans and not take any responsibility for their young." It was a snarl, and I felt my own lip curling. As the product of such a union, I felt that to my core.

Courtland tilted his head. "Your Alpha General doesn't make them take responsibility?"

She snorted but didn't answer. I guess that was answer enough.

But Courtland wasn't done. "Do you have a Pack? Maybe a mate?"

I knew she didn't; so did Courtland, because she didn't scent like she was mated. Sure, she smelled strongly of Radic, and earlier she'd scented of an Alpha, but I didn't think she was mated.

She cut her eyes to him, her cheeks that wonderful rosy shade of pink again. I wondered if I could fuck her until her cheeks went that pink? Both sets of cheeks. She was fucking gorgeous. Soft curves, perfectly sized breasts and those thighs. I wanted to take a bite. I grunted in the back, and Pryce looked over his shoulder at me. There was something heated in his eyes, and I assumed he was picking up my pheromones. I'd love to fuck his pretty pink lips too, have those baby blue eyes staring up at me while he was on his knees, but I had a feeling that was just one more thing he hadn't experienced.

I wasn't the right person for someone's first time. I was rough, and wild. I wasn't someone you waded gently into sex with. I was a plunge into dark, shark-infested waters.

Bonnie looked over at Courtland quickly. "Radic is my lover."

Courtland clicked his tongue, but if you were looking at his face and didn't know him? You'd think he had no interest in the girl at all. "I would be a fool not to know that. Your scents are so intertwined, it would be easy to mistake you as mates. But I don't think that's true."

She curled her lip. "Am I only valued and respected if I am some Alpha's property?"

A low rumble filled the car. "A good Alpha doesn't own his Pack like property. A good Alpha is *owned* by his Pack. I give each member of my Pack a piece of myself, until I am the Pack."

The rest of the ride was silent. We drove past small, average homes and giant mansions. This place managed to have everything, including a school. When we pulled up in front of a large two-story home, I let out a low whistle. I'd been expecting a dump, but this place was kinda nice. Made of stone and logs, it managed to melt into the horizon.

"Nice digs."

Bonnie looked over at me. "Used to be dorms for teen Manix, so there should be plenty of room for you guys and your friends." She paused, nodding at the equally big house next door. "That's the Sanctum. I'll be right back. I just have to grab some things."

Courtland nodded, and we both watched her skip

down through the large front yards. When she made it to the door, three big Alphas came out. She spoke to them too softly for me to hear, but all three of their heads snapped toward us. The low growl that emitted from Courtland's chest was more a feel than a sound, and I put my hand on his back.

"Easy, man. She never said she didn't have a Pack. What are the chances a girl that beautiful would be single?"

"Radic isn't part of their Pack. She said they were lovers."

I shook my head. "Means nothing, man. Don't start drama where we don't need it." Even as I tried to be the voice of reason, my wolf wanted to race down there and chew off the hand of the Alpha who was touching her.

"She makes me feel..." Pryce said softly, trailing off when he couldn't find the right words. Hell, maybe he didn't need more words, because I knew what he meant; she made me *feel* too.

And that? Well, that scared the hell out of me.

The last few days had been an overwhelming whirlwind of crazy. We'd driven for three days, only stopping every few hours to switch drivers. I'd seen things I'd never seen before, like mountain ranges with snowy tips. Alpacas. How had I become a nearly thirty-year-old man who had never seen an alpaca?

Because I'd been a chattel for nearly my whole life, much like an alpaca.

Everyone was very careful with me, trying to not overload me—Courtland and Dominic especially. With those two, I felt like I could be brave. Which was insane, because I'd known them less than a freaking week. But they'd been great with the babies, and great with me. I couldn't fault their actions. We'd stayed in Missoula for two days while Courtland came up with a plan to approach the leaders of this town. I didn't think this was the plan though.

Dominic showed me how to unlatch the baby seats so I could take the whole thing inside without pulling them out. They were sleeping, and their bodies needed as much of that as they could get, at least according to the doctor.

Courtland took one of the carriers and Dominic took the other, and they ushered me into the house. "Shouldn't we wait for Bonnie?" I asked quietly, because it felt almost sacrilegious to say her name. I wasn't sure why, but I felt like I needed to whisper it or something. It was insane, the things she made me feel. At least with these two, I'd had nearly a week to cultivate some kind of rapport with them.

But with Bonnie, it had been almost instantaneous. From the moment she ran into my back, and I'd wrapped my hands around her arms and felt her warmth against me, I'd wanted her fiercely. My Beast had wanted her just as bad.

Courtland touched my spine, and I made myself relax. My Manix enjoyed the contact from them, but the man? I'd spent my whole life being touched and tortured, and it would take me a while to not flinch every time someone laid a hand on me.

But not with Bonnie. She'd hugged me and it was like... I don't know. Like she was soothing my wounds from the inside out. I wanted to never let her go, but I also wanted to run away and hide.

"Bonnie knows where we are. She will come back when she's ready." Courtland seemed so sure, and I envied him the ability to walk into a room and know that everything would end the way he wanted it to. Like there was no uncertainty in his life.

I nodded, but took in his cool expression from the corner of my eye. This Alpha, he scared me as much as he made me feel safe. He was like a statue, unfeeling, but I kept remembering his burning eyes as he rescued me from the facility. The way he'd claimed me as his in the Legion offices. I didn't know where I stood and it was making my Beast angsty. He knew what he wanted, but I hadn't been around any others of my kind. Not really. What if this was how I would feel around all Manix Alphas?

Life was so confusing and strange and frustrating. All of it except her.

The inside of the house was loud already, the noises of men and teenagers bouncing off the walls like a cacophony of sound that hurt my ears. I was so used to silence. But I found I enjoyed the noise, I just had to adjust.

"Rosa?" Courtland yelled, and the spitfire teen—the one who had started everything back when she was a newborn—appeared. She smiled happily at me and cooed at the babies. She was another one who knew her place in the world, who could walk into a room and know that she was in control of it. It wasn't because she was Alpha though. Maybe it was just because Courtland was her role model.

"Hey guys, how did it go with the doctor?"

Courtland nodded. "We have a course of action."

She raised an eyebrow. "Well, that doesn't sound like a cure, but we'll take it. I'm just getting the kids settled and then Radic said he'll get dinner sent up for us until we can get some groceries."

The front door opened and closed again, and I looked over Rosa's shoulder. Bonnie was there, holding two canvas backpacks.

"What are you guys staring..." Rosa looked over her shoulder and then back at us, her grin so huge it could only mean trouble. "Oh, I see. Is this your 'course of action?'" she teased Courtland, laughing and dancing away as Dominic swiped at her. She bounded up to Bonnie, wrapping her in her arms. "Hi, I'm Rosa. Are you my new mommy?"

Courtland growled, which just made Rosa laugh harder. The sounds of a teenage brawl deeper in the house caught her attention.

"Winston! I swear to god if you are hitting Luca again, I'm going to kick your ass," she bellowed, sprinting back into the bowels of the house. Bonnie just stood there, looking slightly mussed, as if she'd just walked through a natural disaster event.

Dominic laughed. "That's Rosa, she's our ward. Well, one of them."

Courtland nodded, his lips twitching in what was almost a smile. "Also, Naja's sibling. It is… complicated."

Yeah, that was an understatement. Our whole group was complicated.

Bonnie just shook her head dazedly, then shrugged, walking further into the house. She looked between Courtland and me. "Take your shirts off."

Courtland blinked. "Excuse me?"

She raised a single brow. "Shirt. Off. Please?"

Dominic had started to chuckle, but I could see him tamping it down. "You heard the lady. Get naked."

She cut him a glare. "I didn't say get naked. I said to take their shirts off." She held up a contraption that I had originally thought was a backpack but was actually some kind of harness thing.

"Baby carriers. There's a method of holding a baby, usually preterm babies but I think it will work for these two, where they are pressed to your chest for long periods of time. It helps with heart rate and breathing regulation, as well as bonding. I think this will help with Doc's suggestion. Now, shirts off. You"— she pointed to Dominic—"help me take the babies' clothes off, except their diapers. It has to be skin-to-skin."

As Dominic hopped to it, I looked at Courtland. He

was appraising me with his dark eyes. "Only if you are comfortable. I am sure someone else could soothe them this way if Bonnie says it's needed. Dominic or Radic, maybe?"

Bonnie was looking between us, her brow scrunched as she tried to work out what was wrong in this situation. Honestly, I didn't know what was wrong. It was just a body, and the babies were mine. These people had probably seen hundreds of half-naked torsos in their lives.

I was being stupid.

I peeled off my sweater and then my shirt, but the whole time I was watching Courtland undress. He did it slowly, methodically, and it was oddly mesmerizing. First, his tailored jacket was folded over the back of a chair. Then his long, strong fingers unbuttoned the vest of his three-piece suit. It was beautiful, hugging his body like a second skin, showcasing his wide shoulders and his slim waist. Once that was unbuttoned, it was placed on top of his jacket. Cufflinks next, his biceps flexing. Then those fingers went to work on the buttons of his shirt. Slowly, methodically working his way down, revealing warm flesh with every button freed until he reached the button of his pants.

Was this foreplay? Because it felt like foreplay. My eyes flicked up, and they snagged on his own. The darkness that was usually so cool suddenly seemed molten, and my breath shuddered in my chest. My whole body felt hot and tingly, and I made a low noise in my throat that made everyone's eyes snap to me. Even Bonnie looked at me with something that looked like lust, before she shook her head.

I flushed bright red when Radic appeared from somewhere in the house, taking in the scene. Bonnie dragged her eyes to him, and then realized how it looked, flushing as pink as me. "We're trying Kangaroo Care to improve their vitals," she squeaked out, and Radic's eyes swept between us. He cleared his throat, walking closer to Bonnie, but I could see the hard bulge in his pants, smell the arousal coming from Bonnie. Fuck, all this because I made a noise?

"It was the sound of need, Omega," Courtland said matter-of-factly. "We are made to appease all your needs, biologically speaking."

Dominic grunted. "Speak for yourself. I'm hard as a rock and it has nothing to do with Manix biology, and everything to do with the giant cock he's packing in those chinos." Courtland frowned at his Beta wolf, and I flushed a little more.

Bonnie cleared her throat. "Well, nothing kills the mood like crotch goblins. Come here, Pryce." I walked toward her quickly, and took the harness she was holding out. "It clips on the side around your waist. Put one of the straps over your shoulder."

I clipped it up, following her instructions like a good little Omega. She scooped up One, and held her to my chest. I placed my hands on her back instinctively, clutching her close to my chest. She was so fucking small. Two months old and still the size of a newborn. Bonnie arranged her on my chest, her legs frogged up, her face to the side, and the baby let out a small shuddering breath that sounded like a relieved sigh. Bonnie hooked the other strap over my shoulder. As her fingers worked the back clip, I shuddered. But it wasn't in disgust. No, I wanted to feel those fingers running over other parts of my body.

Did I imagine that she just ran her fingers down my spine because she wanted to?

She cleared her throat, stepping back in front of me. "They have a special insert in there to make sure they don't accidentally fall out the side. We don't often get babies this small at the Sanctum, but the other families around here donate stuff we might need." She stepped over to Courtland, and hesitated. He took the carrier from her hands and put it on like he'd done it every day of his life. When she passed him Two, he held my son to his chest like he'd protect him forever. I swallowed the lump in my throat. I'd always tried hard not to think of the offspring as mine. But they were. They were my children, and the sight of the giant Alpha, holding an infant that wasn't even as big as one of his pecs, was making my Omega go crazy.

He watched Bonnie as she arranged the baby, like a predator waiting for prey to climb happily into his jaws. I would go willingly, if I was honest with myself. It didn't even look like Bonnie was breathing, as she quickly buckled the baby in. It might have been my imagination, but Two seemed to have more color to his cheeks already.

Bonnie stepped away, and her chest was heaving. I could smell her juices in the air, which was making my dick painfully hard.

A loud bang had us all jumping, and I realized Radic had clapped really loudly. "Why don't I show you guys to your rooms?"

Dominic gave him a wolfish grin that promised pleasure like he'd never felt before, if only he'd come into his den. "I think that's an amazing idea, Beta. Lead the way."

This whole day had felt like a fever dream. From the moment a rogue Alpha walked into the office, to my sacking, right up until I walked into the room to see my girlfriend surrounded by half-naked men, causing me to feel *aroused*. Not jealous, angry, threatened, or you know, any of those normal possessive traits that were probably toxic but I normally just couldn't help. Like the idea of her half-naked with the Fletcher-Wiley-Reid Pack? That sent me into a full rage.

Yet the fact that she just ran her fingers across this completely unknown Alpha's back? It just made me unbelievably hard.

Clearing my throat, I ushered everyone toward the stairs, before stepping forward and grabbing Bonnie's hand. She was taking the whole thing well, which I knew she would because Bonnie was tough as hell, despite her gooey insides. But if she was anything like me, the pheromones these guys were throwing off would have her floundering.

She gripped my fingers tightly, and I knew I was right. I searched her scent for fear or worry, but all I got back? Heat. Fuck, she smelled like that one time we'd trapped ourselves in her apartment for six days and fucked until we couldn't fuck anymore. Lust to the extreme.

I cleared my throat again, giving my best tour of the house. Courtland's Pack had already settled in, and if I didn't already spend so much time at the Sanctum, I might have found their loud boisterousness off-putting. But they were regular kids, albeit ones who didn't flinch at all at the semi-automatics held by all of Courtland's soldiers.

There were twelve of those in all, though the third-in-command, Antonio, said not all of them would stay. Once they were happy with Prince's security, they would leave. When I'd asked who the Prince was, they'd laughed. Loren—who smelled of witch—had said Courtland was referred to as the Prince, and they were his Court. An obvious play on names, but Courtland had never introduced himself that way. I decided to do some research when I was back at my apartment tonight.

We stopped at a light-filled room. "We should make

this one the nursery. It'll get good warmth in the morning, plenty of sunshine, and I can put my bed over there," Bonnie said firmly, and my eyes whipped to hers.

"Your what?"

Pryce, the softly spoken Omega whose need had made my own flare to life earlier, answered. "The doctor wants Bonnie to stay and monitor the babies. He seems to trust her."

I didn't take my eyes off her, and she looked back at me defiantly. Loving an independent woman was hard sometimes. "He should trust her. He raised her." Fucking hell, Doc. When he'd asked for her assistance, I didn't think he'd be setting her up as a live-in nurse.

My whole body tensed, and Courtland sighed. "We should get all this out in the open, yes?"

How he seemed just as authoritative half-naked with a baby strapped to his chest as he did pinning the Alpha General down in a three-piece suit was beyond me, but he did.

Dominic grinned, rocking back on his heels. "Oh, this should be good."

Courtland gave him a droll look. "I think we are all aware of the simmering sexual tension between us, no?"

I watched all their faces—Dominic's grin, Pryce's confused nod, and Bonnie's tense shoulders. I held her tightly to my side, but said, "Yes."

Courtland paused, his eyes lingering on Bonnie. "Yes," she whispered.

I heard the happy hum that emitted from Courtland's chest. "I expected as much. Pryce, may I tell them?"

Tell us what? Shit, this was all so confusing.

Pryce nodded, and Courtland continued. "My men and I rescued Pryce, as well as several other captives, from a government research facility a week ago."

Bonnie gasped. "But where are the others?"

Dominic shrugged. "Some had family, some we dropped off at places on the way here with enough cash to get them started."

"Pryce had lived in that facility for fifteen years."

"Sixteen," the Omega corrected.

I stared at Pryce. Holy fucking shit. How? "I'm so sorry," I said softly, and he smiled. It was a brittle smile, like he didn't know how to react. I didn't know how to react either.

"So things are confusing for him right now. He had limited contact with other people—let alone other Manix—in there. Some experiences are overwhelming, and I would request that we take things slow with him. We can introduce him to other people at a moderated pace, so he can ascertain his feelings."

I blinked. "Are you giving us the birds and the bees talk right now?"

"No. I was letting you know that despite my assertions about him being Pack, Pryce is free to make his own choices. And while I hope he chooses to stay with us, I am not about to rush him."

His eyes caught mine as he moved closer, and I felt myself unconsciously back up while still leaning toward him. He was all predator in that moment, and I wanted him to fuck me so bad that my dick was throbbing.

"But you"—his eyes slid to Bonnie—"both of you, I want to fuck until you are begging me for more, pledging yourself to me on your knees because I make you come so good. Because I can take care of you, protect you, and make you orgasm every day." He stepped closer until I was backed up against the wall, and Bonnie dropped my hand as she pressed her palms against her own thundering heart. "And all you have to do is say you'll be mine."

He put a hand on my chest and slid it up toward the column of my throat. He leaned down so his lips were barely an inch from mine, and squeezed my throat gently. "Think about it," he breathed, and then he was moving away, taking his towering presence with him. I stared as he drifted toward Bonnie, and I saw her knees go weak, but he was there, catching her with strong arms. "And you? Will you think about it?"

She looked up at him with eyes too big in her face. "Yes," she squeaked out, and he gave her a smile that made me moan. He tilted her chin up, leaning in to kiss her softly, dragging her bottom lip between his teeth.

"Mmm. That's my good girl."

She sucked in air like she'd run a marathon, and the smell of her arousal blanketed the room. Holy shit.

I looked at Pryce who was staring at us all like we were aliens. "Was that foreplay?" he whispered to Dominic, who just laughed.

"That was definitely foreplay, or else my dick is broken."

As one, we all looked down at the impressive bulge in his tactical pants. Hell, even Dominic looked at his own dick. Courtland laughed, and we all joined in, breaking the tense moment.

As if to remind us what the fuck we were doing, one of the babies let out a weak cry. Fuck. How did I forget that the man trying to seduce me was holding a damn infant?

My face flushed red, and I stepped toward the door like I was going to run away. And maybe that was a good idea, because the longer I was in the presence of these men, the harder it was to remember that I barely knew them, and that I was in a committed relationship with my best friend, and that they were fucking strangers trying to take over the town.

"We should continue with the tour. I'll get someone

to bring over some cribs from the Sanctum." My voice sounded raspy and unused. I hadn't felt this nervous since I was a teen trying to work up the courage to climb into Bonnie's bed.

Courtland gave a rumbling noise from his chest again, thrumming, and waved a hand. "Lead on, Beta."

Bonnie had said I should get used to having an infant attached to my chest like a limpet. I think perhaps the Beta female just liked seeing me without a shirt. But I'd held the first baby for several hours, and then Bonnie had put them both down to sleep. When they'd awoken, they'd fed slightly, and I'd had the other one placed in this carrier that I was somehow going to have to incorporate into my suit. I wondered if I could find a tailor in this town who would just create me a three-piece suit with an infant pouch built in.

"Not going to lie, Prince, but having a baby holster attached to your chest really messes with your commanding image," Loren joked, but before he could finish his sentence, I had my gun out and pointed between his eyes.

He raised his eyebrows, holding up his hands. "Listen, I know you're still scary as fuck. Pretty sure you could decimate half this town with six babies strapped to your chest. It just makes you look softer. Happier, maybe? It's not a bad thing."

I dropped my gun. To be honest, what I really wanted was to flop back on the couch and have a nap right along with the baby on my chest.

Loren and Antonio had been with me the longest of any of the Prince's Court. Almost as long as Dominic, but not quite. We both knew I wouldn't shoot him for being mouthy, or he would have been dead a hundred times over by now.

I huffed out a breath. "Will you stay or go?"

Loren shrugged and ran a hand over the soft tuft of baby hair that was exposed. "Depends a lot on how the town receives you as their new Alpha General. You might have need of my services for a while yet, hey?"

I gave him an intense stare. It was the type I usually reserved for people I wanted to intimidate, but I wanted him to know how serious I was in making my next offer. "You could stay here. You're always welcome at my side."

Loren laughed. "Nah, thanks though. You're pretty and all, but I'm not about to let you fuck me to join your Pack."

I frowned. "That's not what I meant. Besides, you don't have to be a lover to join a Pack."

He continued to shake his head. "I'm not here for the Pack life, Court. You know that. Maybe I'll head out on my own, find myself a pretty girl who looks at me with those big eyes the way Bonnie the Beta looks at you." He fluttered his eyelashes, and I bared my teeth at him, but I could still hear the regret in his tone. I didn't want Loren to leave, and neither did Dominic. We were friends. Brothers, even more so than the rest of my men except Antonio.

I inclined my head as his words sunk in. I didn't say that I'd miss him, even though I would. I'd miss all of them, but we would all get over the severing of our ties eventually. "And the others?"

"Alvaro is talking about starting a Pack, and the other shifters seem happy with the idea. Taking some of that money we saved and never used, maybe buying a huge parcel of land. They asked Dominic to go with them, lead them maybe, but he won't."

No, he wouldn't. Despite the fact that we weren't the same species, Dominic and I were bonded by blood and pain. There was no severing that connection.

"And Antonio?"

Loren picked at his nails. "He has his own demons to chase in the good old US of A, apparently."

None of them would stay, and in a way, I had expected it. They wouldn't be happy here, sitting on their asses in some idyllic little town filled with Manix.

I'd thought perhaps Loren, but I guessed wrong. As long as they didn't all go together, raising hell across the continent, I was happy. But I guess they wouldn't be my responsibility anymore either.

"What are you going to do about the challenge? We both know you could take that old fuck in a fight easily, but he doesnt seem like the kind to just follow the rules and lie down, you know?"

Yeah, I knew his type too well. "A leader is only a leader while people are following him. They can follow him through fear or love, and given the looks on the faces of some of those soldiers this morning? He isn't a beloved ruler." I paused as the plan continued to work itself through my brain. "So, I will win the position and then get them to love me."

Loren burst out laughing, and I raised a brow. "Sorry, but if our enemies could see you now. Planning to rule people with love. No offense, because I love the hell out of you man, but that has never been in your arsenal of tricks."

As if on cue, there was a heavy knock at the door. "I'll get it," another of my men yelled from somewhere else in the house.

I smiled at Loren. "Ah, but I have a secret weapon." I was moving toward the front door, Loren on my heels, when I saw the tiny powerhouse that was my half-sister.

"Courtland! What the hell?!" Naja shouted, and this time I let myself grin.

Behind her were both of her Alphas, and they eyed me coolly. I'd done my research before I arrived, of course. Gatlin, Naja's primary Alpha, was the bastard son of the current Alpha General. But from all accounts, and what I'd seen in the weeks after her rescue, there was no love lost between father and son. Finlo was from an old and respected family, but he'd stuck his middle finger up at the authorities and created a Pack with Gatlin.

"Surprise?" I said drolly, and they all looked at me with incredulity.

Naja just gaped. "You better start from the beginning, because none of this shit makes sense. Like, why is there a fucking baby strapped to your chest? And can I please hold it, though you'd think after having a whole litter at home that I wouldn't have baby fever anymore but fuck me, it's like it's sent me into overdrive."

One corner of my lip tipped up as I reached back and unclipped the harness. I was a quick study and had managed to work out how to get this thing on and off without Bonnie's help, not that I'd tell her that. I quite liked her touching me with soft fingers.

I handed over the baby, which really needed a name. I was trying to respect Pryce's wishes, but a baby needed a name, and I refused to let these two live anything but long and happy lives.

Naja cooed, cradling the still bare baby to her chest. She looked up at Finlo. "Give me your sweater so this little angel isn't cold." To his credit, he peeled off his sweater and wrapped it around the young immediately. They were good mates for her. If I didn't think that was the truth, I would have torn her away from them in a heartbeat. But they loved her and treated her like the queen she was, so I was happy enough with her choices.

"What's his name?"

I shrugged. "It's complicated."

"That's an awfully long name for a baby this small, Courtland," she said drily, and I couldn't help my smile. Yes, she was definitely related to me. "Why doesn't the baby have a name?"

"Not my place to name it."

"Whose place is it then?"

A throat cleared behind me. "Mine." I looked over my shoulder at Pryce, whose cheeks were pink but he was standing tall.

Gatlin frowned, and looked between us both before bowing his head reverently. "Omega." Finlo did the same. Good, Pryce deserved all that reverence and more. Behind him was Bonnie, and she smiled at the two big Alphas.

"Hi Gat, hey Finlo." She stepped closer to my sister. "Hi, we haven't met yet because these guys have been keeping you trapped up in the mountains. I'm Bonnie. I run the Sanctum next door."

Naja smiled pleasantly at her, before suddenly frowning. "The Sanctum? Like the place they put Ellar and you when you arrived in Maxton, Gatlin? The place where they used to kick the shit out of Ellar?" My sister's eyes flashed back toward Bonnie, who held up her hands.

"Hey, way before my time. I don't stand for that shit anymore." She cast an imploring look at Gatlin and Finlo. "Tell her."

Finlo laughed, reaching out to grab Bonnie in a side hug. "Nah, Bonnie is one of the good ones."

I was growling before I even realized, and both of Naja's Alphas pushed in front of Bonnie and Naja. That made my Beast even madder. I tried to push it down, but the sight of another Alpha with his hands on *my* Beta, even if I hadn't claimed her yet, had sent my Beast out of control.

Apparently, Bonnie got the idea though, because she stepped around Finlo's back and in front of me. Gripping my chin, she dragged my face down to hers. I thought she might whisper something reassuring, but I was sorely disappointed. "Cut it the fuck out."

Loren snorted from beside me, and I cut my eyes

toward him to see that he had his hand on his gun but hadn't drawn it.

Bonnie gave me a furious look. "We'll talk about this later. I have no interest in any Alpha, least of all these two. I once saw Finlo drink so much moonshine, he vomited and shit his pants simultaneously. You can't come back from that."

Naja laughed, and Finlo gave Bonnie a betrayed look. "You swore that you wouldn't tell a soul."

Bonnie just raised an eyebrow. "That was before you got all he-man up in here."

I looked between the Alphas and Bonnie. "Mine," I growled.

Gatlin, whose power may have rivaled mine, looked at me impassively. "Bonnie belongs to herself. When she says she's yours, then I'll respect it. You don't just take what you want—that isn't how it works in Maxton."

Naja began to giggle, then her giggle turned into a full-blown belly laugh. "Says the man who stole me from a stripclub in nothing but a thong?" My sister looked up at me, the mirth leaving her face as she gave me a dead-eyed stare so like my own. "You force her into anything, I will castrate you and wear your balls as earrings, got it?"

I swallowed down a laugh and nodded. "You have my word."

Gatlin stared at me a little more, and I met his eyes,

refusing to look away. If we battled for dominance, it would be a close thing. Finally, he nodded his head.

"Okay, let's see if we can't help you wrestle leadership of the Manix from that crusty old fuckbag."

Well. Okay then.

---



While Gatlin kept Courtland busy talking logistics and gunpowder plots, I snuck away to find Radic. Every part of me tingled from Courtland's Beast trying to claim me in front of Gat and Fin, and I needed to shake it off.

Fucking Alphas. They confused everything. I needed to find Rad and figure out what was going on—between us, in the town, I don't know. I was so damn confused. But mostly, I was horny and I needed relief, before the lustful wench inside me took over completely and I no longer had any control.

I saw him sitting in the office on his laptop, probably wrangling the town from his position of Beta. He'd always been so underappreciated. It wasn't the Alpha General, or even most of the Legion Generals, who kept things afloat in town. It was Radic, from his pokey little office, making sure people were fed, things were done, and that our people got what they needed to survive.

I stepped into the office and shut the door. Radic looked up, his eyes widening a little. I must have looked like a hot mess, but I didn't care. He was out of his chair and around the desk in a split second, and I was dragged against a hard chest.

I lurched for his lips and we slammed together, his hands clutching at my ass as his tongue tangled with mine. I wrapped my arms around his neck because my knees felt weak. I was so fucking ready; I'd been walking around in a constant state of arousal since Courtland and Pryce had taken off their shirts in the foyer.

We had so much to talk about, but the words had escaped me at that moment. When he picked me up and deposited me on the desk, all thoughts were gone. He dragged my blouse up over my head, and lifted my breasts from my bra. My nipples were achingly hard as he wrapped his lips around one nipple and sucked hard, making me arch closer to his face.

"Radic," I breathed, and he hummed, sending a thrill of pleasure right down to my clit. "Please."

He pulled me off the desk, undressing me quickly, then lifted me back onto it, his body positioned between my thighs. Pushing me back onto my elbows, he dropped to his knees, dragging my ass to the very edge of the desk. Wedging his shoulders between my knees, he dived into my pussy, sucking my clit until I was bucking against his face. God, I was so close already.

A throat cleared near the doorway, and I sat up, snapping my thighs around Radic's head, making him grunt. Ah shit.

"Sorry," I murmured, before looking around his head at Dominic standing in the doorway. He was clutching his dick, which seemed rock hard behind his zipper.

"Is this a private meeting?"

I looked down at Radic, who was still on his knees between my thighs. His eyes were red-hot with lust, but he mouthed, "Up to you."

I looked at the heavily tattooed shifter who was still lingering in the doorway. He hadn't stepped any closer, wasn't trying to force his desires onto us. And he was hot as fuck. "Take your shirt off," I murmured, and the grin he gave me made me impossibly wetter. Radic groaned, leaning forward again to lap at my pussy eagerly, and I threw back my head. Fuck.

There was something to be said for stumbling into bed with your best friend. The man knew how to get me off in ways that I couldn't even imagine. He knew my pleasure as well as I did.

I forced my eyes back open so I could watch Dominic peel off his shirt. Holy shit, tattoos ran all over his body, right up his throat to the sharp line of his jaw. I wanted to study every inch of him with my fingers, my lips, and my tongue.

He swaggered over, unbuttoning his pants and pulling out his cock. He stroked it firmly as he watched Radic drive me closer to the edge. Knowing we had an audience drove Radic a little crazy too, because he upped his game. He licked and sucked my clit like he was possessed by a sex god, and physics no longer applied.

I panted hard, my head thrown back as my legs shook. "Radic, oh god…" I panted as I came all over his cheeks, my thighs pressed tight to the sides of his head. I met Dominic's eyes as he stroked himself, my eyes falling to his fingers wrapped around the throbbing head of his dick. His dick was girthy, and if I closed my eyes, I could already feel the stretch of the head pushing inside me.

"Can I taste?" he murmured softly, and I nodded, probably a little too eagerly. Radic moved from between my knees and stood, a little off balance. Shit, I hoped I hadn't done too much damage when I'd thigh-slammed him.

Dominic stepped toward him, and instead of coming closer to me, he grabbed Radic's jaw and kissed him. It was a hard kiss, like he was plundering his mouth for the slightest taste of me. Radic's hands moved to grip his hips, and the sight of his pale, smooth skin against the angry dark tattoos of Dominic's hips did something for me. I was going to come again just watching them kiss.

Finally, Dominic dragged himself away, breathing just as heavily as Radic. "Damn, I want to fuck the hell out of you right now, but Courtland would have my balls," he croaked out, his voice rough.

He sauntered toward me, falling to his knees gracefully. I didn't know what it was about this man, this shifter, that made me so fucking hot. It might be the tattoos, or the smirk, or maybe even the fact that he didn't have a shirt on but still had a knife strapped to his chest in a soft black holster.

He was dangerous, and it oozed from his pores. Not because he'd just take what he wanted—he'd proven he wasn't about that, by asking permission twice now. No, he had that air of unpredictable violence that would scare me if I was his enemy. It was hard to think of him that way right now, as he looked up at me with molten chocolate-colored eyes from between my knees.

He didn't break eye contact as he licked the remnants of my release from one thigh, and then the other one, his straight brown hair falling over his forehead. I forgot to suck in oxygen as I felt the puff of his breath against my damp lips. He inhaled deeply, and a low rumbling in his chest echoed around the room.

"Why do you smell of home, pretty Beta?" he whispered softly, then he ran the flat of his tongue from my entrance to my clit.

Oh shit. I hadn't expected to come again. Thought I'd be too sensitive, but the wild pleasure shooting through my body was proving me wrong. He pulled away, and then dragged me to the floor. "I don't think it's fair that you get to come twice, and our hard-working friend here just has to watch, do you?" I shook my head, and he grinned. "Mmm, that's my good girl."

Well. Fucking set me on fire, because those words burned me up. He just grinned at me as if he knew his effect, which he probably did.

"Grab the chair, Radic." Rad grabbed the office chair and rolled it over. "Now take off your pants and sit down. Your girl is going to take care of you."

I sat on my knees, my butt resting on my heels, and looked over my shoulder at him. He was smiling, but it wasn't lustful at that moment.

"Look at you. It's like you were made for him, and you don't even know it." He shook his head, and then reached out to stroke Radic's cock. I moaned, a long, embarrassingly high-pitched sound.

Dominic laughed. "Oh, you like to watch that, beautiful Bonnie?" He sat up on his knees and moved fluidly toward Radic, pushing his knees apart as far as possible. Then he wrapped impossibly perfect lips around Radic's cock and sucked him down deep.

I wasn't sure which of us moaned loudest, and

there was no way a whole house of Manix hadn't heard it. Dominic pulled away, his face full of mischief as he looked up into Radic's slack face.

"Eat many popsicles growing up?" Rad asked in a strangled voice, probably trying to cut the tension.

Dominic shook his head. "Nah, but I did suck a lot of dick." A laugh burst out of me, and Dominic grinned over his shoulder. "Come over here and show me how good that pretty mouth looks around his cock." Yep, there went the mirth, rapidly replaced by raging lust.

I crawled over to Radic on my hands and knees, who was looking between me and Dominic as if he'd just won the lottery. I uncurled my body as I rested my hands on Radic's strong thighs. He'd unbuttoned his shirt, and I took in the hard planes of his chest and abs. He was frowning down at me, probably trying to read if I was into this or not.

Holy shit, I was into it.

I grinned, and then slid him in my mouth, suctioning my cheeks. He threw back his head and moaned, wrapping his fingers in my hair as he bucked up into my mouth slightly. He might know what I liked, but that went both ways, and Radic? He liked it a little rough.

Uncovering my teeth a little, I let them scrape back up his cock. "Oh, fuck," he breathed, gripping my hair a little tighter.

Done with watching, Dominic spread my knees a little and lay on his back, until I was balanced precariously over his face. "Fuck, I love these thighs," he groaned, lifting himself up slightly on his elbows so he could bite the fleshy part of my inner thigh. "Now ride my face like I'm a mechanical bull, baby."

A sane woman didn't say no to that. I didn't have your normal chubby girl hang-ups anymore, even though they'd added another facet to my teenage angst. I wasn't worried about my weight, or the fact he might suffocate on my thick thighs.

I looked down between my body and Rad's, at Dominic's head peeking happily out of my thighs. He'd probably like to die that way, in fact.

Rad tugged gently on my hair again, as if drawing my attention back to his straining dick. I gave him an apologetic look as I slid back down his length, moaning as I came back up because apparently, Dominic had decided it was time to go back to work too.

His tongue swirled, and I moved faster up and down Rad's cock, until I was bouncing on Dominic's face. Dominic moved up to suck my clit, and thrust his fingers inside me fast and hard, curling them to get all the good spots while driving me crazy.

My movements got messy and haphazard, but that didn't matter because Radic was losing it too. He gripped my head in both hands, thrusting up until I gagged around his cock and he came down my throat in hot bursts.

"Fuck, Bonnie," he moaned, slumping back in the office chair.

Dominic took that as permission to drag me away and pull me tighter to his face, and I did what I'd been asked. I rode his face as his tongue stroked and thrust, until I was coming all over again, my nails digging into Radic's thighs, leaving pink crescent marks on his skin.

I lifted myself off his face, but Dominic didn't let me roll away. Instead, he just moved me down his body until I was straddling his lower abs. He rolled us both to the side, burying his face between my breasts.

"Fuck, your body is glorious," he said with a happy sigh. He pressed my boobs together around his cheeks, and blew a raspberry between them. "Honestly, who invented tits? I want to shake that man's hand. They are everything good in the world." He moved his head to the left, biting my breast and making me gasp. I realized he was giving me a damn hickey on my boob. When he was done, he looked up at me and grinned. "So you don't forget me."

He rolled onto his back and then sat up. I blinked at him, looking between him and Radic, as if I was supposed to know what happened next. I felt a little bit exposed at that moment. Well, obviously a lot exposed, because I was lying on the office carpet naked. But vulnerable, maybe?

"Is that it, then? Just this once?" I kept my voice even, like I didn't give a shit, which I probably shouldn't. I didn't know this guy from a hole in the ground.

But Dominic laughed loudly. "Oh, no, baby. You don't get rid of me that easily." He leaned over me, sliding his hand down over my hip and around to cup my pussy. "I intend to fuck this over and over until you can barely remember your name." He kissed me softly, and he tasted like my release. When he pulled away, he looked up at Radic, and that mischief was back in his eyes. "You too." Heaving a sigh, he sat up. "It's just that I'm about to get my ass kicked in five... four... three... two..." He pointed at the door just as it slammed open, and I rolled onto my front quickly.

A furious looking Courtland was standing there, a slightly confused—and, judging by the tent in his pants, really aroused—Pryce behind him.

Courtland pointed at Dominic. "Out. Now."

His voice was more Beast than man, making goosebumps tingle all over my skin. Dominic just grinned, ran his hand over my ass one more time, and then strutted out of there, shirtless and with his dick out.

Once he'd left the office, Courtland's heated gaze seared me as his eyes took in every inch of my body and then Radic's. He turned on his heel, shutting the door softly behind him. I slumped onto the carpet, my jello muscles not able to hold me up anymore.

"Hey Bon?" Radic murmured, and I turned my head toward him.

"Mmm?"

"I don't think we are in Kansas anymore."

I shook my head. We weren't in Kansas, or Maxton, or anywhere that the normal rules applied. We'd taken a strong left turn down the rabbit hole, ended up at the bottom of Mary Poppins' carpet bag, and I wasn't sure I wanted to find my way out.

---

## 13

DOMINIC

I snagged my shirt on the way out of the room, trying to keep my pleasure to myself. But it was hard when I still smelled of Bonnie. I could feel the thunderous anger of Courtland behind me, and I was prepped for a fight. Not that I thought it would really come to that. Courtland was mad at me, but I didn't think it was anger so much as jealousy.

When I went to turn left to my designated bedroom, Courtland's growl stilled my feet. Well, maybe he was a little angry too.

"Outside, Beta."

Oops. Looks like we were going to settle this the old-fashioned way. I swaggered outside like I hadn't done anything wrong—which I maintained I hadn't. Just because Court had wanted the Beta pair, didn't mean they were his property.

I'd asked. They'd agreed. It was all above board. Kinda.

Once we were out beneath the pink rays of the setting sun, Court pointed a long finger at me. "Shift."

I gave him the finger back. "No, asshole. I am not fighting with you about this."

He wasn't listening though. I didn't worry about an audience, because the men knew better than to watch while we fought. Courtland could switch his anger to one of them on a dime, and no one was willing to take that chance for the sake of some useless gossip.

He just looked at me coolly. "Do you know what it was like, to sit in a strategy meeting about over-throwing a fucking governing body, while I could hear the sweet little moans of the Beta from the floor above? Or the pure fuck-me pheromones they were both sending down those stairs? I found Pryce stroking himself outside the door of the office." He pulled back his lips and snarled. "Other people heard you having sex with both of my Betas before I had even tasted them. Do you know how offensive that is?"

I snorted. Yeah, I knew I was right. He was jealous. "One, I asked and they enthusiastically consented. You aren't the Little Prince anymore, Courtland. You don't get to take what you want and then leave the leftovers for everyone else."

He was in front of me in a second, his hand around my throat. I resisted the urge to purr, because we needed to have this conversation, and I didn't mean the one about my blue balls. "You knew I wanted them."

I shook my head, but didn't pull out of his grip. "You aren't hearing me. You aren't the Prince in his fucking court now. You are a man, an Alpha, choosing his Pack." He shook his head, but I pushed closer so he couldn't deny it to himself. "You are. And I always thought that when you decided to settle down, there'd be a place for me. That I would be your Beta."

His hand slid from my throat. "There is. You are."

I stepped away, shaking my head. "No, I don't think I am. Because this was enough for me while we had a role to play, Court. When you had to be the stone-cold killer without attachments, and I had to be your crazy fucking sidekick. But we aren't running drugs in a conservative country anymore. We are in Maxton, motherfucking Montana. I'm no longer just your faithful hound. And if that's how you'll always see me, rather than someone in your Pack, then I can't stay."

I turned away, walking back toward the house. I built up my walls, because I'd said my piece, but I didn't know how Courtland would react. He wasn't an easy man to read, even for a shifter.

"Stop!"

My feet slowed, and I desperately wanted to stop, to do what he said, but I pushed past the urge. I opened the door and stepped through, closing it softly behind me. I didn't realize I was breathing hard until I was on the stairs. I was happy that there wasn't anyone on my way up the stairs, so I didn't have to put on my jovial face and pretend like I wasn't hurting a little that there were no footsteps coming up the stairs behind me.

I pushed into the room that I'd made mine. Well, not really, because the only decorating I'd done in the short amount of time we'd been here was to spread a multitude of weapons across the bed. It was probably all the decorating I'd ever do.

I could go, lead Federico and Alvaro's Pack like they'd asked, after Courtland was secure here. Because despite the things I'd just said, I was loyal to that fucker like no one else.

The door slammed open, and Courtland was there. I hadn't even heard his footsteps in the hall.

"Jesus fucking christ, Courtland. Get a bell or something."

Instead of answering, he reached out one huge hand and dragged me into his body. He caught my face in a tight grip and kissed me punishingly hard.

Holy fuck.

He spun until I was pressed into the bedroom door, trapped between an angry Manix and a hard place. His lips were unforgiving as he fucked me with his tongue, one hand back around my throat and the other gripping my bicep.

I groaned as I kissed him back, thrusting my cock against his body. He pulled back when we both needed to breathe, and I stared. I couldn't form words, my mind a jumble of confused thoughts.

His hand slid up to my hair and he gripped it tight. "You think I didn't know? You think I didn't want to fuck you too? Didn't think that every time you went home with one of the whores, that I didn't hate that it wasn't me fucking you?"

"Court..."

He tugged at my hair hard, the pain running through my scalp making me pant. "I'm not finished. You don't think I saw the way you looked at me? That I didn't know what you wanted from me?" He leaned close so his lips brushed mine as he said, "You are fucking mine, Dominic. You don't get to walk away. I am your Alpha, and you are my Beta. I will give you everything you need. Protect you as you protect me. Fuck you how I know you want it. Because that's the real secret, isn't it? That there's a part of you that wants me to take away all your decisions, all your power, until you're just here for my pleasure."

I sucked back the gasp that threatened to leave my lips. Because he wasn't wrong. I wanted him to bend me to his will. To make me crawl if that's what he wanted.

I nodded, but he shook his head. "I want the words, Dom. I want you to tell me that you're mine. That you'll do what I ask, as soon as I ask it."

I wanted to shout yes, but you know, communication was key. "Just to be clear, you want to be my dominant?"

"Yes. Always Prince to you..." He paused, his voice dropping low that I could feel it in my bones. "Puppy."

Fuck, I was going to come in my pants. "Only within these walls, and only between us. The men have to respect me, and I don't..." Fuck, I didn't know what I was trying to say. "With the Betas, and Pryce, I want to be someone different. With you though..." I fell to my knees, my thighs spread apart as I rested on my heels, my hands on my thighs. There'd never been an Alpha for me other than Courtland, but I'd learned what pleased him. "I'm yours, Prince. Because you might know what I need, but I know what you want too. You need this control more than anyone." I looked up at him imploringly. "Those Betas are perfect for us both. Don't cut me out."

He stepped closer, squatting down before me. I looked into those dark abysses, like the type of pools you'd drown in because you got disorientated. He smiled. "Ah, Puppy. This is just the beginning." Then he stood and left, leaving me there on my knees, confused. Unpredictable asshole.

Fuck, this was going to be fun.

**14**

---



I didn't know how to turn on the television. Or the oven. Or use the cellphone. I slumped back on the couch, determined to teach myself. Pressing the big red button—that was always a good plan. The television blared to life, the blue glow casting a halo of light in the darkness. But it was too loud. I mashed the red button again, and the light disappeared.

"Pryce?"

I startled at Bonnie's soft voice, looking over my shoulder to see her silhouetted in the hall light. "I'm sorry. I didn't mean to wake you." I was glad she couldn't see the flush of my embarrassment in the darkness.

She stepped into the room, making her way over to the couch. "It's time for the babies to feed. I was just heading down to the kitchen to warm their bottles."

I swallowed hard. That was why I was here too. I'd tried to work the microwave, but it was high-tech. Too high-tech. I blew out a breath. I was floundering in the modern world, and I didn't want to ask for help because then they'd know I was defective. They wouldn't look at me the way they did now. Like they wanted me.

Bonnie was watching my face carefully. "Do you need help?"

It grated at me to nod, but of all the people who could offer me help, I was most likely to take it from her. There was something about Bonnie that was non-judgemental. She hit the red button again, turning on the television, but then she immediately started mashing another button.

"This is the volume. And if you click this button here in the middle, it will link you into a streaming service so you can flick through things until you find what you like. Hang on, I'll just use my account."

Her fingers flew across the buttons as she entered her password into the field on the television. A menu popped up with what I assumed were different movies. Under the 'Recommended for you' section were two pictures. One showed a couple in the snow, staring at each other with exasperated interest. The other one had the words *Most Wanted* on a dark, ominous picture. They seemed polar opposites, and I could see the slight pink of Bonnie's cheeks in the light from the hall.

"Uh, just flick through stuff until you find something you like, I guess?" She pressed a bunch of buttons, showing me how to navigate, and then stepped away. "I'll go feed the babies. Goodnight, Pryce."

I chewed my bottom lip but gave her a stiff wave. "Night, Bonnie."

She left on soft feet, and I slumped back into the couch, happy to go back to wallowing in my self-pity. I couldn't decide what I wanted, so I settled on a cop show with fake laughter in the background so I could at least pretend I was normal, laughing when they laughed.

I was an episode in, and it was kinda funny, when I felt eyes on me again. I looked over my shoulder to see Bonnie standing in the doorway once more.

"Pryce? You still awake?"

I paused the show. "Yep." Sleep didn't come easily to me, never had. Sleep made you vulnerable.

I felt her hesitance, heard the slight increase of her heart rate, before she sucked in a deep breath and walked into the room. "I know Courtland said you'd been through some... stuff." I stiffened, but she put a hand up. "I don't want to know anything you don't want to talk about. But, uh, Manix? We are Pack animals, traditionally. Touch with fellow Manix is as important for you and your healing as it is for the babies."

I tilted my head at her, still reading her body language with my senses. Her heart rate was raised, and she smelled a little worried. About me? Under the worry though, was the scent of Radic and Dominic. Memories of the noises they'd been making, the scent of sex that had slid beneath the closed office door hit me again. I bit my tongue to stop myself getting hard, because that would be even more embarrassing than Courtland busting me with my hand on my dick and then telling everyone about it.

So I shook my head at her. "I don't like to be touched."

Bonnie nodded understandingly. "That's okay too. Maybe I'll sit and keep you company?"

I paused, looking around the darkened room lit only by the glow of the television. It was kind of depressing to sit in the dark by yourself. "If you don't want to go back to bed, you're welcome to sit."

She gave me a smile so radiant it was like she'd reached into my chest and squeezed. She grabbed a throw blanket off an armchair and slid onto the couch beside me, careful not to touch me.

I turned the show back on, and we both watched it in silence. Well, she watched the show and I watched her. Her throaty laughs made my lips curl of their own accord, and watching her snuggle down into the soft blanket made me want to drag her into my arms, despite my previous declaration.

Was she right? Was this empty void in my chest meant to be filled with a Pack? I'd felt better in the last week, with Courtland and Dominic, and all the teens. Though it could be just like, I don't know... What was the obsession you got with the person who saved you? Hero worship?

I moved my hand toward the fingers I could see just poking out of the blanket. I slid my fingertips over her knuckles, and her body tensed, but she didn't turn to look at me. So I laid my hand on top, and felt the warmth of her skin seep into mine. She felt warmer than normal, or was that just the connection she was talking about?

We sat like that, connected by the slightest of touches, no more personal than a handshake, but she was right. I did kind of feel better. Less alone.

Eventually, Bonnie's breathing evened out and she began to slump to the side. When I looked over, I realized she was asleep. She looked so young when she was asleep, her lips slightly parted and her face free from lines. She kept sliding further and further to the side, so I scooted closer to prop her up. Although maybe I should have let her fall to the side; lying down had to be more comfortable than sleeping upright, right?

Ugh, I was so tired of not knowing any of the

answers to anything. Her head fell against my shoulder, and I tucked the blanket back around her tightly. I sat as still as possible, but lying against the curve of my shoulder couldn't be comfortable. I should probably wake her and send her off to bed.

But instead of following my own sound advice, I lifted my arm and wrapped it around her shoulders, so her head fell to my chest. Her body slumped against mine, the hot puff of her sleeping breaths flowing across my shirt.

I squeezed her gently closer, and breathed. Like an actual, fully relaxed breath. Holy shit. She'd been right. My Beast reached out and wrapped around hers, like it was seeking comfort from her, and providing her comfort in return.

Lightness trickled into the dark abyss in my chest, and I let myself ease into her hold too. I could get used to this. The feel of a soft body pressed along mine.

Ah shit, no. No thoughts of how soft she felt. Or how good she smelled. Just platonic physical contact for medicinal purposes. I rested my head back against the couch, soaking in the warmth of the woman beside me, but trying to pretend she was just a really beautiful hot water bottle.

Ugh.

Three episodes later, I'd managed to convince myself that her body was just an extension of mine and nothing to get hard over. Another episode after that dirty rotten lie, I fell asleep too.

I woke to the sound of voices, and for a moment, panic consumed me. I was strapped down again on the table, unable to shake off the restraints across my chest. But the room didn't smell like chemicals; the table was not cold metal. The weight on my chest smelled good and tickled my nose.

I slid my eyes open, and realized I'd lain down on the couch at some point. The morning sun was just peeking through the windows. Bonnie was strewn across my body, her cheek pressed against the top of my abs. There was a little patch of drool cooling on my shirt, and I nearly laughed. That was when I realized my arms weren't restrained, but I did have my hand tangled in her hair. My morning hard-on was pressed tight to her soft stomach.

"I thought you said he didn't like touch," the voice whispered, and I realized it was Radic.

A soft noise that could have been scoff or a murmur of agreement answered him. "We both know our... your girl is special." Hmm, Dominic?

"Leave them be," the last voice, unmistakably Courtland, echoed. "This is good for them both. Radic, would you feed one of the cubs?"

They walked away down the hall, and I was left

alone with Bonnie. God, she was even more beautiful with her hair like a bird's nest and a bit of drool on her bottom lip. How was that even possible?

That wasn't a question I needed an answer to, because I didn't care. I closed my eyes, willed down my hard-on, and went back to sleep.

I was throwing all my faith behind an Alpha I didn't know, which terrified the hell out of me. But my more primal instincts knew he'd be a good leader. I just had to have faith in that gut feeling.

I also needed to forget about what had happened yesterday and concentrate on doing my job, but that was hard when Dominic was acting as my bodyguard today.

He didn't badger me with conversation, and seemed to take his role very seriously. There weren't that many threats in Maxton; this wasn't a battleground. Well, at least not a physical one, unless you were an Alpha. Though if you'd asked me whether the Alpha General would attack me yesterday morning, I would have scoffed, so what the fuck did I really know?

I had to set up a meeting between the Legion

Generals and Courtland, as well as track down Merrick and Murphy to let them know what was going on so the Legion Force didn't end up on our doorstep, armed to the teeth.

Times needed to be arranged, notices sent out, the arena prepped. Yeah, we had an arena for Alpha fights. Not usually for a position this high up, more for fights between feuding family Alphas, but still. It was nice to have somewhere contained, and filled with the appropriate medical equipment to do these things.

"I thought I told you not to come back." The growl came from behind me, making my whole body tense. The Alpha General was throwing around his power, and my Beast was pushing me to fall to my knees and supplicate myself. I gritted my teeth, clenching my fists at my side, and remained standing. But that one small act of defiance was the hardest thing I'd ever done.

Swallowing hard, I muttered, "Not here for you." I hated that I couldn't raise my eyes to look at him. Dominic was there, slotting his body between mine and the Alpha General's.

"Back off, old man, before I fucking slit your wrinkled throat." I could see the flash of throwing knives as they slid from his sleeves.

"This has nothing to do with you. This little worm is still under my authority, and I'll do what I wish with him," the Alpha growled, and even with clenched fists, my hands trembled.

Dominic though? He looked completely unperturbed. "Not anymore. This one is mine. And soon, none of these people will belong to you." He gave a cold laugh. "You'll be mine too, and if you don't learn *your* place soon, I'm really going to enjoy driving home the point."

I felt the hot burn of the Alpha's eyes on my face. "Whoring yourself out, Radic? I expected better of someone with your breeding. Though you've been fucking that dumpy little reject for long enough that maybe it's rubbed off on you—Argh!"

My eyes flicked up to see a fucking knife lodged in the Alpha's shoulder. My eyes whipped between the stormy face of Dominic and the shocked outrage of the Alpha.

"One more word, and the next one goes in your fucking eye," Dominic growled. The Alpha General ripped the knife out of his shoulder and threw it on the ground, and I could feel him beginning to shift.

"What the fuck is going on here?"

I whipped around to see one of the Legion Generals appear, and breathed out a sigh of relief. It was Joshua, who wasn't the biggest fan of the Alpha General anyway, not since he had almost gotten the mother of Joshua's grandcubs killed.

Dominic gave the man a bright smile. "A misunderstanding."

Joshua looked at me, and I sucked in a breath. "There's been a challenge."

He raised an eyebrow. "I'm fully aware of that, son."

I snorted. I liked Joshua; he was old-school but progressive enough not to be stuck in his ways. I would counsel Courtland to keep him on if he could. I shrugged. "The Alpha General doesn't like the side I have chosen. Or my girlfriend, apparently."

Joshua frowned, so I knew that this wasn't the first time the Alpha General had bad-mouthed Bonnie. I knew as much, but I kind of hoped Dominic would make good on his threat and stick a knife in the Alpha's eye.

"I am sure that the Alpha General has misunderstood," Joshua said, though his tone said he didn't think there was any misunderstanding at all. "Come along. We have many things to talk about, Radic, if this challenge is indeed going ahead."

There was a low growl from Dominic, who hadn't taken his eyes from the Alpha. "Oh, it's definitely going ahead." He gave the Alpha a grin. "And once I tell him what you said about the sweet Beta, there's no way you'll walk out of that arena still the Alpha. Your time is up." With that, he turned his back on the Alpha and herded me toward the Legion offices.

God, I hoped Dominic was right.

Joshua followed along behind us, and soon overtook us so he could power toward his office. Joshua was a pretty strong Alpha, and he'd had a lot of strong Alpha sons, as well as Raiden, one of the few male Omegas left. They had a good relationship, even if he did seem a little unsure of what to do with Raiden at times.

He unlocked his office door and stood aside, waving us both in. Shutting the door behind us, he motioned for us to take a seat. "Well, this has been an eventful twenty-four hours, Radic."

I couldn't help the laugh that burst from my chest, because he didn't know half of it. Dominic settled himself in the corner, not trying to insert himself into the conversation. I appreciated that.

"It has been intense, but I have to say, not entirely unwarranted, Sir."

The older Alpha across from me waved a hand. "Please, call me Joshua. I got three phone calls from my sons last night, all with a different account of what exactly happened here. Ezra said it was a hostile takeover, Cody said that your Alpha"—he directed that at Dominic—"came in and slapped down the Alpha General like he was an errant puppy. And Raiden... well, he said that karma had come for the 'arrogant fuck.' That's a direct quote, by the way. I think I might like to hear it from your perspective, Radic. You've been loyal to the Alpha General's office for a number of years, so switching sides so quickly seems out of character."

I recounted the arrival of Courtland and his Pack yesterday, and the Alpha General's response to a request for aid from a fellow Manix. "I don't know about you, but an Alpha who would decide on power plays over getting tiny sick infants medical help, well, he isn't an Alpha I'd want." I paused, because I knew now was the time for candor. "And honestly, Sir, I haven't been happy with the Alpha General's response to a lot of things lately. This was just a nail in the coffin. If you'd seen those infants, you would have known there was no time to waste."

The older man drummed his fingers on his desk. "How did they get in that state to begin with?"

I paused, not wanting to spill secrets that weren't mine to tell, but Dominic spoke up and solved my indecision. "We rescued them and the Omega from a research facility south of the border. They were cross-bred with another full-blooded shifter and, well, your medical professional suggests that the two beasts are fighting a battle that their bodies can't handle."

The older Alpha's eyebrows shot up, but soon enough he was frowning again as he mulled over that statement. And there was a lot there to unpack. Two lost Manix from the same area? What were the chances of that? I had a feeling that there might be a little Legion Force contingent heading to the warmer climates south of the border real soon.

Finally, he nodded. "I'd like to meet with the new

Alpha—before the challenge, if I could. I can probably sway some of the other Generals, because like you, I believe a change in leadership has been warranted for some time now. But I will not hand over the lives of my people to a man I've never met, who I can't be sure has the best interests of us all at heart, not just his own Pack."

Dominic snorted. "If there's something Courtland has, it's a savior complex. None under his care have been harmed in any way."

"And what is it your Pack did before you arrived in Maxton?" Joshua said, a little imperiously.

Dominic just grinned. "Contract logistics."

I shook my head. "They ran drugs and probably other illegal goods across the border. They were criminals."

I could feel the searing heat of Dominic's gaze. "And why do you think that?" He didn't dispute my claim.

Now it was my turn to look imperious. "I've met your men. I've made some deductions. Plus, I'm not an idiot—I can connect the dots. But I think it's best to start this whole thing with truth." Dominic continued to stare at me, and although we were different species and on a similar power level, I had to try really hard not to drop my eyes. His gaze promised retribution later, but there was a slight heat in them that told me I might like it.

Finally, I dragged my eyes away, clearing my throat. "I'll schedule the challenge for this full moon, Sir." Standing, I dipped my head in respect. "I'll set up a formal meeting before then."

Joshua looked around the office. "It might be best if we meet up at the old Sanctum dormitories." He pointed to his ears and then the walls. "I shall bring a gift for the young. The Legion used to give gifts to all new cubs, and unfortunately it's just another tradition that has been pushed to the side for far too long."

I smiled. "I'll pass it by the Alpha, but I think that would be best, Sir."

We said polite goodbyes and left, Dominic trailing just behind me. As we passed the supply closet, Dominic reached out and grabbed me, dragging me into the tiny darkened room. He pressed me against the tower of copy paper, and I let out a small oof. He pressed a leg between my own, and I could feel the hard press of his cock against my thigh.

"Beta, you tempt me more than you fucking should," he growled, gripping my jaw in his hand and kissing me hard. Pulling away with a gasp, he ran his tongue up the sharp line of my jaw. "One day soon, my Alpha is going to fuck you and you will only ever call one man Sir again." His grin was feral and filled with mischief, and then he was gone, leaving me panting and painfully hard surrounded by office supplies.

COURTLAND

The week before the full moon had devolved into a cycle of endless meetings, and I was beginning to miss a time that I could pick up a nine millimeter and let it do the talking for me. Now it was all negotiations and political maneuvering, hand holding and reassuring a bunch of aging Alphas that I was the right choice.

I would never win a Miss Congeniality pageant, and it was beginning to strain my already thin patience. Or maybe it was that Dominic, Bonnie and Radic had been fucking like monkeys and I hadn't yet gotten a taste.

I tapped my finger on my thigh, as another 'concerned' citizen had something they wanted to talk about, which was basically them needing reassurance that I wouldn't steal their business/money/Omegas from them.

"I assure you, I have no interest in taking over the whole of Maxton. Life will continue as it has before, with the exception of less hoarding of resources, and removing the prison bars around this town," I appeased once more.

Radic appeared at the door of the formal sitting room we'd been using for these meetings. He was smiling but his eyes looked worried. "Sir, your next meeting is here."

I didn't have another meeting, but I hurriedly cut the meeting short with... Fuck, I'd forgotten his name already. One of the sheep. A Beta who'd been content with the status quo because it benefitted him.

Once he'd left, I stood as Radic moved into the room. He was pale, and I automatically went for my gun. A brief gust of wind was the only warning I got before there was a huge fucking vampire grabbing my wrist.

"Won't need that," he purred with a faint British accent.

Fuck, I had Baby Two strapped to my chest— would it be dangerous to shift with him attached? My eyes darted quickly to Radic, trying to work out how I could extract us all from this situation.

As if he saw my Beast rising, he raised a hand. "The Convocation is here, Courtland."

I shook my hand out of the vampire's grasp, and I knew he let go because he wanted to, not because he was compelled to. I looked at this big, tattooed bastard. "Since when does Alexander use vampires?"

A light, tinkling laugh echoed from just outside the room. "Alexander doesn't, but he's ancient and cocky and decided that considering you guys were basically extinct, you come under my purview."

A pretty girl with bright red hair wandered in. Behind her were two more vampires. The girl looked like she was eighteen at most, but then my nose filled in the gaps. She was a vampire, though something else niggled at my senses just below the surface.

"I'm not a vampire though."

The girl smiled. "Well, obviously. I'm Raine, Convocation member for Endangered Species." She sat down in the chair opposite me, and honestly, she was about as scary as a fluffy bunny. But the guys surrounding her? The coiled violence that clung to them was making my Beast rage.

"Oh my god. Do you have a baby?" she squealed, and I realized she'd only just seen that the lump across my chest wasn't a gun, but a tiny infant.

I bared my teeth, and the vampires all moved slightly. "Yes." I looked at Radic. "Come and take Two."

The Beta was across the room in a flash, ignoring the menace of the vampires. I unstrapped the baby quickly and passed him over. With my eyes, I told

Radic to move the children and Pryce to a safe place. But I didn't have that kind of history with Radic, so I could only hope he understood my meaning. When he hurried out of the room, I thought he might have.

Raine pouted. "You didn't have to do that. I promise you we are no threat to your Pack, Alpha."

I didn't comment, and the Convocation member sighed. "I have kids too, you know? They are teenagers now, of course—or well, adults, I guess. Same age as I was when I died. So we all just look like friends. Being undead is fucking weird sometimes."

I blinked, and the big tattooed one walked over and stroked her back. She smiled up at him lovingly. Oh. Her mate then.

As if she could read my mind, she looked back at me. "So rude of me. These are my consorts, X, Judge and Lucius."

When she pointed at Lucius, a chill ran down my spine. I had heard of Lucius of the Vampires. God, I hoped it wasn't the same guy, but judging by the Pictish swirl tattoos, I wasn't getting my hopes up. I nodded at her consorts, and worked at keeping my face neutral.

"So, you're probably wondering why we are here?" Raine said, and I raised an eyebrow. "Not a big talker? Well, we got a call from the Alpha General, who told us that an army came into town and deposed him of his role as Alpha, and was holding the town hostage." I opened my mouth to protest, but she waved her hand at me again. "Don't worry, I stopped by his house first, and then the bakery, and then your house, which is filled with what seems to be a variety of shifters and teenagers alike. Not much like a battle-hardened army."

I frowned. "You stopped at the bakery first?"

The one called Judge laughed. "Professional curiosity, isn't that right, Sugar?" He had a slight Southern accent, and eyes that were dead. "Raine owns a bakery in Dark River, up in Canada."

I just continued to blink, and that was when Dominic barrelled into the room, guns raised. He was beside me in an instant, then took in the possible enemies in the room. Frowning, he looked at the girl.

"There's a bunch of armed supes outside, Court. No one is taking shots, but what the fuck is happening right now?" he growled under his breath.

Raine grimaced. "Apologies. Just my Enforcer contingent. Sorry."

I met and held Dom's eyes. "I believe they are checking we aren't a hostile takeover. This is Raine, Convocation member for Endangered Species, and her mates. This is my second-in-command and my Beta, Dominic."

Dominic's mouth fell open. "Is that the motherfucking Executioner?"

My eyes reappraised the giant tattooed vampire. I

only vaguely knew of him, but Dominic was a bit of a killer aficionado.

The tattooed vamp gave us a grin that chilled me to my core. "Aw, you've heard of me?"

Dominic looked at the other vampire. "And Judge! Holy shit."

I pinched the bridge of my nose. "Are you fangirling over vampire assassins while we are surrounded, Beta?"

That snapped him out of it. He tilted his head to the side in submission. "Sorry, Alpha."

Raine stood, and her mates closed in around her. "Look, despite what the Alpha General of this town says, it seems everyone is operating within the law. But if it's okay with you, I will stick around and ensure that the Alpha challenge is above board?"

It was phrased as a question, but it was clear that we had no choice. I nodded, and she gave me a smile that transformed her from curvy, tiny human to something more.

"What are you?" I asked before I could stop myself. Fuck. Straightening my shoulders, I leaned into my outburst. "To be a Convocation member, I mean. Vampires aren't exactly rare—no offense."

Lucius' unblinking eyes felt like bugs crawling across my skin, but Raine rested a hand on his arm. "I'm a succubus," she purred, and the power in it slid over my awareness like a caress.

I looked around at her mates, three of the most insane and feared vampires in supernatural society. "Makes sense now."

Raine laughed. "Right? Someone had to save you all from an ancient vampire-induced massacre." She waved, and then they were all gone.

I slumped back in my chair, because surprisingly, that was as close as I'd ever come to a being that could kill me. The Manix were killing machines, but we could only kill what we could see. Maybe I could take a younger vampire in a fight, but against those three? I'd stand no chance.

"We should check on the Pack," I suggested, getting to my feet. "Rosa!" I yelled as I left my office.

"Up here, Court!" Her voice came from the top of the stairs. Dominic and I took them three at a time, and nearly ran face-first into the business end of an AK-47.

Dominic whipped out a hand and took it from her. "Fucking Goddess, Rosa! What the hell are you doing with an AK?"

My errant ward stuck out her tongue. "Protecting our family, *Dominic.*" She drew out his name like it had fifteen syllables instead of three. "What are you doing? Unarmed and running around with your thumb up your ass?"

"Using diplomacy, child. You should learn some."

They continued to bicker as I walked past them

and into the nursery. Radic was there, already shifted, as well as Loren. My wards were all wrestling around, generally being rowdy—no strangers to violence, or the threat of it. But the adults in the room all looked a little worried.

I thumped Radic on the back, making sure to drag my fingertips across his shoulders. "You did good. They are just here to oversee the challenge. They seem... pleasant."

Dominic snorted, walking over to Bonnie and kissing her casually, like he'd done it a million times before. I envied him badly once more.

I looked at Loren. "We'll tighten security around the house, but her guards are vampires, and we would be helpless to prevent them entering if they were so inclined." He nodded, leaving to enact my orders. I looked at the kids. "Stay in the house, no roaming into town, and be aware of your surroundings."

They generally gave me grumbling teenage agreement, though when someone yelled that there was a Madden Tournament on the Playstation, there was more enthusiasm. Soon, they would all move on, find their own Packs, and I knew that Rosa had been taking them over to meet Naja one or two at a time to introduce them to their sister, and their niece and nephews. Maybe that was why I'd dug my heels in over this whole Alpha thing so badly. Soon I wouldn't be needed at all, and then what the fuck did I do? Run drugs to unscrupulous humans to destroy lives with? Languish around and watch television? No, I wanted to be here, closer to my kin, even though if anyone asked, I would tell them I didn't need anyone.

Pryce looked tense, his hands gripping the edges of the crib. When I was close, I reached a hand toward him. "Omega." It was a command and a reassurance. Such a fine fucking line that I didn't know if I was screwing up or not. But I kept my hand out, giving him the choice on whether or not he took it.

He was a strange being, this Omega. So independent and separate, like he couldn't even wrap his mind around trusting his safety to someone else. He resisted the pull of our bond like it was a betrayal of his body.

But when he placed his hand in mine, my chest swelled with pride. And when I gave it a gentle tug and his body moved toward mine, I wanted to shout with delight. Instead of dragging him into my chest like I so desperately wanted to, I kept an inch or two of space between us. I met his dark eyes, and smiled softly. "You are safe here, Omega." The sound of my voice was all Beast, and Pryce reacted instinctively, curling toward me.

I locked down my control to stop myself from grabbing him up and biting his throat. Marking him as mine. Instead, I let him take his comfort, keeping my touch gentle. He was more damaged than he let on, and it would be my job to make sure that he wasn't overwhelmed.

Soon, when this challenge was over, when he'd had a chance to know other Alphas and Packs, I hoped that he would still choose me. That he would choose the Pack I'd created here. Not out of gratitude for saving him, but out of desire. Out of need. Because he *wanted* to be part of my Pack.

His aqua eyes saw all this, read it on my face, and I found something about his touch calming as well. His Beast was soothing my own; this was why Omegas were so important, so revered in Manix society. They were a rare and calming balance to the Beast that raged within our souls.

"I know, Alpha," he said softly, and then laid his forehead on my shoulder. I didn't move, letting him soak in my strength, forgetting anyone else was in the room at that moment. I stood there and let him work through his demons, letting myself be the life buoy he needed until he learned to float away.

"But what is he like?"

"Will he take the Omegas?"

"Does he want a new Beta?"

Bonnie! Bonnie! Bonnie!

Goddess, it was all I'd heard all day. I should have sent Darius or Radic to town for supplies, because this was unbearable. I preferred when people just ignored me.

I looked at Peter behind the counter of the diner. "He's Alpha, Pete. He's scary as hell, but no more than any other Alpha. He seems..." Well, not nice, but I wouldn't tell Pete that. He needed to think Courtland was a pussycat, otherwise the rumor mill would have him as a killer of kittens by the end of the day, and the Destroyer of All Things Good by next week.

"He's intense and powerful. But he's very gentle

with his young. He's done more to stock the Sanctum in a week than the Alpha General has done in the last five years." I realized everyone was listening. "Look. I've known the guy for a week. I can't vouch that he's a saint. But he is even and fair with his men, rescued a bunch of kids who aren't his own, and doesn't judge me for being rejected by my parents or being unmated, which is a lot more than I can say for a lot of members of this town, especially the Alpha General. So you guys can meet him eventually and make up your own damn minds."

I turned and left, my cheeks pink with embarrassment. Shit. I should have kept my mouth shut. This was why I didn't do politics. I clutched the box of pastries that Dominic had asked me to get. Apparently, the fearsome wolf had a sweet tooth. Though when he'd asked for an eclair, I had a feeling that he had an ulterior purpose for the confection.

I couldn't wait to find out what it was. Although we still hadn't had sex since Courtland had dragged Dominic out of the office a week ago, Dominic hadn't been shy in pulling me into any darkened corner and making me come on his hands until I was biting his chest to muffle my moans.

Didn't want to get spanked by the Alpha. Well... maybe I did. A little.

As if I'd summoned the man himself with my dirty thoughts, he appeared on the footpath with a red-haired vampire who I now knew was the Convocation member for Endangered Species. She was so damn pretty. She laughed and smacked Courtland's arm, and I growled low.

Courtland's eyes found mine immediately, as if my growl had been a call. The vampire turned toward me too, and she looked amused.

I saw another vampire melt from the shadows and honestly, I was impressed, considering he was fucking huge. He looked over at the redhead with mock disapproval. "Nope, I'm with the Manix with the nice boobs. Hands to yourself, Love."

Now Courtland was growling. "Beta, come here." The Alpha in his tone had me flowing toward him without thought, and I didn't stop until I was in touching distance. Courtland eyeballed the big vampire like he had a death wish. "This is Bonnie. Do not look at her breasts. She is mine."

The vampire threw back his head and laughed. "Don't stress it, Armadillo boy. I've got my hands full. More than full. In fact, if I wanted to, I could have my hands full, mouth full, ass—"

The redhead punched him in the stomach. "X!"

The vampire laughed like she hadn't just nailed him hard enough to break a rib, and the woman shook her head.

"Apologies, Alpha, Bonnie. I'm Raine. This guy is barely civilized after like three centuries." She said it so lovingly I thought maybe she enjoyed his barbarity. "He gets a little stir-crazy when we have to be out of our home territory for too long. He misses our other mates."

I expected the big guy to bluster and deny it, but he just shrugged. "Truth. You should see our mate, Tex. Tightest ass in existence," he said wistfully.

Another vampire melted from the shadows like a spectre. "He'd also hate it if he knew you were talking about his ass to strangers, X."

They started to bicker, and Raine rolled her eyes. "Are you looking forward to tomorrow? The waiting is always the hardest."

My heart thudded in my chest. Was I looking forward to the challenge? No. For some reason, the idea of Courtland fighting, possibly dying, filled me with ice-cold fear. The likelihood of him dying was slim, of course. The fights didn't have to be to the death, just until the other party submitted. Courtland was also strong and powerful. Younger and more fight-ready than the Alpha General.

But I'd known the Alpha General my whole life, and the man didn't hold his position with power alone. He did it through fear and underhanded tactics. I wouldn't rest easy until it was over.

As if he sensed my roiling tension, Courtland slid a hand down my spine to rest on my lower back, subtly shifting me toward him. His Alpha vibes wrapped around me like a fluffy blanket, calming my nervous pulse. His pheromones promised everything would be okay, reassuring me like no words could.

"The holding pattern is a bit torturous," I said to Raine, and she gave me a sympathetic smile.

"I can imagine. Okay, I have to go visit the other Alpha now, tell him it's okay to back out, but I have a feeling it will go down about as well as it did with you when we spoke earlier," she chuckled. "Bonnie, it was lovely to meet you."

Then they disappeared like they'd never been there, too fast for even my supernatural eyes. That would be a handy skill to have. Courtland turned to face me. "Are you okay, Beta?"

I nodded, straightening my shoulders. "Of course." He held my eyes with those imperceptibly dark ones. Finally, he nodded.

"Let me carry that for you." He took the box of desserts from my hands, and his nose twitched. "Cake? Let me guess, for Dominic?" A faint smile appeared on his face, and I decided he wasn't jealous anymore.

"Yes."

Courtland made a low humming noise. "He has always been a fan of sweet things."

I grinned back at him, because there was something both terrifying and endearing about Dominic. Like he could make you laugh and moan at the same time. It was basically a superpower.

I chewed my lip as we reached the ATV that I'd parked in the lane between the bakery and the diner. "You aren't?" I asked absently, thinking about what else I could grab to feed the absolute hoard of people living at the dorm house. I'd been going to try and wrangle some bulk burger meat from Pete, but had stomped out of there before I could ask.

Courtland's fingers around my arm snapped me out of my thoughts. "I didn't say that, Bonnie."

Looking down the street, he gave me a quick, mischievous grin. I was suddenly in his arms and he was moving me back into a small doorway in the lane. Probably the back entrance to the bakery.

Courtland set me on my feet and took a step away. "I'm about to get out a cake, probably something coated in chocolate cream, and then I'm going to smear it across your breasts so I can lick it off, right here in this alleyway where anyone might walk by. Is that something you'd consent to?"

The hell? I stared at Courtland with wide eyes, as my brain struggled to process what he'd said. He watched me closely, reading me, and when I nodded, he grinned again, closing the distance between us.

"I'm going to need that in words, pretty Beta."

"Yes," I breathed, straining toward his lips.

He thrummed, that soundless Manix purr, deep in his chest. "Yes what?" he whispered against my lips. If I could lean forward, I could take them with mine. But when I tried to taste him, he moved away. "I asked a question, Sweetheart. Yes what?"

"Yes, Alpha," I moaned back.

Then he kissed me, and it was like something inside me slid into place. Like it had been mashed into a reasonably working order, but never sat just right until Courtland had kissed me. His tongue stroked mine, and it was a languid, confident movement. Like we had all the time in the world to stand here and make out.

His hands slid up my arms to my face, his strong hands holding my chin still as he sucked at my lips, before tilting my head to the side to lick along my jaw and down my throat. My knees shook as he closed his lips over my pulse point, a low rumbling hum in the back of his throat making me moan loudly and my Beast batter against the walls of her cage.

After an excruciatingly long moment, he moved on to my collarbone. He straightened, and I realized he was still holding the box of pastries.

"What to do with these?" He opened it, pulling out a cupcake with pink frosting, dusted with edible glitter. "Yes, this will do nicely." He closed the box again, and placed it on top of my head. "Hold this here with both hands."

I stared at him, his eyes molten with lust. I did as I was told, reaching up to hold both sides of the box sitting on my head.

"Don't let it drop, Sweetness, or I will have to spank this pretty ass until it is as pink as this frosting. Do you understand?"

My voice was shaky when I said, "Yes, Sir."

The smile he gave me almost made me drop the box already. "Mmm, that's my girl." Wetness flooded between my thighs at his words. I was not ready for the full force of Courtland's... whatever the hell this was. It was all-consuming.

He tugged the scoop neck of my skater-style dress, making a happy noise when it stretched down under my bra. "Perfect. The damn vampire was correct on one front—you do have the most delicious breasts." He tugged my bra cups down, making my breasts spill over, and he gave another happy growl. Standing back, he grabbed the cupcake like it was an artist's brush and dragged it down over my heaving chest. He ran it over the soft curve of one breast, swirling it around my nipple and then back up and down to the other. Leaning forward, he swirled his tongue around my nipple, then sucked it firmly into his mouth.

I moaned loudly, the sound echoing down the alley. He popped my nipple from his mouth and then began to run his tongue up my chest, lapping at the frosting trail he'd left behind.

"Mmm, Beta. This is delicious. You should taste it. Open wide." He peeled back the wrapper and placed the cupcake to my lips. "Take a bite, Sweetness, but not all the way through. This will keep you quiet until we're finished and I've tasted my fill."

Unconsciously doing what I was told again—because damn it, I didn't want him to stop—I bit into the cupcake and held it in my mouth. Happy, he returned to licking and sucking the frosting from my skin, until he reached the other nipple.

Finally, he sucked at that nipple too, the sensation shooting straight to my pussy. This time, my moan was muffled by cake as I resisted biting down. I clutched the box on my head with tight fingers, and I was pretty sure it was going to be crushed by the time Courtland was finished.

A huge hand wrapped around my thigh, and he slid his fingers higher, pushing the hem of my dress with it. His mouth didn't lift from my breast even as he brushed his fingertips under the edge of my underwear. He pulled back slightly, though he seemed mesmerized by my frosting-coated breasts. "Tell me yes." It was a command, but it was from the man, not the Alpha.

"Myeffff," I said, in a muffled moan because I had a cupcake stuffed in my mouth, but curling hopefully toward his fingers, willing them to relieve the ache in my clenching core, got the point across.

His fingers brushed my swollen clit and I moaned, biting through the cupcake. It fell from my lips and bounced off Courtland's head. His lips popped off my breast, and I froze. He uncurled his body slightly so he was looking down at me again, though his fingertip was still absently circling my clit, making my brain and my vision fuzzy.

He leaned forward and kissed me, lapping at the frosting on my lips the way he'd just done my breasts. "Bad girl," he chastised. "You dropped your gag."

I swallowed the remainder of the cupcake before I choked to death of raw lust. "Sorry, Sir."

He growled low. "We are just going to have to go fast and hard, and I'll make you pay for that later."

As if to bring home his point, he slammed two fingers inside me, stretching me and making me shout. Removing his fingers again, he clicked his tongue. "Quiet, Beta, or I'll have to stop."

I might just die if he did, so I clamped my lips shut and, when he slid his fingers back inside, I rode them in silence. The only sounds in the alleyway were the buzz of ATVs and the faint hum of voices inside the bakery.

Courtland read my body until he was pleasuring it like he'd been mastering it for decades, and when his teeth scraped over that spot on my neck again, I came hard, biting down on my lip to silence the scream that wanted to burst out of my throat. Courtland stroked his way through the pulsing of my orgasm, drawing it out until my knees were shaking so hard, I was pretty sure he was holding me upright like a damn puppet.

He curled his fingers out of me, making me squeak out one more gasp of pleasure. Withdrawing his hand from up my skirt, he held up shining fingers coated in my release, and smirked with satisfaction. Moving my hands—which were still clutching the cake box—down from my head, he opened the lid of the box, pulling out the eclair.

In a movement that was more pornographic than I could imagine, he slid his cum-covered fingers into Dominic's eclair, the grin of mischief on his face making him look a decade younger. He pulled them back out, licking off the cream.

"Delicious." Taking the cake box from me, he wrapped an arm around my back, holding me steady. "Let's go home, shall we? Wouldn't want the pastries to spoil." He winked, and I swear, I nearly swooned.

As he ushered me back up the alleyway, I knew I was never going to look at a cupcake the same way again.

## 18

DOMINIC

The crowd was roiling, the arena filled with Manix and a smattering of other supernaturals. The vamps and this Convocation chick's protection detail were dotted around the arena. I'd made Rosa stay home with the kids, and it helped that Courtland gave her responsibility for the babies. Otherwise the crafty little shit would have just stuck them in front of the Playstation and snuck out.

Courtland looked entirely relaxed; his shoulders were loose and he was smiling at Bonnie. Yeah, something had happened between those two yesterday, and it wasn't just because she came home with flushed cheeks, smelling of sex. And it wasn't just because my fucking eclair tasted of her.

No, they seemed more at ease in each other's space. They were definitely going to fuck any day now, and I knew that Courtland was holding back due to this stupid fucking fight. I wasn't sure whether I was annoyed that we had to go through the formalities, or ready to see my Alpha shed some blood. Either way, I wished we could skip the fucking performance, spill some blood and go home already, because my wolf was feeling angsty and it wanted to fight or fuck. Or maybe both.

Courtland looked over at me, and his eyes conveyed what he was thinking as clearly as if he'd said it. We'd been together so long, we didn't actually need words anymore.

*If anything happens, you know what to do.*

I snorted. *If you lose to this geriatric old fuck, I will laugh my ass off as they put you in the ground.*

He gave me the finger, but his lips twitched. Soon, he'd shut down completely, turn into the cold and emotionless Alpha he needed to be. Still, Court's eyebrows drew together. Oh, we were going to have serious silent conversations. His eyes flicked to Pryce, who'd insisted on being here, and Bonnie, who was holding his hand.

Ah, we better have this conversation out loud. Stepping closer, I shook my head. "They'll be fine, man. She's lived here forever, has Radic, and people love her."

Court sniffed. "I don't like it. If it goes bad, or he gets lucky, try to convince them to leave with you. I don't trust that there won't be repercussions for choosing the side they did."

I nodded, because I knew he wouldn't focus until I promised. He nodded back, and started to unbutton the crisp white shirt he was wearing. Only Courtland would wear a business suit to a death match. He wore that shit like some men wore Kevlar.

One of the old Alphas who made up the Legion Generals—stupid fucking name, by the way—stood and walked into the middle of the arena. Actually, it might've been Joshua, who I'd gone to see with Radic the other day. He seemed alright; some of those old fucks had to go though, and soon. They were literally killing off their species with their prejudice.

"As you will know by now, there has been a challenge to the leadership of the Manix. The other Legion Generals and I have met with the contender and have decided that his claim is valid. Both parties have been given the opportunity to relinquish the challenge, but both have refused. The winner of today's challenge will be Alpha General."

There was an indistinct murmur of voices that traveled around the arena at Joshua's words, but no one protested. That was interesting in itself.

"The winner will be by submission or death. No weapons, though shifting is permitted. The person who leaves this arena victorious will lead our species into the future." His words weighed heavy on the crowd, and he turned to nod toward us, before indicating the Alpha General should enter the ring as well. The Alpha General shucked his clothes, shifting as he entered the ring.

I had to admit, he was more impressive in this form. He was a big fuck, probably bordering on seven feet, and I could understand why the people of Maxton had sat on their asses for so long. I still wasn't worried though. I'd seen Court's Beast in full killer mode. He'd obliterate this guy.

Court's face was impassive as he slid off his dress pants, folding them neatly like he had all the time in the world. Completely uncaring that he was standing mostly naked in front of hundreds of people, except for some tight boxer shorts—because no one wanted their dick out in a fight.

I mean, I wouldn't be ashamed of being almost naked either in his position because the man was beautiful. He had a long, sleek body, like a competitive swimmer or something. Broad across the shoulders, muscular right down to the V of his hips. His skin was flawless, and honestly, he made my mouth water. Judging by the scent of lust in our small group, I wasn't the only one.

I looked over at Pryce, who was curling and uncurling his hand like he wanted to reach out and touch. As down as I was for that, Courtland needed his head in the game. I was used to his shift, but there was an audible gasp in the crowd as his Beast unfurled from the body of the man.

I stepped up close, though he towered over me by at least a foot and a half now. "He favors his right. The man has a slight weakness in his left knee that probably carries over to the Beast. Get it done so we can go home, Court. Don't play."

The Beast gave me a feral grin, his fangs so sharp they almost cut his slightly thinner bottom lip. Courtland might be cool as fucking Siberia, but the Beast inside him was anything but. I had no doubt in my mind that this overgrown armadillo/cat/hyena hybrid thing that they called a Manix was going to paint this arena with blood before he was done and relinquished control back to the man.

"I mean it, Court. We need these people to respect you, not have PTSD every time you're within a ten foot radius."

He snorted. "I've got it, Beta. I'm in control." Yeah, now it was my turn to snort, but the Beast was done with the chit-chat, swaggering into the center of the ring like it was already his domain.

Joshua looked between them both, and I could tell he wanted to shift too or get the fuck out of dodge. I'd suggest the latter. He indicated they should face each other in the arena. "May the best Alpha succeed to lead the Pack," he announced, then hotfooted it back to his seat. Smart Manix.

The arena fell completely silent as the two Alphas circled each other. The scent of Pryce's distress was tickling my nose, and I looked over my shoulder to see that Radic had come to bracket his other side, Bonnie clutching Pryce's hand so tightly it was hard to tell who was supporting whom.

I put both hands on the railing that ran the length of the arena and watched. The two Alphas stared each other down as they circled, the amount of Alpha power radiating off the two of them intense. I had no doubt that half the arena's inhabitants would be on the ground, baring their throats before the end of the fight.

The Alpha General looked tense, his body strung so tightly that it was making his movements almost jerky, whereas Courtland looked entirely relaxed, like this was just another day. I could tell that was pissing the Alpha General off too.

"Aren't you going to attack, reject?"

I almost laughed at his taunt, because if this fool thought he could taunt Courtland into anything, he was sorely mistaken. Courtland ignored his words, continuing to stand there completely nonchalantly. Honestly, I wouldn't be surprised if he started picking his claws in boredom.

The Alpha General smirked. "You're right. You aren't that reject. No, if anyone is a reject, it's that little bitch who's now covered in your scent like a common whore."

The growl of rage that bellowed from Courtland's chest, followed by a swell of Alpha aggression, made the lesser Betas in the crowd whimper and fall to their knees.

So, maybe I'd been wrong about not giving in to taunts, because in a move that was more like a blur than anything else, Courtland was in front of the Alpha General, whose face was comically surprised. Courtland grabbed him around the throat, throwing him across the sand. Oh, it was on now. Any thought of a diplomatic sparing had flown out the window.

The old Alpha was on his feet quickly and he flew at Courtland in a whirl of claws and fangs, one of the two cutting a huge gash down Court's shoulder. The smell of first blood riled the audience, and there was the odd cheer here and there as the old Alpha inflicted a second cut. I wasn't worried, as Court dodged the next two swipes. His huge hands were weapons as he stepped into the old Alpha's space, slicing him open across the chest.

Dragging my eyes from the fight, I checked on our guys, who were strategically placed around the arena watching for an ambush. I didn't trust this old fuck one bit. I noticed the vamps, as well as the Convocation member's guards, were doing the same thing, when they could drag their eyes from the fight.

Claws and feet flew, and the smell of blood started to perfume the air. I could spot the moment that

Courtland's Beast stopped playing though. His claws became impossible to follow, let alone dodge, but I noted the old Alpha had gotten some good shots in too. A slice in Courtland's abdomen looked deep, so deep that he was probably only a fraction of an inch from having his insides be his outsides.

Finally, in what seemed like only seconds of battle but had to be more like minutes, Courtland had battered the old Alpha to the ground, and towered over him. "Surrender."

The old Alpha began scrabbling backwards toward the center of the ring, bleeding profusely, and beaten down beyond doubt, but at least he wasn't dead. "No," he croaked, continuing to crab crawl backwards with zero dignity. It was fucking sad.

Courtland shook his head and landed a punishing blow to his midsection, driving him further into the middle of the ring. "Surrender."

The old Alpha—I should have learned his name, but didn't care enough to bother—slumped back onto the sand. "I surrender."

Courtland inclined his head, turning toward the Legion Generals and the crowd. "I am your new Alpha," he roared, and I watched the scene with pride. The defeated Alpha was still on his back, but he didn't look too upset.

Which was weird.

His hand slid under the sand and I saw the glint of

metal, as he lifted the barrel of the gun to Courtland's turned back.

I had my gun out and pointed at the fucking coward when suddenly, he wasn't there anymore.

Well, his head was there. My eyes searched the arena and I saw the headless corpse of the previous Alpha in the arms of one of the vampires.

Fucking Lucius.

Holy shit.

In one hand, he held the detached wrist of the old Alpha, still clutching the gun, and he had his other hand buried in the Alpha's ribcage, holding him up like a side of beef on a hook.

"Lucius!" Raine, that was her name, hissed at the ancient vampire, whose face was somehow smeared in blood, like he'd stopped for a sip in that nanosecond it had taken to kill a fully grown, extremely powerful Manix.

"What? He broke the rules. A coward's act deserves a coward's end." Lucius grinned, and his teeth were stained red. "Plus, he's kind of delicious and I wanted to taste a Manix before we had to go home and you said I couldn't taste anyone innocent." He said all this in a monotone voice like it was entirely reasonable. Shrugging, he dropped the body of the Alpha General to the ground, and I watched the crowd for any other attacks. It looked fine.

Well, everyone looked completely shell-shocked, but fine.

Courtland snarled at the vampire, who just watched him impassively. "I am Alpha."

Suddenly, the fucking Executioner was there, grinning as he grabbed the crazy as fuck vampire. "Yeah, mate. You're the Alpha. We got you. You're welcome, by the way," he said with a wink, before turning to Lucius. "Let's go home." Then they both disappeared.

Raine pinched the bridge of her nose. "Sorry about that. Congrats, I guess? I'll be in touch." Then she was gone too.

One of the Legion Generals stood, kneeling on the sand. Theodore, that was his name. Not a bad guy. "Alpha," he said loud and clear, and the other Legion Generals followed suit. We'd still have to keep an eye on them, despite their pledging of allegiance.

In a wave, every person in the arena knelt, and I looked over my shoulder to see Radic, a pale-faced Bonnie, and a trembling Pryce all doing the same thing. I'd pledged my loyalty to Courtland a long time ago, but I sank to my knees as well.

Later, I would show him what else I could do while on my knees, but right now he needed a show of respect.

Courtland spun in a circle, taking in his new subjects and then strode out of the arena, blood still streaming down his front. I knew the look in his eye though. I looked at Bonnie.

"Get him to the infirmary before he collapses in front of them all," I murmured, and she rushed toward him, hovering close to him but not touching him as she asked questions in a low, calm voice.

I turned to Radic and Pryce. "His Beast and bloodlust are riding him hard, and once he's patched up, he's going to want to fight or fuck. My money is on the latter. So if you don't want to be in that position—and to clarify, that position is bent over with a dick in your ass—I suggest you head home now. One of the men will take you, to make sure there are no repercussions from today. If you're cool, I'll meet you in the infirmary."

With that, I turned and jogged toward the small building that was acting as an infirmary. To be honest, it wasn't just Courtland whose blood was pounding with bloodlust. Watching the man I'd wanted so bad for so long almost die by a bullet to the back had my wolf baying, and I was barely holding on as it was with the scent of blood and gore in here. No, there was only one place for me to be right now, and that was with my Alpha.

Post-fight orgy, here I fucking come.

## 19

I watched Dominic's shoulders as he jogged away, disappearing into the crowd before my brain even had time to catch up with his words. Radic remained beside me, but he seemed torn. He didn't want to leave me, that much was obvious, but the heavy scent of lust pouring off him told me he wanted whatever it was that Dominic was offering.

To be honest, I wanted it too. But I was scared. Not of Courtland or the sex or anything like that. I was scared of the unknown, I guess. Of taking a step that I couldn't take back. Of being trapped in another wrong decision.

Radic reached out a hand but dropped it, still respecting my boundaries. "I'll take you home, Omega." His eyes screamed for permission to take care of me like a good Beta should, even though it warred with the other instincts that were probably turning his blood to fire right now.

I shook my head. "Don't you want to be in there? With Bonnie and the guys?"

He only hesitated briefly. "You don't understand, Pryce. The smell of your distress is like a beacon to me and every other Manix in this arena. Please let me take you home? Bonnie..." He hesitated. "Bonnie can take care of herself, I promise."

I tilted my head at him. "What if I said I wanted to follow them and take part in whatever is going on down there?"

Radic hesitated again. "I would attempt to talk you out of it," he said with a sigh. "Look, I'm about to make some assumptions, okay? I'm going to say that you've never been really intimate with a person"—he paused —"at least with your consent. That's why you're uncomfortable with physical contact. Believe me, a fully beasted out Alpha Manix is not the way you want to experience lovemaking for the first time. It's wild and frenzied, and sometimes brutal." He reached out and grabbed my hand, his icy blue eyes meeting mine. "You've experienced enough brutality. And Courtland would never forgive himself. But ultimately, the choice is yours, Pryce. You have all the choices."

I swallowed hard, letting him hold my hand, and the instinctive urge to pull away told me he was right. But I hated that he was right. I stood there for a little longer, and I could see some of Courtland's men lingering around. They'd want to be protecting Courtland too, while he was injured at least, because he'd just proved beyond anyone's doubt that he could handle himself. My Omega was basically panting at the thought of having him, but the man was still shying away.

"What if I wanted to just watch?"

Radic blinked. Swallowing hard, he nodded. "Okay. We'll watch it together."

I shook my head, because now I felt like a needy asshole. "I don't want you to, uh, miss out."

He grinned, and I realized just how handsome he was. He wasn't the broody handsome of Courtland, or the charismatic sexy of Dominic. He was just classically beautiful. "Don't worry about it. I have a feeling there's going to be plenty more orgies in our future." He tugged on my hand, pulling me through the slow moving crowd. We headed through a gate and into a small building that I assumed must be the infirmary.

He knocked on the door and Dominic was there, his gun at his side but a grin on his face.

"Decided to join us? Don't worry, you haven't missed the festivities. Bonnie and the Doc are just patching him up; apparently that last swipe nearly perforated his intestines."

He was smiling, but I could see the worry lining his face. If there was one thing of which I was certain, since my life had been well and truly turned upside down in the last month, it was that Dominic was absolutely devoted to his Alpha. He would jump in front of a moving bullet for the man, and I didn't think it was just Pack loyalty. He loved him. Like, soul-deep loved him, and I'd never say it to the man himself, but it was the type of love that I aspired to have one day. Maybe with him, if he had enough love left over to share.

Dominic tilted his head, trying to read me. Then he stepped forward, grinned and kissed me. It was soft and delicate—not something I'd ever associated with him—but it was also full of promise.

"Don't be scared, Omega."

Radic shook his head. "We're spectating today, Dominic."

Have you ever seen a fully grown man, completely covered in tattoos and scars, pout like a child? Dominic jutted out his full lower lip, although his eyes were laughing. "No fun. Next time, though," he purred, and I knew it was a promise. "I'll put on my best performance, just so you know what you're getting yourself into. Rad here already knows." He leaned over to kiss the Beta, giving me a wink.

Radic shook his head again as the door to the clinic opened and a blood-splattered but now patched up human Courtland stumbled out, Bonnie close behind like she was willing to catch him if he fell.

Although he was human again, the aura of his

Alpha was still suffocatingly present in the room. Doc strode out after him, his leather doctor's bag in his hand. He looked between us all and raised an eyebrow. "Goddess, there are enough sex pheromones in this room to kill a horse." He looked between Bonnie and Courtland. "Do not rip open those staples because I'm not putting them back in," he warned, but I figured it was an empty threat. The guy was gruff, but I'd seen him handle the cubs. He was soft-hearted.

With one more shake of his head, the doctor left the room, slamming the door shut and Radic lurched toward it to lock it.

For a moment, we all stand there as still as statues. Courtland was still naked, and the hard length of his cock was nearly touching the stitches across his abdomen. He was so fucking powerful that it was beautiful. No, not beautiful—that was the wrong adjective. Majestic? Insanely hot?

I grew hard behind the sweats I was wearing, and his eyes snapped to mine. "Omega," he growled, his voice still entirely Manix and his expression a little feral. He stalked toward me, but suddenly Radic was there, standing in front of me.

"Move," Courtland growled, and I could see Radic's back twitch as his own Beast wanted to obey.

"Alpha," he said, his head bowed. "The Omega doesn't want to participate. He just wants to watch." He lifted his head, meeting Courtland's eyes briefly.

"Courtland. This isn't the way anyone should start a relationship."

Courtland froze, his eyes moving past Radic to me. "Is this true?" I nodded, because my mouth was so dry that I couldn't have spoken if I tried. Courtland reached out and wrapped his hand around Radic's throat, using his long fingers to tilt up the head of the Beta Manix. Bonnie and Dominic had drifted closer, like they weren't sure if they needed to step in.

"Good, taking care of our Omega, protecting him, even from me," Courtland whispered softly, then leaned forward to kiss him with complete possession. Radic was his, just from that kiss alone, and I could see it in both of their body language.

Courtland finally drew away, the look on his face primal. He let go of Radic's throat, and Radic stumbled away like his legs no longer worked. Then Courtland was in front of me, kissing me softly. "Soon, Omega, when the lust isn't riding me so hard, I will make you mine," he murmured against my lips before turning away, his grin feral as he faced the other two people in the room.

We felt like a Pack, and I knew my Omega was beginning to feel that way, despite what my head said. My Beast wanted to reach out and steady Radic, wanted to hold him close to me, to watch what was about to happen next. Bonnie looked somewhere between scared and crazily turned on.

"Mmm, my Betas. Kneel." There was power in his words, but no compulsion. He would dominate them, but only for as long as they'd permit it.

I was surprised as hell when Dominic dropped to his knees like he'd been waiting for the command his whole life. He dropped his chin but it did nothing to hide his grin.

"Holy shit, Dominic's a sub. I didn't see that coming," Radic whispered, but his eyes were on Bonnie. She was looking at Dominic and Courtland, her gaze flicking between them like she couldn't quite believe her eyes.

Courtland stilled. "Kneel, Beta," he said softly, and it was an invitation more than a command. That seemed to decide for her though, because in the next moment, she was kneeling on the floor beside Dominic, her butt resting on her heels. She didn't drop her eyes though, and Dominic reached out to grab her hand, dragging it into his lap so he could stroke the spot between her thumb and forefinger.

Courtland rumbled low in his chest, and I got impossibly harder. This was it.

## 20

BONNIE

My heart felt like it was going to thump right out of my chest, despite the soothing feel of Dominic's hand around mine. Courtland looked primal and every part of me was quaking with need. Or maybe fear. Or maybe an intoxicating mix of both. He strolled over, the Beast barely contained in his human form. He squatted down before me, still naked as the day he was born, and hard as a rock.

"This is how it goes, Bonnie. Anytime you want to stop, you say... " He looked at Dominic. "What's your safe word?"

The man in question frowned. "I've never used one. No one has ever gone far enough that I thought I'd need one."

Courtland smiled. "How about cupcake?" I had a

vivid flashback to his tongue lapping at my breasts and his fingers stroking my core, and nodded. He smirked like he was remembering the same damn thing. "Excellent." He stroked my cheek. "This is about pleasure, Bonnie. About giving up control just for a moment, for letting pleasure take over without external worries or fear. I may be in control, but it's you, Sweetheart, who has all the power right now. Do you remember what to call me?"

"Yes, Sir."

Dominic sucked in a breath beside me, and I looked over to see him watching us, his eyes almost molten with need.

Courtland stood, making me face to dick with him. And it was a really impressive dick. Almost majestic. Could a dick be majestic?

He held out a hand to me, and I took it. Pulling me to my feet, he dragged me to his chest and kissed me. It wasn't a soft kiss like the ones he'd just given Pryce and Radic. No, it was a kiss that claimed me as his once more, and I knew, deep down in my soul, that he was right. He was my Alpha, though I wasn't ready to admit it yet. I wasn't ready to become someone's Beta, even if I couldn't remember why I didn't want that right at this moment.

Finally he stepped away from me, his eyes hooded. "Strip."

The Alpha possessiveness was back in his voice,

and I slowly unbuttoned the front of my sundress. I could feel the warm slide of Dominic's hand up the inside of my leg, and I looked down to see him staring at me with so much hunger that it was intoxicating.

"Take her underwear off, Pu-Dominic," Courtland said, cutting off his words. Hmmm, pet names? I desperately wanted to see the dynamic between these two as a spectator. A fly on the wall. But who was I kidding? There was no way I could even think about these two together without getting wet. I couldn't be a non-participant.

My eyes shot past Courtland to Radic and Pryce, who were both staring like they couldn't bear to look away. Radic bit his lip hungrily, and I could see he had his palm pressed tightly to his dick, like it could relieve the pressure building there. Pryce's eyes were darting around like he was trying to see all of us at once, and was unwilling to miss a thing. When his eyes connected with mine, I gave him a quick reassuring smile.

My smile turned into a gasp as the soft brush of Dominic's hands finally reached my pussy. I looked down and he was kneeling at my feet, grinning up at me, my dress now pushed all the way up over my hips.

"Uh-uh, Dom. Not with your hands. With your teeth," Courtland chastised, drawing my gaze back to his. When I was locked in its impenetrable darkness once more, he smiled softly, holding my eyes even as the scrape of Dominic's stubble slid against my skin, and his breath cooled my overheated folds.

I wanted to watch but I couldn't drag my eyes away from Courtland's, and it was probably a good thing. Because, you know in porn when they slowly remove the underwear from the hot female with a thigh gap and they just slide down her legs? That didn't work for me. I had some seriously chunky thighs, which I loved and so did Radic, but my comfortable granny panties didn't just magically fall to the floor. Nah, Dominic worked for it.

Normally I'd be mortified, but the look in Courtland's eyes chased away any self-doubt. He looked at me like I was the fucking sun—if the sun had an ass he wanted to sink his teeth into. I stepped out of my underwear, and squeaked as Dominic ran his tongue back up past my knees until his face was pressed in the junction of my thighs.

"I think I could die here," he said wistfully, and I couldn't help the burst of laughter that came out at the sound of pure happiness in his voice. At least, I laughed until he spread my knees and slid his tongue against my clit. I immediately locked my hands in his hair, holding him there as he lapped and sucked against my clit.

"Enough, Dom." Courtland's voice was like a whip crack in the room, and both of us turned to watch him as he swaggered close. He was stroking his cock, and it was mesmerizing. He bent down close to Dominic's ear. "I didn't say to taste, Puppy," he breathed in his ear so low I knew I wasn't meant to hear it. He tilted his head up and kissed him, sucking at Dominic's lips and tongue, like he was stealing the taste of me. "Go sit over there. You can taste when I say you can taste. You touch when I say you can touch. Do you understand?"

"Yes, Sir."

Dominic crawled a few feet away, but he was grinning again. Courtland shook his head, and there was a touch of the man back in his manner, rather than all Beast. Well, I felt that way until he tugged my dress roughly over my head and then kissed me. Holy shit, did he kiss me. His tongue didn't coax, it demanded. He slid his hand down between our bodies, brushing my clit with his palm before thrusting two fingers inside me. Oh god.

"So wet, pretty Beta. So soft." He curled his fingers, and I mewled for him. Legitimately mewled. When he slid his fingers out, I whined. But not for long. He picked me up easily, notching his cock at my entrance, and I wrapped my legs around his waist as he slammed himself inside me with a grunt that was pure Beast.

He took a few steps forward until I was pressed against a wall. I didn't even care that the rough stone at my back was scraping me, and didn't care that his hand in my hair was almost too tight. I liked the pain as an anchor, because when he thrust into me again, I screamed as pleasure felt like it was electrifying me from the inside.

"Mine. My Beta," he grunted, as he slammed into me over and over. I knew that if I opened my mouth at that moment, I wouldn't have disagreed at all. I felt like I was his. Like he was claiming me.

The pleasure was too intense to fear that feeling right now. All I could do was wrap my legs around his waist and meet his thrusts. The Beast was in control now, and my Manix was rising up to meet him stroke for stroke, thrust for thrust.

I leaned forward and sucked hard at his chest, scraping my teeth over the skin, and he shuddered, pressing closer into me and pounding harder until I was coming on his cock.

"That's it, good girl," he breathed into my ear. "I bet you could take my knot, couldn't you, pretty Beta?" I froze, because the thought both terrified me and thrilled me. I was beginning to think that was how it would always be with Courtland, burning so hot that I might spontaneously combust.

"Cupcake," I whispered from a dry throat.

He stopped immediately, the Beast receding so quickly it was like sucking all the oxygen from the room. He stilled, his hands holding me close. "What's wrong?"

I swallowed hard, and for some reason I wanted to cry. "I don't want... I can't take your knot."

"No, Sweetheart. Not today. We're not there yet, I understand." He kissed me gently, a brush of his lips across mine. "Now I need you to give me one more orgasm, and then I'm going to fuck the brat right out of Dominic over there. Okay?"

I swallowed hard, my brain automatically showing a slideshow of what Dominic and Courtland making love would look like, and I clenched hard around Courtland's cock. He groaned, pressing his forehead to mine.

"As fucking brain-melting as feeling your tight little pussy clench on my dick is, I'm going to need the words, Sweetheart."

"Please, Alpha," I moaned, as his dick twitched inside me.

He slid out and then back in torturously slow. "Mmm, as much as I like it when you moan Alpha like that, that's not the right word," he murmured, the head of his cock notched just at my entrance, the steady push stretching me deliciously. "Say it again. Properly now."

"Yes, Sir," I breathed, and he slammed inside, making me scream. He groaned, resting his head against the wall above my head, buried balls deep inside me.

"Your delicious little core is going to make me come," he chastised. "And we can't have that yet. Dominic," he called, and immediately Dominic was there. His eyes were hot and somehow he was naked already. Leaning forward, he stole a kiss, making Courtland huff. "I'll punish you for that later. Right now, I want you to make our girl come twice on your cock. Do not stop until she's come two times. Do you understand, Dominic?"

Dominic held my eyes as he replied, "Yes, Sir. I've been dying for this all night."

Courtland lifted me off his cock, and I whimpered at the loss, but I needn't have worried because in a second, he and Dominic had switched places and Dominic was inside me. He felt different, thicker, and it stretched so nice, filling me until I was sure there was no room for him to move inside me.

But he proved me wrong. He wasn't as tall, so he wedged me against the wall and sucked at my nipples as he slid in and out of me in long, lazy strokes. Not the pounding claiming of Courtland's lovemaking. No, this was the slow, insanity-inducing build to something earth-shattering. Dominic was grinning around my nipple as he dropped me up and down on his cock, hitting all the perfect places. Every. Damn. Time. It should be a physical impossibility but I was a moaning, shaking mess before I could even blink.

He stretched up, kissing me hard. "That's one. Think you can give me another one, pretty girl?" I shook my head, but I didn't mean it, because already his hand had slipped between us and was tapping my sensitive clit.

Oh, shit.

A rough growl of pleasure came from behind Dominic. Suddenly, Courtland was pressed tight to Dominic's back. He grabbed his face, turning Dom's head so he could kiss him over his shoulder. "You sure about this, Dominic? This is the..." He paused, but it was heavy with meaning. They had history, these two, and it weighed between them like an anvil.

Dominic smiled. "This is perfect." As if to punctuate the words, he gave a short, sharp thrust inside me, making me moan. Dominic met my eyes and repeated, "Perfect."

Courtland unwrapped my legs from around Dominic's waist, holding my thighs easily as he slotted his body tight against Dominic's. Then he moved his hand beneath us and slid two fingers inside me underneath Dominic's cock, and my brain failed.

"Holy fucking shit, oh god," Dominic groaned as Courtland stroked us both. When he removed his hand, it was soaked. He thrummed so hard, I could feel it through Dominic's body.

"Thank you, Beta, for your slick. It will make this..."

I could tell the exact moment he slid his cock into Dominic, because I saw Dom's eyes roll backwards with bliss. For a moment, Dominic clutched me like I was the last buoy in a tsunami of pleasure, and Courtland slowly fucked us both. Oh, Goddess.

But Courtland stilled. "Dominic. Two orgasms for our girl, or no one gets to come."

"Yes, Sir," Dominic breathed, and then started fucking against Courtland until he was bouncing between us, impaling himself on Courtland's cock, before driving deep into me.

It wasn't long before the orgasm was a blinding burst of pleasure, waiting just there out of reach. "Please, please, please," I chanted, and I didn't need to ask twice. Courtland grabbed Dominic's hips and fucked me with Dominic's body, slamming into him until we were all slamming into the wall so hard I was worried we'd go through it.

My orgasm burst through me, unlike anything I'd ever experienced. I was a screaming, clawing animal as pleasure touched every nerve ending, making every inch of me tingle and thrum. Dominic pushed back, pulling out of me to come all over my stomach, even as Courtland continued to fuck him until he too was growling his release.

I wasn't sure which one of us collapsed, but Dominic clutched me close and took the brunt of our descent to the ground, though Courtland was quick to catch his head so it didn't bang into the concrete. I looked up into the eyes of Courtland the man, not Courtland the Manix.

"Thank you, Betas."

Dominic winked. "Any fucking time."

Someone made a choking noise, and I looked over to see Radic dragging his hand up and down Pryce's cock, his hand covered in the Omega's release. Pryce looked flushed and confused, though his hand was over Radic's, like he was holding his hand there. They weren't touching anywhere else, and they were fully clothed. Radic's dick looked painfully hard in his jeans. I'd take care of that when I got home, so he knew that despite the fact that I'd just been tag-teamed by these two, I loved him first and foremost.

Shit, maybe the former Alpha General was right. Maybe I was a whore. But I didn't give a single fuck right now.

## 21

RADIC

The weeks after the dominance fight were tense but liberating. Everyone had been on edge, with this unknown force sitting ominously in the background like a guillotine. That was until a switch flipped in Courtland and he became the ultimate damn politician, shaking hands and kissing babies. Telling little old ladies that they were safe in their homes.

It was fucking exhausting for me on the sidelines, but I knew all this pleasant, hand-holding politics was beginning to stress Courtland out. With the higher-ups and the Legion Force, he was more the commanding Alpha I'd seen before the challenge. He chastised the Legion Generals for sitting on their fucking hands as the Sanctum was paid for out of Bonnie's pockets, and the million other little things they'd been letting slide, and for what? To line the town coffers? Or better still, their own pockets?

The Legion Force went back into combat training immediately, and Courtland used his own men—at least the ones who weren't watching his back—to ensure that they were back to battle readiness.

Bonnie had moved back into the Sanctum, though she shared her time between the two homes. Courtland's little Pack of tiger shifters had joined with the Sanctum misfits, and from what Terra, their teacher, told me, they'd started a coup to overthrow the power structure of the school. Having met Rosa, I expected nothing less. She had a finely tuned sense of justice, considering she'd grown up in a cartel compound. Or maybe it was because of that.

Some of Courtland's men had left to return to Mexico, or to move on to other adventures, now they were happy their mentor was secure. I could tell that even though he kept a stoic face, every time one of them waved goodbye, Courtland was sad. Not that he said anything, or even conveyed it in his facial expressions. No, it was more that he became a little withdrawn. Although he guarded everyone tensely, he hadn't made a move to pursue anything physical with any of us since the post-fight insanity. At least, not with Bonnie or Pryce.

I looked at Pryce across the kitchen bench, where Bonnie was teaching him to bake a cake. Whilst Courtland had pulled away, Pryce had been opening up more and more, especially with Bonnie, and I liked to think, a little with me. He now accepted the casual affection that Pack life was all about. He accepted the pats on the back, and held Bonnie's hand, and happily snuggled between us while we watched a movie. Sometimes, Dominic would be there too, his head on Bonnie's lap so she could stroke his short hair.

Pryce still used the babies like a shield though, stopping himself from getting closer to us all, like a reminder that shitty things happen every day. Speaking of which, Two was strapped to my chest, and if I wasn't wrong, felt a little heavier. Still way too small for his age, but much healthier. There was hardly a time they weren't attached to one of us, and they now ate like normal Manix babies.

It was beginning to sound weird calling them One and Two. One was somewhere with Courtland, strapped to his chest. One had always been the weaker of the two, so she spent the most time strapped to Courtland. Doc said it was probably because the beasts inside her were both Alpha, so they fought harder. But when she was with Courtland, you wouldn't know it. She looked much better.

"Pryce? I think it's time."

Pryce looked up at me with a frown. "Time for what?" Yeah, I'd probably have to be more specific, considering there were so many decisions for the Omega; it must be overwhelming.

"Time to give them names."

He froze, not even stirring the cake batter anymore. "Radic..." His voice was barely more than a whisper. "I can't."

I stood, coming around the other side of the bench. "I can't promise they'll be okay, even though I truly believe it. But not giving them names isn't what's helping them grow. They are your flesh and blood, and even without names, you love them. *We* love them. They deserve names."

He dropped his eyes and continued to stir his cake, long after it was thoroughly combined. The scent of his distress made a whine bubble up low in my throat. I hated that he was hurting, that he'd had to experience whatever bad memories plagued him over and over.

Eventually, the scent drew Courtland and Dominic from the office. "What is wrong?"

I thought I'd be immune to the sight of the man without a shirt on, the new pink scar slowly beginning to fade until soon it wouldn't exist anymore. He had One strapped to his chest, his hand gently pressed to the baby's back, protecting her even now.

I was silent, ashamed that I'd caused Pryce any distress, but Bonnie reached across the counter and gripped my hand in hers. "Radic suggested Pryce name the babies. It's time."

Courtland didn't say anything but his eyes took us all in, before he nodded. "Radic is right, Omega. It is time. I made you a promise, and it's one I intend to keep. These two?" He indicated the baby that was strapped to his chest. "They are Pack, and they deserve the respect of names. We won't rush you, but you should think about it." He paused, and for the first time since I'd met him, looked almost uncomfortable. "You should also think about if you'd like to become part of *my* Pack. If you don't desire it, we can work out how to set you up in your own home, so you feel more comfortable exploring what Maxton has to offer." He meant other Packs, ones that weren't ours, and my heart tugged painfully.

I wouldn't admit it to even Bonnie, but I wanted to be in this Pack and I was just waiting for Courtland to ask. I knew in my bones that Bonnie wanted it too. But if I had to choose between Courtland and Pryce? My Beast whined at the thought, and Bonnie's hand tightened on mine.

Courtland looked at me, his eyes pulled tight in something that looked a lot like sadness. "The Beta will be able to facilitate some more social gatherings so you and your Beast can experience more of the social scene here in Maxton." Courtland unstrapped the baby from his chest gently, and handed her to Dominic. When he'd divested himself of One, he looked at me. "That's an order, Beta."

I shook my head. "We aren't a Pack yet, Alpha." There was a whine in my voice, and I wanted him to make it better, right now.

He grunted. "Then consider it an order from the Alpha General."

The wolf shifter just looked between us all forlornly, like he could see paradise just drifting away, after being almost in our grasp.

Pryce cleared his throat. "Gabriel and Georgia. I want to name them Gabriel and Georgia. After my parents. They were good people. They protected each other and me the best they could." He paused, his scent so fucking sad it made me want to cry, his eyes watching bad memories that played in the distance. "Yeah. Gabriel and Georgia."

Courtland gave him a tight smile. "Excellent names, Pryce." He turned and left, his scent also as distressed as I'd ever smelled it.

I looked down at little Gabriel. My Alpha General had given me an order, and even if I hated it, I would do it. Not because he was an Alpha, but because I knew that we couldn't move on until we'd worked this out.

. . .

"Hey Radic, who's your friend?"

I gritted my teeth as Wilkie turned up at our table, and my hands clenched beneath the table. Fucking Wilkie. "This is Pryce."

I was short with my answer, and I didn't care if I was unduly swaying Pryce with my reaction. I hated this smug, arrogant fuck. His Betas were mostly nice enough, although they were well and truly ground beneath Wilkie's boot heel. I looked past his shoulder at Susannah, his female Beta. She was in a short dress and sky high heels, but I gritted my teeth and growled low at the finger-shaped bruises around her arms. Susannah snarled at me. "Fuck off, Radic. None of your business."

She flounced away, one of the other Betas with her. Quinn wasn't a bad guy, but he was way down the totem pole of Wilkie's Pack. The Alpha in question ratcheted up the Alpha vibes he was throwing off. I searched the bar for Dominic and Loren, who had come to guard us, I guess, but were under strict instructions not to interfere unless we were in danger.

"Let me buy you a drink, Omega?" Wilkie purred, and I winced under the weight of his Alpha command.

Bonnie appeared behind him, her lip curled back in obvious loathing. "Fuck off, Wilkie. No one wants you or your sleazy fucking drinks."

Wilkie raised himself to his full height and towered over Bonnie. "No one asked you, you fat whore."

I saw how much his words hurt her, despite the way she lifted her chin. He raised his hand and wrapped it around her arm, the same place there were bruises on Susannah's arms, dragging her closer. I stood, but Susannah was already there, shoving Bonnie away.

"Hands off," she growled, like Bonnie had chosen to get mauled by this asshole.

Suddenly, there was a knife at Wilkie's throat. Dominic had a feral grin on his face and a murderous glint in his eye. Why did I find that so fucking arousing?

"I would love nothing—and I mean *nothing*—more than to slice your throat right now. And that includes getting my dick sucked. Because I can get a blow job any day, but ridding this town of a fucking scum sucker like you is a once-in-a-lifetime experience."

Wilkie's Betas edged closer, but I saw Murphy and Merrick closing in. Their eyes dropped to Susannah's bruises too, and Murphy curled a lip.

"Everything okay over here?" he called, though his eyes said *do you want me to hold him while you slit his throat?*

Susannah had grown up with most of us. We were all within a few years of each other during high school, including Merrick and Murphy. Susannah had been a bitch, but she'd lost her mom and had to raise her Omega baby brother. We cut her some slack. Then she up and joined the Pack of the first Alpha who asked. That sleazeball happened to be Wilkie, an Alpha twenty years her senior who knew exactly what he was offering when he poached a vulnerable female Beta straight out of high school, especially with her connection to Raiden and to Joshua, a Legion Alpha.

And since then, Susannah had been stuck. You could see it in her eyes as she stared at Bonnie, her mouth twisted in a possessive snarl that didn't reach her eyes. No, I was pretty sure Susannah was protecting Bonnie, and that made me irrationally angry. What the fuck was happening over there in Wilkie's Pack?

Now, she clung to Wilkie's arm like a limpet. "Everything is fine, right Wilks?" she cooed, and you'd have to be an idiot to miss the sound of desperation in her voice.

Luckily for us all, Wilkie was an idiot. "Sure." He looked around at us all, before his eyes settled on Pryce. "I will be seeing you again, Omega."

Dominic laughed. "Only if he comes to spit on your grave. Now, fucking move."

We all watched as Susannah and Quinn ushered the rest of Wilkie's Pack away, and there was a tension in our group that remained. Murphy growled low. "I hate that fucker."

I snorted, because I was pretty sure that was a widely held sentiment. Pryce was watching the two Alphas curiously, and my heart thudded in my chest. Fuck. Unlike Wilkie, I liked Merrick and Murphy. They were good Alphas, strong and trustworthy. Kind too, which wasn't a trait you found much amongst Manix Alphas.

I cleared my throat. "Pryce, this is Murphy and Merrick. They are Alphas in the Legion Force."

They both looked down at Pryce with the kind of intensity that seared along your skin, before bowing their heads respectively. "Omega," Murphy murmured. "We didn't mean to interfere with your night out."

Bonnie patted Merrick on the back. "No, it's fine. Come and sit with us. You'll keep the riff-raff away." She looked up at me, her eyes imploring me to not interfere. If Pryce didn't choose us, choose Courtland, then Merrick and Murphy were the best of us who didn't already have Omegas, or even Betas.

They'd be a good match for Pryce, but not as good as us. Not as good as the Pack that Courtland was creating. I was angry at Courtland for not just asking Pryce, but I understood logically that he was doing it because it was what Pryce deserved. He deserved to experience the world, and dating, before he got locked down to a Pack. We'd all had decades to figure out what we wanted.

I just wished it wasn't necessary, because I knew in my soul that we were what was best for him. We just had to convince him too.

My eyelids felt like sandpaper as I assisted Pryce in taking the cubs to visit the doctor. Too many sleepless nights as Radic and Bonnie took my Omega out to experience the world. It wasn't that I worried the Betas were trying to woo Pryce in any other direction but mine, but still, it grated knowing that they were all out there, unclaimed. It made my Beast angsty. Hell, it made the man angsty as well.

Pryce looked happier however, more secure in himself. That was what I wanted for him most. It helped that the cubs, Gabriel and Georgia, were flourishing. The Doc, Bonnie's adoptive father, had been correct. Being with dominant members of one species had helped. I wouldn't feel secure until they were healthy children like any other Manix babes, but I breathed a little easier. They moved more, ate better. Still small, but alert. Their breathing was better and you would not know that they'd been so close to death a month earlier.

I started to wear all my dress shirts open at the neck because I was so used to having a child strapped to my chest. Not going to lie, it definitely didn't hurt my image with the general population in the days after the dominance fight.

Not with the Legion though. If I did one thing while I was Alpha General of this town, it would be to whip the Legion Force into something to be proud of. They would fear me or respect me, but either way, they would be better protectors of arguably the last Manix colony in the world.

Arguably, because up until a few months ago, I'd thought I was the last Manix in the world. Well, Naja and I.

"You seem very comfortable with that cub, Alpha," Doc teased, holding out his hands to take Georgia from me.

I snorted, handing over the baby gently. "They don't expect much from me, other than warmth and the odd bottle. It is Pryce and Bonnie who do most of the work."

Doc gave a low hum, raising a single eyebrow. "Indeed. But a lot of Alphas would do a lot less."

"I am not most Alphas."

Doc laughed as he placed Georgia on the scales. "I think that is abundantly obvious. Ah, well done little cherub, you have put on a whole pound since arriving. Aren't you just a little achiever, hmm? I wonder if you will be my grandcubs?" he whispered to the baby conspiratorially. "I see the way your Papa and Alpha look at my Bonnie. I am sure they wouldn't just be playing with my girl's affections, don't you agree?"

Pryce flushed, and it was my turn to raise an eyebrow at the older Manix. "I assure you, Doctor, that I feel a lot of affection for your daughter." Blood or not, Bonnie was his daughter. The doctor might be gruff, but there was obviously love there too. "Pryce is discovering himself, and we aren't rushing him."

Doc stood, holding Georgia to his chest. "As it should be. I am only teasing, Omega. A happy Omega means a happy Pack, so don't let anyone pressure you into anything. You don't *need* a Pack, unless you want one."

I choked on my tongue, but kept my Beast in check. He revolted at the very thought that Pryce wouldn't be ours.

Doc handed me Georgia. "Bonnie holds you both in high regard, that much I know. Now, Alpha, how is that stomach wound healing up?"

Another twenty minutes of fussing, we were finally able to leave with the Doctor's blessing. "Come,

Omega. Let me get you something to eat." I ushered him outside and down toward the diner.

He nodded, shifting the baby on his chest. "I, uh, have a date tonight with the Alphas Merrick and Murphy. But there's still time."

I hated them. I mean, I didn't before right now—they were good men and some of the few capable Manix in the Legion Force—but I was absolutely demoting them to the worst shit-kicker jobs I could think of.

"That sounds... exciting," I murmured, forcing my tone to be neutral. Hell, it probably bordered on uninterested.

As I held the door to the diner open, I was aware that all conversation stopped. I was used to it now, but I missed how it was with my men, that casual camaraderie. Most of them had left to find new things to do—separately of course—except Loren and Dominic. I knew Loren would leave sooner or later too; he wasn't a man made to sit still.

It would take time to get used to this pedestal power, where I was far above everyone and they somehow revered me as much as they feared me.

I hated that too.

The diner owner, a fidgety Beta male named Pete, appeared from the kitchen. "Alpha General. It's good to see you again." Pete seemed nice enough, not prone to genuflection at my appearance. He turned to Pryce. "It's good to see you as well, Omega. And the little ones." He stepped closer so he could coo at Georgia. "Aren't you the prettiest little biscuit that's ever seen the side of a griddle?"

I blinked, because I wasn't sure if that was a compliment or a threat. Given the man's wide grin, I was going to go with a compliment.

"Hey, Alpha General. Come and sit with us." The voice that called to us was laced with sarcasm, and I knew it could only be one person. My sister, Naja.

I turned and winced internally at the sight of her Alpha, Gatlin. Also known as the son of the man who'd had his head ripped off because of me. I hadn't been ignoring them specifically, but I hadn't been searching them out either.

I guided Pryce over and Naja stood, smiling at both of us, before reaching out her hands. "Gimme gimme," she demanded, shaking her hands toward Gabriel.

Seven, her Beta, rolled his eyes. "We have enough of those at home, remember? We were coming out for a cub-free lunch."

Naja made a rude noise and pointed to me. "Gimme One as well."

I was impressed that she knew the difference between the babies, but Pryce smiled proudly. "They have names now. Georgia and Gabriel."

Gatlin gave him a soft look. "That's very good, Omega. They look like they're doing much better." You didn't need to be an Alpha to sense it wasn't just the babies doing better, but no one said anything.

Naja easily juggled both babies in her arms. "Gah, they are so cute. I swear our cubs just grow like weeds." She kissed the top of both babies' heads. "You will too now, you sweet little things."

Gatlin shook his head. "Sorry, we think perhaps she's going into heat again soon. She's been a bit baby-crazy, nesting and things."

I raised an eyebrow, because I didn't know much about Manix biology but I did know it was meant to be only once every year. And given the age of the cubs, it hadn't been a whole year yet.

Pryce frowned. "Is that what that faint scent is? It makes me feel... anxious? No, that's not right. I'm sorry, I don't mean to offend you."

I put my hand on Pryce's, calming him with my Alpha vibes. "It's okay, Omega. We all understand what you mean. When a female Omega goes into heat, it creates that sense of urgency in all Alpha and Omegas in the general vicinity, and even the Betas. Except relatives." I sensed nothing.

"Will you try for another litter?"

Naja literally gasped. "Hush your mouth, Courtland De Léon. We have a bunch of four-month-olds at home right now. We do not want to add another litter to that. No way. It's going to be difficult, and probably a little, uh, tense for a week or so, but no, we aren't going to try for another pregnancy."

Someone sighed around the table, and I noticed their whole group had tensed, but tried in vain to look relaxed.

"The hard thing will be saying no to the other Omegas who come to beg for a chance to sire a litter. Some of them are so worthy, Court. And I feel so bad saying no. But..."

I lifted my hand, because I understood. "It has always been an Omega's choice, and just because you are the last female Omega, doesn't mean that negates your choice. Besides, as Alpha General, I have to think of the long-term health of the Manix, and having a whole generation of half-sibling Manix would lead to some... undesirable results."

Seven snorted. "I don't know, an extra arm or head might come in handy during battle." Naja elbowed him in the ribs.

I shook my head. "I know the doctor is looking into genetic reasons why we stopped producing Omega females. I am not of the opinion that the Manix are a superior race, unlike my predecessor. I will put the wellbeing of my people now, over the racial purity of future generations."

Pryce sucked in a breath, and I reached out to grip his fingers. I knew he was having flashbacks to that wretched research facility.

"Not like that. Always free choice. We aren't free if it is mandated who we can make our mate. But I know that our Omegas especially have urges that need to be fulfilled, so I will try my best to find scientists or some shit who can fix this before it's too late."

I wasn't talking to my sister, or Pryce. I was talking to the entire room. I knew how small towns worked; by the time I paid my bill, this little proclamation would be all around town.

Naja handed me Gabriel. "Anything we can do to help, let us know. Doc wants to run some tests when I go into heat this time, and I think that perhaps the guys won't turn into growling assholes and actually let him, considering we aren't trying to... you know."

"Whelp?" I suggested.

She pointed a finger at me. "Gross, Courtland. No."

Pryce laughed, and then Pete was coming over to take our order. I enjoyed this downtime with my Omega and my sister. I felt like I had made the right decisions, that I had always been working toward this point. Like fate had been guiding me to this moment, which was pretty self-important, and Dominic would definitely make fun of me for the sentiment. We ate and chatted about business with Gatlin, and about the rowdy teens with Naja. Rosa had been taking them all over to bond with Naja and Louisa, and I could tell it was healing for all of them, but especially Naja.

Once I finished, I stood, and they all stood with me.

Literally every person in the room, in some weird display of subservience that made me as uncomfortable as hell. Well, all except Naja who was laughing at me with her eyes, and Gatlin, who was daring me to make him stand. He didn't know that this was the last thing I wanted.

I turned to the room. "Sit. That level of... whatever the fuck this is, is unnecessary. You are warriors, not fucking sheep. Now, sit." I put the Alpha in my voice then, and they all did what they were told.

Seven raised an eyebrow. "You know you literally just contradicted yourself, right?"

I gave him a dead-eye stare, then looked pointedly at the baby in Naja's arms. "Can you give me my other cub?"

Naja gave me a shit-eating grin. "*Your* cub, Alpha? I don't see a ring on Pryce's finger."

I frowned. "Manix do not use wedding bands."

Naja sighed. "It's no fun teasing you when you have no idea what I'm talking about." She handed the baby back to Pryce. "Now the babies are doing better and can probably keep up with mine, you should bring them around for playdates. Bring your pretty Betas." I growled low in my chest, making everyone snap their heads toward me. Naja just threw her head back and laughed.

"You seem to have fallen into the annoying younger

sibling role very easily. I shouldn't let Rosa spend so much time over there," I growled.

That just made Naja laugh harder. "If you think you *let* Rosa do anything, you are delusional. She's a wild one."

I sighed, rubbing my temples. "You have no idea."

I hustled Pryce out of the diner and over to Bonnie's van. I liked their ATV rules in Maxton, but I also preferred to be able to strap the cubs into proper seats.

"Let's go, Omega. You have a date tonight, I believe."

Pryce looked at me for a long time, and I locked my shit down tight. Finally, he sighed. "Yes."

This was weird. I felt like one of those sitcom characters who was an exaggeration of an awkward virgin. I didn't know how to date, didn't even have a personal style when it came to clothes. I didn't really know what I liked, and the idea of being on a date without Bonnie or Radic, or even Dominic in the background, was making me feel anxious.

I couldn't fault the Alphas who were taking me out though. They'd been perfectly polite and attentive, without being overbearing. They'd brought me to a restaurant, somewhere with alfresco dining so I didn't feel trapped. They held the conversation when I'd been too socially inept to make small talk. They'd been so kind.

"Would you like dessert? Or we could go for a walk? There's a nice little dock that goes out onto the lake if you would like to see it?"

I felt like shit. Like I was a broken Omega, destined to disappoint everyone. But I could fake it. "That would be great, thanks."

Merrick went and paid, while Murphy ushered me outside. We walked down the street; it was quiet this time of the night, and the stars were especially beautiful. I didn't think I'd ever get tired of gazing at the night sky. Fluorescent lights still triggered me a little. I'd never said anything, but all the fluorescent overhead lights in the kitchen of the Sanctum dorm house we'd made a home had been quietly removed and replaced by industrial hanging lights. No one had mentioned it or made a big deal about it, but I appreciated it anyway.

"You can be happy with them, you know?"

I looked over at Murphy, though he wasn't looking at me. "Excuse me?"

He turned then, smiling sadly. "I know they were the first Pack that you encountered outside of... wherever you were, but that doesn't negate your feelings. Do you want to choose them because you feel thankful, or because they make your heart hammer in your chest?"

I didn't say anything, because I wasn't sure what to say. It felt rude to talk about the Alpha you were living with to the Alpha you were on a date with right now. So I shrugged and we continued walking, Merrick jogging to catch up.

"So, why don't you guys already have an Omega?" That felt rude to ask as well, but it was a legitimate question.

Maxton wasn't very big, so the walk to the edge of the water wasn't far. Merrick sighed. "There aren't many Omegas around, and they always get the choice —which we entirely agree with," he hurried to add. "And I guess, two Alpha bachelors with no Betas, who work as Legion grunts and live in barracks isn't some-thing that would appeal to a lot of Omegas."

"Not to say Omegas are snobbish or anything," Murphy interjected. "I'm sure that if we'd really connected with an Omega, it wouldn't have mattered. But we haven't had that kind of connection and we don't have a lot to offer without it."

I frowned, because that seemed wrong. "You're both very nice."

Merrick laughed. "Thank you for that, Omega. But nice doesn't send an Omega into rut now, does it?"

He looked over at Murphy, who gave him a warm smile. "We are happy as a pair. We aren't pushing for it to happen—we believe the Goddess will find us an Omega when she's ready. I'm thinking that it might not be you though, am I right?"

Guilt washed over me again. "I'm sorry."

Merrick nudged me with my shoulder. "Don't be. Besides, I don't think I could compete with your Alpha. Holy fucking hotness, that guy has some serious power. Honestly, I cracked an extremely inappropriate boner during his leadership fight with the old Alpha."

Murphy snorted. "That's definitely inappropriate."

And just like that, the weirdness disappeared. Merrick and Murphy were genuinely lovely guys, and if I had been born in Maxton, been raised here, they were the type of Alphas I would have chosen in a heartbeat.

We sat on the dock in the middle of the lake, and I found myself talking to them like I would other guys my age. Not like Alphas or potential mates, but like friends. I told them about the facility, and the babies. Not just Gabriel and Georgia, but all the ones who came before them. The slight night breeze whisked away the acrid smell of their anger when they realized I'd been in that facility since I was a child, and they didn't push me to reveal anything I didn't want to. Maybe that was why I told them so much. There was no expectation, and honestly, it was nice to unload on strangers. Maybe this was why people had therapists?

While I trusted Courtland and Dominic, and now Bonnie and Radic, more than I had any real right to, I still kind of wanted them to want me. With Merrick and Murphy, I wasn't trying to impress them, and they seemed only too willing to take my damage and shoulder it for me. Unfair of me, but still somehow therapeutic.

When the moon was high in the sky, I smiled at them both. "I better be getting home before they start to worry. I had a nice time. I'm sorry…" I let the words drift away.

"Anytime, Pryce. You let us know if they aren't treating you right over there."

A laugh burst from my chest at the thought. "They treat me wonderfully, but if that changes, I'm pretty sure Bonnie will kick their ass."

That made them both chuckle. "You're not wrong. Bonnie is not shy when it comes to protecting someone she's decided to care for. It's why what she does in the Sanctum is so important. I hope your Alpha won't make her give that up," Murphy said, a little too loud.

I frowned, but shook my head. "He's not either of our Alpha yet."

Now it was Merrick's turn to laugh. "Yet, Omega. I feel like your bonding is written in the stars. This is the closest Bonnie has ever come to settling down. Even Radic couldn't persuade her to give any Alphas a try. Obviously, she was waiting for you and the Alpha General."

Something about the idea of Bonnie waiting for me made my heart leap in my chest. "I hope so."

We'd made it to the end of the pier now, and they both turned to me. "We would offer you a lift home, but your escort has been hiding in the shadows for at least an hour. Maybe even longer and we just missed it with the wind shift," Merrick said conspiratorially, and I frowned, confused. Well, at least until Dominic appeared from the tree line.

"I was a little worried that our best of the best were broken hacks as well," he snarked. "Glad to see I was wrong."

Murphy tapped his nose. "You're good, wolf, but nothing gets past my nose." He turned to me. "I had an excellent night, Pryce. Don't be a stranger." He leaned over and kissed my cheek, and Merrick patted my back. Dominic growled low as they walked away, but he didn't start anything.

"Checking up on me?" I asked lightly, trying to tell my stupid heart not to be happy that he was here. He'd interrupted my date—kind of, anyway.

He shook his head. "Just making sure they were respecting you properly, that's all."

I looked at the ground so he didn't see me smile. "Did you run down here?" Dominic nodded. "Do you, maybe, want to run back?"

He cocked his head to the side in what was a very wolfish gesture, and nodded. "Sure."

I paused. "I, uh, might shift and run in my Manix form."

Dominic paused, because I hadn't shifted into my Manix form since they rescued me. My Beast had stayed below the surface, squished into the human skin. "Have you run since you got out?"

I shook my head. You'd think that would have been the first thing I'd wanted to do once I was released, but the outdoors had scared me. I felt like such a weak shit for even feeling like that, but I'd spent so long inside four walls that all this expanse—including the night sky that I now loved so much—scared the hell out of me in those first few weeks.

It had been Bonnie who'd helped, and like the fluorescent lights, she'd done so without really making a big deal of it. It started by taking the babies, as well as the kids from the Sanctum, on long walks. Bonnie said kids needed fresh air and good exercise, so off we'd go. And I was so busy panicking about the one who insisted on climbing the tree, or the one jumping off huge boulders, to worry too much about being outside. Bonnie had taken my natural protective, nurturing instincts and used them to help heal me. She was truly something else.

Dominic started peeling off his clothes. "I hope you wore your tighty-whities, Omega, otherwise you're gonna be flopping all over the place."

I laughed, glad I was too. A naked run through the woods might be too much for me just yet. I unbuttoned my dress shirt—well, Radic's dress shirt, because he'd lent it to me for my date—and folded it neatly. I reached for the button on my jeans but paused to watch Dominic undress.

I'd seen Dom naked dozens of times; the man was supremely comfortable in his skin, and I'd also witnessed that extremely hot moment between him, Bonnie, and Courtland. That moment plagued my dreams, making me wake up soaked with sweat and achingly hard.

Dominic was all hard muscle. Broad shoulders tapered to a narrow waist, and his whole body was covered in tattoos, which he must have paid a fortune for because I knew that most shifters healed too fast for human tattooing methods.

"Like what you see, Omega?" Dominic rumbled, and I flushed. I was glad it was dark and he couldn't see it.

I shed the rest of my clothes, keeping on my underwear, and when I looked up, Dominic was giving me a heated once-over. "Like what you see, Beta?" I snarked back at him, but he just took a step closer to me.

"Yes." Leaning down, he licked my nipple, before giving it a gentle bite that went straight to my cock. "Leave your clothes over here. We'll pick them up in the morning." Then he shifted, and where was once a sexy ass man was now a huge red wolf.

I'd seen wolf shifters in the facility. It had been the first thing they'd tried to cross me with. But Dominic was absolutely beautiful, and his wolf knew it too. He stalked around me, his tail wagging slowly. I ran a hand over his fur, which was coarse along his back but softer around his sides. He spun, snuffling my hand and giving a yip. Guess it was time to run.

It was a weird sensation. I'd run before, of course, but on treadmills. I'd never had the wind on my face like this, or the earth beneath my feet. My heart started to thump as I followed the big red wolf through the trees, slightly uphill, until my breath was burning in my chest.

Dominic doubled back, running in a circle around my legs and yipping again. He was definitely mocking me.

"Hey, don't judge me asshole," I panted, and he made a noise that might have been a wolfish version of a laugh before bounding back off again. I raced to catch up and, not going to lie, I was kind of happy when I saw the lights of the house up ahead. But I'd never felt more alive than I did right now, with a pounding heart, in my Beast form, my cheeks stinging from the cool mountain air.

Before we stepped out into the light around the house, Dominic shifted back. Completely, utterly naked. He was grinning wildly as he stepped closer to me. In my full shift, I stood a head taller than him, but I didn't want to tower over him right now. I shifted back, glad once more that my underwear had enough stretch in them to not tear off.

I could feel the tension in the air around Dominic and me, and the way he was looking at me told me his thoughts all too clearly. I braced myself for his kiss, because it felt inevitable, but when it came, it wasn't hard and brash like the man himself. It was a gentle whisper of a kiss.

"So fucking glorious watching you run, Omega. I want to drop to my knees and worship your cock the way it deserves to be worshipped."

My dick, hearing its name, perked up, growing hard. Well, harder. It was impossible to look at a naked, rippling Dominic and not have a semi.

Dominic sighed, stepping away. "But I'm not the right person for any of your firsts, Pryce. You need someone gentle like Bonnie, or powerful like Courtland. We're the right Pack for you, for each other. I just need everyone else to pull their heads out of their asses and see it too," he grumbled under his breath.

The burn of rejection stung me, despite knowing somewhat that he was right. Sensing my negative feelings, Dominic stepped into my space once more and rubbed his hand along my cock. "I might not be first time material, Omega, but I intend to be the best second time—or hell, two hundredth time—you've ever had. But you've got to choose. They won't make a move until you choose."

I chewed my lip and nodded. He gave me that smile that was full of mischief and waved me toward the house. "Let's go home. A hundred bucks says they're all still awake, pretending to be busy but really waiting around for you to get home safely."

Turns out, I owed Dominic a hundred dollars.

I was walking down the hall—well, slinking actually, because it was a habit now. Stick to the shadows, stay low, even within the confines of a house filled with people I trusted and respected.

The sound of Courtland's voice, that I almost knew better than I knew my own, slowed my steps. "Do you like that, sweet Beta? You aren't all sweet though, are you?"

There was a heady moan, and when I tiptoed out of the shadows, I caught the flex of Courtland's hips as he fucked Radic in a darkened corner on the top floor. They were so caught up in what they were doing in that darkened corner, they hadn't even heard me walk up.

Cocking my head, I made sure there was no one on this floor who shouldn't be here. The kids were the next floor down, so that was fine. The men that were left were on the ground floor, the first line of defense.

Up here on the top level? There was just us, and apparently Courtland was making good use of the privacy. I couldn't hear what he was murmuring in Radic's ear, but I could smell the raw primal perfume of their sex and it made me hard as a rock.

But this wasn't my playtime, so I dodged around them as quietly as possible. I could have been a marching band with how much attention Radic was paying to his surroundings, but Courtland's head snapped toward me.

I winked and made an entirely inappropriate thrusting motion, making Courtland grin. That smile meant everything to me. Way more than it should. I moved down the hall on silent feet, listening to the rest of the household settle down for bed. Well, if I listened hard enough, I could still hear the dull thud of Courtland's hips against the hard muscles of Radic's ass too.

I paused outside my room, a discontent settling in my bones. I didn't want to be alone tonight. Turning, I walked over to the door three down from mine. Bonnie's room, now that she didn't have to bunk in with the babies.

Knocking lightly on the door, I heard her soft voice telling me to come in. I pushed open the door and realized our errant Omega had beaten me to it. Lying on her bed under the covers, the television paused in the background, I found Bonnie and Pryce snuggled together.

"Am I interrupting something?" I said, waggling my eyebrows.

Bonnie snorted and threw a pillow at my face. "We are watching The Shawshank Redemption, Dominic, not porn."

I grinned, giving a stern mental talk to my fluttering heart, and telling it to calm its tits. "Is there room for one more?"

Bonnie smiled at me widely, scooching closer to Pryce so there was space on her other side. I skipped over and started peeling off my clothes.

"No funny stuff tonight, Dominic. We're just watching a movie."

I pressed a hand to my chest like I was a silver screen damsel. "My fair Bonnie, I had no intention of getting up to anything deviant at all. Just some good old-fashioned Pack snuggles."

In that moment, I found it was the truth. I just wanted to cuddle into Bonnie's warm body, brush my fingers over Pryce's strong forearms and just *be*. Wasting no more time, I bundled Bonnie into my arms until she was pressed to my chest. I threw my leg over hers until my foot was brushing Pryce's calf muscle.

This was perfect.

"Anyone ever told you that you're a bed hog?"

Bonnie protested, but I didn't miss the way she rubbed her cheek over my chest, scent marking me.

"Can't say I've snuggled in bed with anyone before."

Bonnie reared back to stare at me. "Really?

I nuzzled my face into her hair, mostly so she'd stop looking at me like that. "Not much time to snuggle during my previous career choice. Or people to snuggle with."

Bonnie raised her eyebrows. "Not even Courtland?"

I snorted. "Especially not Courtland."

We were silent for a little while, just watching the movie. I'd seen this one before of course—it was a classic—but it was interesting watching Pryce's reaction to it. Bonnie's thumb rubbed absently over my forearm, and I was somewhat regretting my promise not to initiate any funny stuff.

"How did you come to be in Courtland's... group? Gang? Cartel?"

I shifted slightly so I could look at them both properly. "Someone left me with Courtland's dad as collateral for a shipment. Needless to say, they didn't pay, and Court's Abuela raised me."

It wasn't really a big deal. Where we came from, people were a commodity. Did I hate whoever had disregarded me with a bunch of drug dealers without a thought? Absolutely, to my very marrow.

Did I get lucky that Courtland's family were who

they were, and not someone with far, far worse intentions? Absolutely, and I thanked the Goddess it was them every day.

I looked down into Bonnie's horrified face. "It's not that bad, babe, I promise. I had a good life, filled with violence and fucking." I gave a small, mirthless laugh. "It's not what I'd want now, but it wasn't a bad life. I had Courtland, and his family. My family. I was mostly happy, or at least too stupid or drunk to realize I wasn't happy."

She nodded, her big blue eyes a little too shiny. "And what is it you want now?"

I squeezed her tightly, soaking in her warmth and her softness like it could chase away all the barbs and sharp edges of my past. "This. This is what I want, right here." I looked at Pryce. "With you both, if I can, but there's no pressure. I think I'd like you to be happy more than I want to hoard you for myself."

We were silent again, and I'd wondered if I'd ruined the moment with my big mouth once more, but Bonnie only held me tighter. I breathed her in like she was a balm to heal everything, to heal all of us, which was a lot of pressure to put on a single Beta. She wasn't responsible for fixing any of us, but if anyone could, it would be her.

After about ten minutes, I felt Pryce's strong fingers come up to tentatively grip mine where they rested on Bonnie's hip, and I tried to suppress the massive grin that threatened to crack my face in half. Instead, I twisted his fingers in mine and continued to watch the guy fool them all and tunnel his way out of prison.

"It's funny, don't you think?" Bonnie said a little sleepily.

I dragged my nose up over her cheek, like I could just breathe her into my lungs forever and be happy. "What's funny?"

"That we were kinda just dumped like we didn't mean anything." She said it lightly, but there was pain in her voice.

"They don't matter. Want me to eat them?"

She laughed and shoved at my head. "No, dumbass. I just think it's funny how the three of us have that in common. Not that I am comparing my experience to yours, Pryce."

Pryce looked up at us from his pillow. "My parents loved me. They just thought they were doing something good for me. That I was being taken to go to a good school, somewhere where I wouldn't be living in a cave and eating dirt, you know?"

Fuck, that was rough. They'd been so fucking epically wrong, even if their hearts had been in the right place. "Do you want to find them?"

Pryce shook his head. "No. I barely remember them now, or where I lived before, and if they knew? No one should have that on their conscience. Better they think that I got a good education, found a nice girl and had a bunch of kids."

I squeezed his hand. I once again wanted to go back in time, tell Courtland that he needed to take Pryce with him that day, no matter what. But there was nothing I could do about that now; I could only ensure his future was better.

"Well, Omega, you're halfway there, right? You have your head right next to the breasts of a very nice girl, you have two kids that are absolutely gorgeous—all that's left is a good education and finding what you want to do in life."

Bonnie let out a small laugh, but she ran her fingers through his dark hair. "No pressure, Pryce. You do whatever you want to do, and we'll be here to support you when you work it out."

With that, we went back to watching the movie.

We must have all fallen asleep at some point, because when I woke up next, it was a mess of limbs. Bonnie's cheek was stuck to my chest, and Pryce was spread out like a starfish, with his leg flung over the both of us.

Trying to figure out what'd woken me up, I searched the shadows of the room, and my heart thudded out of my chest when I saw a dark figure standing in the corner. But then all my senses came back online and I realized it was Courtland.

"Have fun?" I teased softly, and was rewarded with a flash of teeth in the moonlight.

"He is something special, that is for sure."

Bonnie frowned, like she could hear his voice but was too deeply asleep to differentiate a dream from reality.

I stroked her hair softly, smiling at Pryce's soft snores. "It's time, Courtland. Make them Pack or cut them loose. They aren't the only ones catching feelings." Let him think I meant him and not me.

"I know. I will." With that, he snuck back out of the room, and I pulled both Bonnie and Pryce closer to me, even though they were basically plastered to me as it was.

This was perfect, and I never wanted to give it up.

## 25

BONNIE

Dragging myself out of bed on Monday was harder than normal. It wasn't just because I was curled around Radic, or because at some point in the night Pryce had slipped into my bed and quite frankly snored like a freight train.

I think I was just actually exhausted.

I tried to twist my way out of the tangle of limbs without waking either of them, but when Radic's arm snaked out to pull me against his chest, I just sighed and went with it. Snuggling into his arms was always like going home. That warm, calming feeling that let you know you were exactly where you were supposed to be.

He nuzzled my neck. "Morning, baby."

I melted like a puddle. Radic's rough morning voice was like liquid ecstasy. I loved it.

"Morning."

Pryce snored softly, making us both quietly laugh. Rad kissed my cheeks and pulled back a bit so he could see my face. Whatever he saw there made a small line appear on his brow. "Are you doing okay, Bon?"

I nodded, leaning down to kiss his full lips that had no right being so naturally plump and pink on a man. "Just tired, I think. It's been a crazy couple of months."

Wearing just a pair of stretchy boylegs and a tank top, I could feel Radic's morning wood pressed against me. I briefly thought about putting that hard-on to good use, but it felt wrong with Pryce sleeping in the bed next to us. Besides, I really was feeling stupidly exhausted.

"I better get up and head over to relieve Darius at the Sanctum. They've really stepped up the last couple of weeks but I miss the kids."

Radic kissed me softly, his hands roaming up and down my back in soothing lines. "I'll come with you."

I smiled, and swung a leg over him so I could stand up beside the bed. "It's okay. Stay and snuggle with the Omega. It's..." I struggled to find a word that fit how I felt about Pryce. Devoted, maybe? "Nice." That was inadequate, but it would do.

Being with Pryce felt right. Like we were meant to be connected, skin-to-skin, heart-to-heart. It hadn't been hard to cement that feeling either. Over the course of the last couple of days, Pryce had been by my side all the time, like he couldn't bear to be apart from me. I think he was feeling a little emotionally tumultuous with all the Alphas he'd been meeting and the decision he thought he had to make.

Radic frowned at me some more, but I kissed it away and headed to the bathroom. I wasn't the only one who was tired. Radic had been working his ass off to help Courtland settle into his new role as Alpha General, being the familiar face to smooth over the less welcoming responses of the townspeople. Everyone loved Radic—me most of all. He was an easy man to love.

I showered in the bathroom instead of my ensuite so I didn't wake the guys up again, and ran into Courtland. He leaned forward and kissed me, and for the second time in a single morning, I felt my insides melt.

"Good morning, Bonnie," he rumbled and I swear, it made my clit feel like a concert speaker.

"Morning, Court." I still flushed when I saw him, and honestly, I was a little gobsmacked every time we had sex that he'd chosen me. Of all the beautiful Betas in Maxton—and there were some real beauties—he'd decided on me.

He kissed me again lightly, before moving his hand down to the small of my back and leading me through to the kitchen. "Sit, Beta. I'll make you breakfast."

I sat at the small kitchen table and watched this

giant Alpha make me a grilled cheese, which was kind of adorable. He moved around the kitchen with the same easy confidence as he did everything.

"Are you sleeping okay? Do you want me to talk to Pryce about moving back into his own room?" he asked as he sliced cheese.

I shook my head. "No, I like having him there."

Courtland held my eyes for a moment then nodded. "I appreciate you taking care of our Omega."

My heart stuttered in my chest at his use of the word *our*. "Is he ours?" I asked softly, watching him chew his full lower lip, the first sign of anything less than the absolute confidence I'd always seen from him.

"That depends on both of you. Do you want to be mine?"

This felt like too big a topic to be having over a fried sandwich, but then, when was a good time? We were Manix. We didn't do rings and proposals. I stared at him for a long time, and then dropped my eyes.

"I'm not sure... I mean, I'm not what most Alphas—most *men*—are looking for. I know, you haven't known me long, but I'm opinionated. I'm not very submissive—"

"I'm going to politely disagree with you on that one. You were beautifully submissive when the need arose," he said firmly, and his lips curled a little at the memory.

My body flushed, and my cheeks were probably

pinker than cotton candy. "I mean, outside of the bedroom. I won't bow and scrape just because you're my Alpha." I swallowed hard. "You don't have to take me just because you want Radic. I won't stand in his way, if he's the one you actually want. He's... everything."

Courtland frowned, putting the knife down and stepping around the island counter. He walked over to me, stooping down low so he could grip my chin. "Beta, I need you to listen to me really well right now, okay?" He put a bit of Alpha in that command, so I nodded. "You are perfect. I do not need slaves, or yes-men. I need a partner, someone who isn't afraid to tell me when I'm being an arrogant asshole, with a heart big enough to care for Pryce and who can take Dominic's damage. I need a Beta with the capacity to love us all, to care for us all. A mother for our cubs, a lover for these fucking cold mountain nights. Seriously, how is it so damn cold in these mountains?" he muttered, and I choked out a laugh. "You aren't an add-on to Radic, although I would very much love him in the Pack too. No Bonnie, you are the main prize. Will you be my Beta?"

I blinked up at him, and my eyes burned with tears, even though I really didn't know why I wanted to cry. Happiness? Overwhelming emotion? "Yes. I mean, I have to talk to Radic; we are a package—"

"Yes!"

I turned around to see a grinning Radic. He flushed under our combined gaze. "Sorry, I didn't mean to eavesdrop, but if you want my thoughts, Bon, the answer is yes."

I smiled so wide that I thought my face would crack. Happiness filled my chest as I nodded. "Yes. Please."

Courtland leaned forward and kissed me hard, a possessive kiss that branded my very soul. When he finally pulled away, he gave me a rare smile, one that lit up his eyes like they were on fire. "Thank you, Beta. I will do my best to be an Alpha worthy of your mateship."

Then he stepped forward and kissed Radic with a searing heat that made my panties flood. Jesus. I'd never get over them kissing like that, like it was a war and only one of them would submit. It was always Radic but man, he looked like he enjoyed the battle.

Courtland pulled away, and pointed to the seat beside me. "Sit, let me take care of you both."

I didn't think my heart could feel any fuller than it did at that moment.


Courtland walked me to the Sanctum, even though it was less than twenty feet away. He held my hand and I couldn't lie, it felt really nice.

Opening the front door with my key, I stuck my head through.

"Knock, knock!"

The sound of thundering feet was like a balm to my soul as tiny bodies ran down the hall toward me. I felt bad that I hadn't spent as much time here as I normally did—which was basically all the time—but now everything was more settled, I might have to move back in permanently. It was something I'd have to discuss with Courtland eventually, because as much as I was psyched to be in a Pack now, these kids needed me. To most of them, Darius and I were the only family they had.

"BONNIE!" came the tiny screams, and even the baby was waving his hands around.

"Hello, guys. Have you been good?" I said, scooping up Duncan from where he threw himself at my legs. I snuggled his cheek and he clung to me, compounding my guilt.

I didn't feel so bad about the older kids. The force of Rosa had well and truly melded the two households together, and I saw more of the teens now than I ever did when we all lived under one roof. But the younger ones had stayed with Darius and his Alphas when I wasn't here, and I'd missed them.

Darius appeared, bowing his head at Courtland. "Alpha General."

Courtland dipped his chin. "Omega," he murmured respectfully. "Please, call me Courtland."

Darius looked from where Courtland's hand rested on my back and then back up toward us both. "Courtland it is. Are you here for the day, Bon?"

I nodded, grimacing. "Sorry for being MIA, Darius. I can't thank you enough for stepping up."

Darius stepped forward and hugged me tightly. "Girl, you needed the break anyway, even without the historical change in leadership." He pulled back a little. "Are you sure you don't need more rest? You look a little peaky." He inhaled deeply, his pupils blowing wide. "And your scent is off."

Courtland frowned, leaning closer until his nose was buried in my neck, sucking in my scent. I flushed, my whole body heating up at the feel of his lips over my thrumming pulse. When he pulled away, the flush remained.

"The Omega is correct. You smell... strange."

Actually, the flush was getting worse, going from warmth to a tingle, and then a burn.

"Bonnie?" Darius barked, but he was dancing in my vision, black dots clouding the edges. I thrust Duncan at Courtland, and as soon as he had hold of the toddler, the blackness consumed my vision and my knees collapsed.

I went down into oblivion with their shouts echoing around the darkness.

## 26

RADIC

I ran through the streets, banging into people but not caring. I hadn't even put the phone back on the hook. Dominic's panicked voice telling me that Bonnie had collapsed was like a banshee scream, and I'd just dropped the handset and run.

My Beast roared with the need to shift, but it would take too much time to get out of my clothes. I ran through the alley between the diner and the bakery, and jumped fences to cut through people's backyards, the need to hurry pounding through my brain like a chant.

Hurry. Hurry. Hurry.

I burst through the door of Doc's office, and it was crowded with people. Pryce and Dominic were there, and Dominic had his arm around Pryce's waist, holding him steady. There was no sign of Bonnie or

Courtland. For some reason, Naja and Gatlin were there too, as well as Raiden.

"Where is she? What happened?" I gasped, and Dominic stepped toward me, grabbing me up in his arms.

"It's okay, man. She's in there with Doc, and Courtland is with her. She lost consciousness and she still hasn't woken up."

I pushed past him and into the treatment room, but my feet skidded to a stop like I'd hit a brick wall. Bonnie lay on the bed, her face completely washed of color. She looked gray. She was unconscious and it was like someone putting my heart in a meat grinder and turning the handle slowly.

"Doc, what happened?"

Doc's face was equally as panicked. "I don't know, Radic. I've never seen it before. I'm doing some bloodwork, but she won't wake up. It's like she's suffered some kind of brain trauma but all her responses are perfectly fine. She's burning up, and until I gave her some relief, she was scrunched over in pain." He seemed rattled, and Doc was never rattled. Courtland's low rumbling growl from the corner made all my skin prickle. Doc threw up his hands in exasperation. "Get out. Get out! I can't think when you're sitting there staring. Go wait in the waiting room and I will come out when I've figured something out."

The man looked devastated that he didn't know

what was wrong with his adopted daughter. But I knew enough about how he worked to know he'd work better if we weren't in the room. I put my hand in Courtland's, pulling him softly toward the door.

"Come on, Alpha. If anyone loves Bonnie more than us, it's Doc. He'll find out what's wrong with her, but the weight of your Alpha pheromones aren't helping."

Courtland stared at Bonnie, and I did too. I stepped forward and kissed her forehead, because I *needed* to. Her skin was so hot, it nearly burned. Courtland trailed his fingers over her cheek and we both moved to the door. This was as far as we would go though; I couldn't leave until she woke up. I needed to see her eyes.

Naja was still there, and I realized she and Raiden were holding Georgia and Gabriel, as Dominic gave instructions. "Your Alphas need to have skin-to-skin contact with them for at least a few hours and their special formula is at the house. I've messaged Rosa to collect it for you."

Gatlin reached out and squeezed his arm. "It will be okay. Bonnie is one of the strongest females I know; whatever this is, she'll pull through. Until you know what's going on, we will take care of the cubs like they're our own. You do not need to worry about your young, Omega." He looked up at Courtland. "Alpha General."

Courtland swallowed hard. "Gatlin. Thank you."

Gatlin shrugged. "When you became Alpha General, you didn't just inherit problems. You inherited a Pack. This is what the Manix do."

Naja threw her arms around Courtland, the baby pressed between them. "Keep me updated. Let us know if you need anything, anything at all. Finlo's sister, Terra, is going to take some meals over to Rosa and the kids, so don't stress about them either. Concentrate on Bonnie."

Raiden came over and hugged me, and then they all left. I slumped against the wall, lost about what to do. Bonnie would know. Bonnie would have been on top of all this shit, but I was flailing because without her, I didn't even know who I was. We'd been a team forever.

Courtland reached out and dragged me closer. "She will be fine, Beta," he said firmly, like the world wouldn't dare to let us have such happiness in one moment and then rip it from us literally hours later.

We were fucking Manix. We didn't get sick, not really. Not until we were so old that our bodies started to wear out completely. I'd just thought she was sleep-deprived or stressed. Even if that was what it had been, why hadn't I paid more attention to her needs, instead of my own? I felt like utter shit, and no matter what words Courtland was murmuring to me, I knew this was partially my fault. These guys didn't know her like I did. I should have seen the signs.

Pryce took two big steps toward me, and then I was encompassed in his arms too. "The smell of your fear and turmoil is heavy, Radic. You are not to blame for this," he whispered in my ear as he nuzzled my jaw. "If you are culpable, then so am I. Something had been nagging at me for a week or more, making me *need* to be close to her, and I ignored it. Ignored my instincts because I didn't know what it was."

I just nodded, staring at the bare white walls covered in faded medical posters for things like poison ivy and ticks. There was nothing that said what to do if the woman you loved just collapsed with a mystery illness.

"Enough, both of you. We could not have predicted this; there is no one to blame." I nodded at Courtland's words, but he was wrong. Dominic was unusually quiet where he stood, propped against a wall. We all fell into silence, listening to every bump and scrape, every beep and swear word that emitted from the room beside us.

I slumped against the wall, sliding down to the ground. I wasn't moving until either she woke up or Doc knew what was wrong with her. I was prepared to wait forever if I needed to.

·  ·  ·

When the door finally opened to the treatment room, everyone stood and rushed Doc.

"Hold up. Look, I've got her stabilized, brought her temperature back down and given her pain relief. She seems to be resting well. But she still hasn't woken and I don't know why." He ran his hand through his graying hair with a frustrated sigh. "I've run every test I can think of and come up with nothing. With your permission, Alpha General, I would like to call in an old colleague of mine, from quite a time ago."

"Anything, Doc."

Doc's face was hard. "He's a Lycanthrope."

I gasped, and they all looked toward me, puzzled. Now it was my turn to be confused. "Lycanthropes and Manix were traditionally enemies. Historically speaking. There aren't enough of them left, or us for that matter, for a blood feud to still exist. Still, they are the enemies in old wives' tales." I looked at their blank looks. "Well, in Maxton anyway."

Courtland raised an eyebrow. "I thought they were extinct, but I don't care about some fucking feud from ancient times when she's in there possibly dying." Doc nodded again and disappeared into his office, leaving us alone again.

"I want to stay with her," I told them, my jaw clenched.

Courtland stroked a hand down my spine. "Of

course. One of us will be with her at all times, Radic. She won't be alone. You have a Pack now to share the load."

I didn't say anything, pushing into the treatment room. Doc would move her into the infirmary soon, keeping the treatment room open, though I don't know how he'd cope. Doc loved Bonnie, and he didn't even *like* most people. This would be his worst nightmare.

I moved over to where she lay. Her cheeks were still flushed but when I reached out to touch her, she didn't burn anymore. I realized the rest of the guys were at my back when Dominic's tattooed hand reached over and stroked her arm.

"She looks like Sleeping Beauty," he murmured. "She does smell wrong though."

I inhaled deeply and I had to agree. It was raw and sweet all at once, and it wasn't like her scent at all. What the hell did that mean? We all stood around, staring down at the woman who undoubtedly had the biggest heart of us all.

She was attached to wires and machines that monitored everything, and the machines beeped softly. This morning, I'd been kissing her in bed and now she was here, in a coma.

Each of the guys hugged me tight. "We'll come and relieve you tonight," Courtland told me. I opened my mouth to protest and he waved it away. "You need rest too, Radic. We do not need both of you here in hospital beds."

I ground my teeth but eventually nodded. He was right, and he was pulling rank as my Alpha, even if we hadn't swapped mate marks yet.

Courtland leaned forward, kissing me softly. "Tell Doc to call me if he needs anything, but assume that if it helps Bonnie, the answer is always yes. Do not wait for my permission."

They each kissed Bonnie, Pryce lingering like he couldn't make himself move away, until Courtland bundled him under his arm and led him out. I pulled a chair up to the side of the bed and prayed to a Goddess, begging her not to be this cruel.

## 27

COURTLAND

Three days later, Bonnie still hadn't woken and we were all on edge. Tired, anxious and it was beginning to wear on us all. Radic was taking it the hardest, which was understandable. For him, Bonnie had been a constant by his side for his entire life. The uncertainty of her situation was driving him slowly crazy, and there was nothing I could do or say to help.

That was it in a nutshell, really. No one had told me that when I formed a Pack, this helplessness would become a part of me. I felt out of control, and I hated it.

I sat across from the Legion Generals as we discussed the minutiae of running the town on a day-to-day basis. Most of the stuff I just signed off on, but I didn't want them to get complacent, thinking that I wasn't watching. It wasn't too late for a challenge to be thrown down, especially if I was distracted by Bonnie's condition.

"Alpha General, if you need to be with your Pack at this time, we would understand." If this had come from anyone else but Joshua, I would suspect that he was trying to get rid of me. But he was one of the few Alpha Generals I liked, and he seemed to have the welfare of his people at heart. I couldn't say that for all of the Generals.

"Absolutely, you should be at home taking care of your Omega and your Pack," Eldridge added, his face imploring but fake. I ground my teeth but kept my face blank. The majority of these men didn't give a shit about Bonnie.

I gave Eldridge a tight smile. "Thank you, but there is not much any of us can do right now, and being busy helps."

Joshua nodded, and his face was creased in under-standing. I remember Radic telling me his wife had died in childbirth, one of the few ways a Manix could die naturally. The thought of losing Bonnie so soon made my heart restrict in my chest. But I couldn't show any weakness in front of these men. Instead, I put on a mask and went about my day.

By close of business though, my soul felt bruised. I stopped in at the infirmary on the way home, which was actually just a few small rooms at the back of Doc's house. It held medical equipment and a bed, but otherwise it looked like a normal bedroom. Drawers and a mirror, lace curtains. Art on the walls. There was nothing sterile about the place.

Pryce lay with his head on her stomach, his eyes closed as he dozed. He had her hand wrapped in his, like he needed to be as connected with her as possible without actually climbing in beside her. I leaned beside the door for a little bit, just watching them both. Pryce was taking her sickness hard as well, and I knew it was PTSD. He'd seen too many people die.

I scented Doc coming up beside me. "His presence seems to balance her out a bit. Not that I'd suggest he becomes a medicinal treatment; the Omega needs his rest too. But her body responds to his presence more than anyone else's. Even yours, Alpha."

Some things in our biology were strange, but the connection between a Beta and her Omega was not one of them. Even unconscious, their souls reached toward each other.

"Any news?" I asked softly so I didn't wake Pryce. Doc was right—he needed the rest.

"Alistair should be here tomorrow. He's bringing his adopted daughter. She's human, but I've heard of her. She's quite the prodigy."

I frowned slightly at the idea of a human in the world of supernaturals, though I wasn't biased like some of the older shifters I'd met. I didn't believe humans were a plague, or sheep—or worse, food. They had such a short amount of time in which to make a mark. Sometimes they did this through doing amazing things. And sometimes they did it by being the evilest beings to walk the earth. Sometimes they just lived basic lives, doing what all living creatures were put on the earth to do. Survive and procreate. There was nothing wrong with that. Most lived in blissful ignorance of the supernatural world's existence, and it was better that way.

"Anything they need, I'll cover it." I had the money, but what good was money if I couldn't use it to keep my Pack healthy and happy?

Doc snorted. "Anything she needed, I'd just go over your head anyway. No offense, Alpha."

I almost smiled. I liked Bonnie's adopted dad. A lot. "I asked her to join my Pack. Right before she collapsed. She accepted."

Doc's head whipped toward me, and I guessed Radic hadn't said anything to the man. He stared at me long and hard, before finally nodding. "It was always going to have to be a strong Alpha who mated my daughter. She isn't one to pander to power, and still, too many Alphas believe that because of their designation, they are gods. Radic as well?" He said it like they were a package deal, which I guess they kind of were, and I nodded. "Good. That boy has had so many offers from Alphas, but none of them wanted Bonnie too. She is respected around town, but always seen as somewhat defective." A low growl ran through his tone, and I found my own echoing it. She was perfection; it was this town that was defective.

We were silent, both gazing at the pale figure of Bonnie in the bed, and fear tried to claw its way up my spine. I pushed it down, straightening my shoulders. "I will take Pryce home, and either Dominic or I will be back down to sit with her."

Doc shook his head. "You should rest too. Bonnie will be fine for a night. I'm here if anything goes wrong."

"If she wakes, I want someone to be with her, whether it is tonight or in a month or in a year. She won't be alone."

Doc didn't argue anymore, just nodded. "Okay, Alpha." He gave a sad smile. "Yes, my Bonnie did choose the right one."

I couldn't even feel happy at his approval, not while Bonnie still slumbered. I walked over and stroked Pryce's face, waking him gently. "Come, Omega. I will take you home."

He blinked groggily, his eyes going straight to Bonnie, and I could see the moment he realised she was still in her unnatural sleep. The hope slowly drained from his face and sadness took its place. "I don't think I can leave her, Court," he whispered, and my heart ached at the pain in his voice.

"You need to rest too. You can come back tomorrow. Dominic or I will be down to sit with her, I promise."

Pryce swallowed hard, but he stood, stretching out his cramped muscles. He leaned forward and kissed her softly on the lips, and then stilled. His whole body shuddered as he straightened. "Bonnie made me watch these old kids cartoon where the prince wakes the princess with a kiss. Guess I'm not a prince."

I led him from the room, trying not to look back as we left. It wasn't just Pryce who was feeling that insatiable pull to her, who struggled to leave her alone. Bonnie had become our heart somehow, and without her, we were merely animated corpses.

When Pryce was at the door, I rushed back and kissed Bonnie softly, but she still didn't wake. I was the Black Prince—a villain, not the hero—and I couldn't shake the feeling that I wasn't the Prince she needed after all.

We pulled into the drive of the house just as Naja and her mates arrived. They'd been collecting the cubs on days Pryce wanted to sit with Bonnie, returning them just as the sun set, happy and content.

Naja climbed out first, a baby strapped to her chest. She gave us both a warm smile. "Hey Court, Pryce." She frowned slightly. "Any change?"

I shook my head as Pryce extracted the cub from her arms. Both of her Alphas were loitering behind her, barely taking their eyes off her. I took Georgia from Finlo, and he held my eyes for a long time.

I stared him down, my lip curling back, and Naja huffed. "Fin, cut it the fuck out." She seemed impatient and restless, and I frowned.

"Are you feeling okay?"

Naja waved a hand. "My heat is nearly here and it's making these two hover like boneheads." She paused. "It means that I won't be able to look after the cubs for a week or two. These guys won't let me escape the house for a while, until my heat breaks, and it will be dangerous for you guys to come to the house. Finlo's parents have offered to babysit the cubs if you need it though. I trust them implicitly, with my life and the lives of my own cubs; I'm confident you can do the same. I'll text you their numbers."

"Thank you." We wouldn't take them up on their offer because I wouldn't trust my offspring to strangers, but it was a nice thought. "I appreciate your help over these last few days."

Naja stepped into my arms, ignoring the warning rumbles from her mates. She may have muttered something about not being a hillbilly, but it was muffled by my chest. "It's what family does, brother."

I let myself relax into the hug, just taking the moment to seek comfort without having to give any in return. But just as quickly, I bolstered myself back up and stepped away, looking over her shoulder at Gatlin and Finlo.

"Another doctor is coming from out of town to look at Bonnie." I held their eyes, letting my Alpha power swirl. Might have been an asshole move considering how on edge they were, but I needed them to know how serious I was. "He's Lycanthrope. Radic suggested that it might be an issue for you guys."

The low growl emitting from deep in Gatlin's chest told me Radic was right. Gatlin stepped forward and hefted Naja into his arms. She looked between us, totally confused.

"The hell? Put me down!"

Yeah, the threat of an old enemy this close to Naja's heat was going to send them insane, but better they know now rather than stumble into an incident later that might end in bloodshed. "I'd appreciate if you guys controlled yourselves while they're here, or stay up at your home. Bonnie needs them, and I don't need your Beasts killing what might be Bonnie's hope for survival."

Finlo nodded. "We'll stay away from town until after the heat."

They walked back to their ATV, Naja still hefted over Gatlin's shoulder. "Gatlin, put me down. I have a girls' lunch to go to and I swear I will kick your ass if you caveman me back home," Naja protested. She was still chewing him out as they drove away.

I turned back to the house, ushering Pryce inside. Rosa appeared as soon as the door clicked closed, her face drawn into a mask of concern. "How's Bonnie?"

I shook my head. "No change."

She reached out and took the cub from my arms. "Here, I'll feed the babies."

I looked at the young woman in front of me; it felt like she'd been the squawking baby just yesterday. But the last few days had proven she wasn't a child anymore. She'd picked up the slack for us all, both here with her siblings and helping over at the Sanctum too, according to Darius.

"You're a great kid—you know that, right? I appreciate you helping out more than you know."

She punched me in the arm. "We're family," she said, unintentionally echoing Naja's words. "You literally did the same for me." She looked over at Pryce, her eyes softening. Pryce looked like hell. "Want me to take Gabe as well?"

Pryce shook his head, looking guilty again. "No, I haven't spent enough time with them in the last few days. But I'd appreciate the help feeding them and putting them down."

I kissed Pryce's cheek as he followed Rosa deeper into the house. I needed a shower and to change out of my suit, and then I would head back down to the infirmary. I dragged myself up the stairs to the top floor, loosening my buttons before I even pushed open the door to my room. I eyed my bed with longing, but even if I did lay down, I knew I wouldn't sleep. Instead, my head would just run with a million thoughts.

I peeled off my clothes, folding them roughly and hanging them over the back of the armchair.

Resting my head against the tiles of the ensuite as I turned on the shower, I let myself rest just for a second, trying to remember when I felt this out of control.

Finally warm enough, I stepped into the water and let it wash away the day. Let it wash away the worries like it was the blood of my enemies.

A noise outside the shower caught my attention, and I wiped the fog to see Dominic kneeling on the bathmat in the perfect submissive position. My heart leapt and my dick hardened, and then I felt guilty. I grunted as I pushed my dick down, trying to keep it under control. "Not now, Dominic."

He looked up from his submissive position, his eyes on fire. "Yes, now, Prince. You are so tense you're about to explode. You need this, and I promise you, none of us would begrudge you a moment of release." His chin dipped down. "We both need this control right now, Court."

I flexed my hands, trying to get a grip on my control, but there was nothing. He was right. I needed this, and the Goddess forgive me, I needed to make him hurt.

"Safe word?"

He looked up into my eyes. "Cupcake."

It was like a blow to the gut, but I nodded. "Get in the shower, Puppy."

DOMINIC

I felt like I was gasping for breath underwater and Courtland was my only lifeline. "Get in the shower, Puppy," he growled, and I was on my feet getting undressed before he'd even finished the sentence. Yes. I needed this. I needed someone to take control of this chaos that whirled through my body for just a moment.

I stood in the doorway of the shower, letting my eyes take in the long lines of his back, the hard muscles and the scars. I already knew each one of those scars intimately. Been there when he'd been shot, causing that puckered exit wound in his shoulder. Stitched up the big gash that wrapped around his hip from a machete in a deal gone bad.

I knew those wounds like they were my own, some-times being the one holding his blood in his body until we could get to a healer. We were tied by that blood and so much love, even back then. It felt like we were an inevitability.

"On your knees," he grunted, still not facing me, but I fell to the tiles with a thud. It put me about ass height, and Courtland had a great ass.

"Yes, Prince."

He growled low in his chest and when he turned, his dick was hard and he had his hand wrapped around its length. I ached to reach out and grab it in my own tattooed hand, see the inked darkness wrapped around his golden skin. But that wasn't how this worked. I had to wait patiently for his request.

"Open your mouth for me, Puppy. I want to fuck those pouty lips." My dick pulsed, and I pushed up on my thighs, reaching for his dick eagerly. I ran my tongue up the underside, and he groaned, his head falling back against the tiles.

The need to please him had me desperate to get him in my mouth, and I sucked him down. He was big, the tight ring of muscle around the base of his cock that would inflate into his knot bumped eagerly against my lips, as he grabbed at my head so he could fuck my face.

And I fucking loved it. Like I was finally serving my purpose.

He grunted as his cock hit the back of my throat, his chin dropping to his chest so he could watch me take his dick. "Do you like that? Do you like eating my dick, Puppy?"

I smirked, humming my agreement, making him groan and thrust faster. Yeah, I knew a few tricks too. I rolled his sac in my hand, and I felt them pull up. Oh yeah, ya boy had moves.

Suddenly, he wrenched his dick from my mouth and pulled me to my feet. Pressing me chest first into the wall, he ran his hand down my body like he owned it. Which he did. Hell, he owned more than my body—he owned my soul as well.

He tugged my hands up to the wall, pressing them far above my head. "Keep them here. They come down, I stop."

He gripped my cock, giving it a firm tug, and it basically leapt into his hand like the Puppy he said I was. Fuck me, I would keep my hands up until they fell off if he kept touching me like that.

His other hand dropped down to the firm muscles of my ass, squeezing my glutes with a hum of approval. Then I felt his fingers nudging at my ass, and I rested my head against the tiles as they pushed inside.

Fuck. I wanted to come all over his hand already, as he scissored his fingers inside me, stretching me out, stroking my prostate until I was growling low with pleasure. Then his fingers were gone, replaced with his cock head. He must have soaped up his hand at some point, because his cock slid into me easily, and I groaned so loudly it echoed around the shower stall. My hands dropped an inch and Courtland growled, stopping his slow, shallow thrusts.

"What did I say, Puppy?" he growled, his hand coming up to grip my throat. "Keep your hands up." He didn't let go of my throat as he fucked me then, squeezing tighter as his other hand stroked my dick and he fucked me into the shower tiles.

My arms shook but I wouldn't drop them until he asked. Not if it meant he'd stop. My orgasm fucking exploded out of me in ropes of cum, getting all over the shower wall and Prince's hand. He loosened his fingers on my throat, dropping them to my hips so he could pound into me, and it took all my strength not to go weak in the knees when he came on a roar, dragging his dick out before he knotted me.

He collapsed against me, his entire body bracketing mine as the water washed away the remnants of our fuck. He buried his face in my neck, biting hard but not breaking the skin. "I fucking love you, Dominic. You know that, right?"

My whole body froze, but eventually I relaxed back into his arms. "Love you too, Prince."

He ran his hands over my abs, then pulled away. "Come, Puppy." He stepped out of the shower, and wrapped a towel around his waist before holding one out for me too. "One day soon, I am going to spend all day torturing you with pleasure until you are begging for release, but not today. Right now, our girl is lying in bed alone and I need to go be with her."

Small lines around his eyes showed the strain he was under, and I hated that. I ushered him toward the bedroom, dragging a pair of sleep shorts out of his top drawer. "I'll go sit with Bonnie, Court. You need your rest. You can't protect us all if you're running on fumes."

He looked like he was going to protest so I threw the sleep shorts at his head, and smacked him fair in the face. His low growl sent a thrill of excitement, touched with primordial fear, through my veins.

He leapt toward me, grabbing me up in his arms. "Fucking brat."

I laughed in his face. "Just because I want you to spank my ass and call me Puppy doesn't mean I won't call you on your shit, Court. Rest. Let me take care of our Pack."

He wrapped his arms around me and kissed me, his lips soft against mine. "Okay, Dom. Okay."

I made sure he was tucked in before I left to head to my own room, pulling on my sweats and weapons. I didn't expect any danger, but I was never unprepared. Boy Scouts and I had that in common.

Night had fallen by the time I stepped out of the front door, and I decided to jog to the infirmary. I hadn't shifted in a week, and my wolf was scratching at the door of my control. But I didn't want to shuck my weapons and phone, so a hard run in my human form would have to do.

Maxton was beautiful in the dark, but kinda creepy too. You wouldn't think it would be any more creepy than the desert, but there was something almost alive about the woods in this area. A restless energy swirled through the trees, and it sounded almost like whispered secrets.

I wasn't a believer in that voodoo shit, but I could feel the long-held roots that permeated every inch of these mountains, either from the human history or the supernatural. I'd seen enough in my lifetime to believe in ghosts, and skinwalkers, and Wendigos and shit, and you know where they all lived? In the fucking mountain wilderness.

Only thing out there to bite you in the desert was a fucking scorpion in your bed.

I slowed as I ran past the back of the Legion Force barracks, the flame of a bonfire lighting up the sky and making the air heavy with the scent of smoke. A furtive voice made me stop jogging altogether, something in the tone making my hackles rise.

"... I tell you they aren't happy."

"They're fucking insane is what they are," another voice hissed. "Good way to end up dead. That asshole does not look like he fucks around."

"That's what I mean. That's why we should do what

he says. You know he should have been Alpha General."

The voices faded away, lost to the cacophony of raucous laughter and the scent of smoke.

Interesting. I filed it away in my brain, and I'd remind everyone to be extra vigilant.

I kept jogging, entering the infirmary from the back. The door was locked, but it was easy enough for me to pick. This was Maxton. It didn't exactly have a wild crime rate. I stepped into the darkness, only the small lamp in the corner of Bonnie's room casting any light.

She looked better today. Less pale and like death. The edge of her bed had rails, so I slid the side closest to the monitors up. Then I slipped off my shoes and shirt and climbed in next to her, wrapping her in my body, in my protection. She was soft and warm, and for a moment, I let myself believe she was just asleep, and not comatose.

I woke to the face of a frowning Latina girl. I reached for my gun and pulled it out, aiming it at her. She didn't seem overly perturbed, just looking over her shoulder at whoever was behind her. "I think I found your problem. She seems to be growing a wolf shifter from her hip."

I knew she was joking, but her expression was so

deadpan I was beginning to second-guess myself.

"Stace, did you just crack a joke? Wait til I tell Enit that you're cracking jokes in front of patients now."

The girl frowned again; she couldn't be more than eighteen. "Then she'll be even more put out that she had to stay behind and you got to come. You can deal with our angry girlfriend." She looked back down at me. "You're still holding a gun."

In the next breath, a hand shot out, bent back my wrist and disarmed me in one smooth move. I growled loudly, and another kid—a guy with floppy blond hair—grinned down at me from beside the bed.

"Sorry, man. But I've been dying to try that trick for ages, and I can't have you accidentally shooting my Packmate, you understand?"

Who the fuck were these kids?

Only one way to find out. "Who the fuck are you?" I growled, and then Doc came into the room, clearing his throat loudly.

"Dominic, this is Stacey and her Packmate, Bohdie. And this is Alistair." He pointed behind him to a tall man with blond hair and golden eyes. He smelled like a predator, and my wolf whined low in its chest at the weight of his power. Actually, the blond kid with the teen heartthrob hair was throwing off some serious Alpha juju too. Not a wolf, but definitely powerful.

Alistair stepped forward, thrusting out his hand. "Pleasure to meet you. I was surprised as hell to get a call from a man I thought had been dead for decades." He smiled pleasantly at Doc. "Just when I thought there were no more surprises left in the world—an entire colony of Manix."

I shook his hand. "Thank you for coming."

I moved out of the way so this new doctor could have a look at Bonnie. He was frowning, his stethoscope and penlight getting a good workout as he checked her over. The girl, Stacey, was checking Bonnie's reflexive responses, or at least that's what I thought all the medical jargon was about. She looked at Bonnie intently, and the blond kid came to stand beside me.

"Don't worry, man, Stace is like a genius. Not even an exaggeration. If anyone can work out what's going on with your girl, it's her."

Goddess, I hoped he was right.

I was pacing back and forth in my room, and at this rate, I would wear a track on the floor. I'd had to leave the nursery because my constant movement was keeping the cubs awake. I felt like there was electricity humming through my veins, anxiety in the back of my brain screaming I should head back to Bonnie. I needed to be there. Needed to see her. Needed to touch her skin with mine.

Dominic was down there now, but soon he'd have to go to work. Then I'd go. But who'd stay with the cubs? Maybe I could take them with me. Yeah, that's what I'd do—I'd take them with me. Decision made, I strode out my door and barrelled straight into Courtland. He gripped my shoulders to stop me bouncing off his chest. Courtland was quite a bit taller than me, as apparently Omega Manix tended to be a little more lithe than the behemoth Alphas, and even most of the Betas.

"Omega, are you okay?"

I was nodding before he'd even finished. "Fine. Just going to get the cubs ready. I thought I might take them with me to sit with Bonnie, you know, seeing how Naja can't babysit anymore and I don't really trust anyone else to watch them."

It all regurgitated out at once, making Courtland frown. "Are you okay, Pryce? Sleeping?"

No. Not sleeping, unless I was with Bonnie. It was like I'd become addicted to her, but I didn't know how to explain that to Courtland with his cool, calm control.

"I'm sleeping well enough," I hedged, giving him a tight smile. I went to step around him, but he didn't loosen his grip on my arms.

"Omega," he bit out, the power in his voice instantly stopping my movements. "Pryce, come here." He dragged me into his arms, and started to thrum. The delicate purring sensation instantly soothed something in my chest, and I felt myself melting into him. His Alpha power was heady, like a hit of some kind of narcotic. "Tell me what's wrong."

It wasn't a suggestion. "Being away from Bonnie is making me anxious," I muttered, the sound muffled against his chest.

He hummed low in his chest, his hand stroking up

my back soothingly. "Do you think this is a residual effect of your captivity? PTSD, maybe?"

I mean, it could be. It definitely didn't bring back fond memories. Hell, maybe that was it. "Doesn't matter. I'm not going to stop going to visit her." I set my jaw as I met his eyes, just so he knew I wasn't fucking around.

He pressed his lips together, his eyes inscrutable, but he nodded. "Of course, Omega. Let me help you get the cubs ready for the day. Are you sure you'll be okay caring for them today?"

I resented the insinuation that I couldn't care for them without help, but the look on Courtland's face told me that he was just trying to make things easier for me. The cubs were more lively now, more like they should be at their age.

"We will be fine, but I would appreciate the help getting them prepared." I stepped away, but I paused. Standing on my toes, I kissed him softly. "I was going to choose you, you know? Before Bonnie... I was going to choose you and this Pack. I know you'll probably think it's due to our situation now, but it's not. You were right for me, all of you."

"You say those words like they are the past tense, Pryce."

I shook my head. "No, I still want you all. But if anything happens to Bonnie... If she dies—"

"I won't let that happen," Courtland growled, like he truly believed he could beat death himself.

But I wasn't done. "If something happens to Bonnie, I'm not sure I can..." I trailed off.

I didn't know how to say that I wasn't sure I could ever let myself feel enough again to endure this kind of loss a second time. Bonnie had introduced me to the world, and I wasn't brave enough to let anyone else in if she died.

Courtland pulled me back into his arms and kissed me hard, and in that touch I could feel his fear, but also his determination. "We get our happily ever after, Omega. You, me and Bonnie. Radic and Dominic too. I will make it happen. You can trust me." I licked my lips, unconsciously drawing the taste of him onto my tongue. He caught my chin. "Do you believe me, Omega? Do you believe that I will do anything to ensure our Pack is happy and healthy?"

I nodded, and he kissed me once more. "Yes, Alpha."

"Good." He scraped his lips down my throat, biting softly. "When Bonnie is awake, the first thing I intend to do is make us a family in every sense. Would you like that?" His voice was so low that I knew his Beast was grappling for control.

"Yes, Alpha," I purred back, and he grunted like I'd physically stroked his dick.

Stepping away, he straightened his pants. "Good. Go get ready, Pryce. I'll dress the cubs."

I watched him walk into the nursery, and I couldn't help but creep closer so I could peek through the door. He clutched the rail of the crib, staring down at the babies. And he was smiling. I couldn't hear the soft words he was murmuring to them, but as he lifted Gabriel into his arms, the baby kicked his legs and gurgled, making Courtland laugh.

"Do you want me to be your Alpha? Or I mean, I guess, your Dad. I mean, I don't know much about it— my father gave me a gun for my seventh birthday—but I promise I will protect you from anything that makes you scared."

Yeah. I'd made the right decision. My Beast thrummed in my chest, in total agreement.

My nose twitched at the foreign scents in the infirmary, pushing my Beast back to the edge. I wanted to bundle Bonnie up and take her home, make her a nest, protect her. I felt Courtland stiffen as he caught the scent of strangers too.

"Wait with Bonnie," he said gruffly, and the Alpha order had my feet moving before I even consciously thought about it. When I stepped into the room though, Bonnie wasn't alone. If my nose wasn't wrong, the girl present was a human. Wearing a white lab coat.

Flashbacks hit me hard, of people in coats just like that cutting me to make me bleed. To watch me heal. Of other horrors that my brain had buried deep in my psyche so I couldn't ever dredge them up again.

"Are you okay?" she said, stepping toward me, but I backed away.

No. No. No. I couldn't go back there again. I couldn't. I wouldn't let my cubs be experiments. No.

"Alistair, Bohdie," the girl called. But I didn't see her anymore. No, her face had been transposed with another face—the head researcher. They just called him Smith.

I needed to run, run away and not come back. I couldn't be a prisoner again. I couldn't.

Suddenly, Courtland was there. "Breathe."

It was a command, not a suggestion, and I sucked in a gasping lungful of air. It wasn't until then that I realized my lungs had been burning with the need for oxygen.

Courtland took in the room. "What did you do?" he roared, and then there was yelling and growling. Someone was speaking, but I could barely hear it over the rushing of blood in my head.

"The coat. Lose the coat." Someone rushed past me, and then the sounds of babies crying filtered through my consciousness.

"Hey, Omega. Give me the babies. It's okay now. Breathe." This time Courtland's Alpha command was laced with softness. I swallowed hard as the panic receded. It was the babies crying. And I was crying.

Courtland pried one and then the other cub from my arms, handing them off to Doc. He bared his teeth when the strangers reached for them. "No. Stay where I can see you." He shifted his focus back to me. "Are you with me again, Pryce?"

I nodded, even though my heart felt like it was simultaneously constricting and trying to escape from my chest. He pulled me to his chest and thrummed loudly, for the second time in one morning. I was damaged, broken, and I was inflicting that on everyone around me. I was a fucking failure of an Omega and these guys would be tying themselves to a lodestone.

"Pryce was a captive at a lab for most of his life," he explained, and my body tensed as I waited for their sympathetic hums.

What I didn't expect was an exclaimed, "Holy shit, me too! For study or breeding?"

I whirled around and looked at the girl, who now stood in slacks and a button up shirt, her lab coat gone.

"Excuse me?"

Someone laughed, and it was then I noticed the rest of the people in the room. A tall blond kid, maybe just a little older than Rosa, and another tall blond, though he was far older. And his scent was ... unusual.

"You're the Lycanthrope."

He nodded, his weird golden eyes taking me in. "Yes. Alistair. It is nice to meet you, Pryce. I am sorry that our appearance has caused you discomfort. We aren't strangers to PTSD of this nature."

I swallowed hard again and gave a tiny wave, before my eyes went back to the girl. She looked much younger now that I could take in her appearance without hyperventilating. "You were studied?"

She nodded once. "Yes, when I was very young. But I have an eidetic memory so I don't forget. I was lucky —my main researcher was a good man. He couldn't protect us from everything, but he tried."

The blond kid wrapped his arms around her, giving her a fond kiss on the head the way you would a child. "Who would think that there'd be two of you in the one room?" he murmured, and she looked up at him blankly.

"Statistically, there's quite a high probability given —" He placed his finger on her lips.

"It was rhetorical, Stace."

I crossed the room to Bonnie, stroking my hand over her hair, which was lank and unwashed. I didn't care, inhaling her scent deep into my lungs. I let out a sigh of relief; just being close made me feel better.

But there was something about her scent today that was different. I couldn't work out what it was though.

Stacey stepped closer, and I could feel her

observing our interactions. "I've run some tests, done some bloodwork, but apart from some raised hormone levels and this unconsciousness, I can't find anything in her brain that would cause this. It's like her body has…" She paused, her eyes going comically wide, like she was a cartoon character with an epiphany. "Shit. That's it. It would explain the positive activity in her gamma-aminobutyric acid receptor."

Then she was gone, the Lycanthrope and Doc along with her, after he'd passed the babies back to Courtland.

Courtland's phone rang at that moment, as we all watched her disappear. He passed the babies back to me now that I was calmer, and I took them in my arms, mentally apologising to them for my freakout. They were still fussy and I felt like a shit parent.

Courtland pulled his phone from his pocket. "Yes? What?" He was silent for a second, his brows anchoring down low. "Are you sure? Just the Betas? Okay, I'll be right there. I'll bring Doc." He hung up, his face pinched with concern. "It's some kind of virus. Two more Betas just collapsed into unconsciousness."

Holy shit, what was happening?

Courtland paused at the door. "Will you be okay?"

I nodded. "Yes. Now go!"

I didn't have to tell him twice. He was gone in an instant. I juggled the babies as I walked toward

Bonnie's bed again. I was hopeful that the girl was onto something, because I needed Bonnie back now.

The cubs continued to fuss, and I rocked them both as well as I could.

"Do you want a hand?" I jumped at the voice, and spun to see the young blond guy was still in the corner. "Sorry, didn't mean to scare you. I'm Bohdie, by the way. No one introduced us." He sauntered forward, and I could tell he was a shifter of some sort. "I'm good with babies, but shit with science. So if you need a hand, I could help?"

He smelled like an Alpha, but his face was open and friendly. My Beast said he wasn't a threat, and I really could use the help.

I passed him Gabriel. "Thank you. I'm Pryce."

He held the cub with ease, and the baby quieted immediately. "My mate is an Omega. She's good with kids too. Her name is Enit and she's the most beautiful woman in the world." I smiled at that, because it was obvious he loved her.

For the next three hours, Bohdie told me about his life, mostly about his mate, and I think I made a new friend, all while Maxton was going to hell around us.

I made myself come back to work, otherwise my brain just fixated on Bonnie. On my mistakes. On a future without her. So instead, I chose to lose myself in endless fucking paperwork. Anything to keep my mind off her.

Courtland still hadn't arrived, but he was taking Pryce to sit with Bonnie, and his first appointment wasn't for another three hours. The amount of people who wanted his time had lessened over the last week, and I wasn't sure if it was because word had gotten around about Bonnie, or because he'd fixed all the problems that people had been festering over for the last decade.

Courtland didn't say no to a worthy request. He didn't heckle over funds either, after talking to accounting. Turns out, Maxton was rich as fuck due to some good investments in property and oil in the early twentieth century. You wouldn't have known it from the previous Alpha General though. That guy had kept a tight fist on the money, probably because he still believed in survival of the fittest.

But when I thought of all the times Bonnie had gone without just so she could feed and clothe the kids in the Sanctum, while we'd had funds to keep it well-resourced for a century, well, that made me impossibly angry. I was glad that old fuck was dead.

My phone rang, and I heaved a sigh as I answered it. "Alpha General's office."

"Fuck, Radic, thank god it's you. Something is wrong with Elizabeth." I recognized the voice of John Fairweather, and he was not a man prone to exaggeration.

"What happened?"

"She just collapsed. She was changing out the spark plugs on old Tom's ATV and then she just keeled over. Hit her head pretty bad and made it bleed. She isn't waking up and I can't get hold of Doc."

Cold fear washed over me. "I'll find him right away, John. I'll get him sent up."

I hung up the phone, but no sooner had I put it down, the phone rang again. I dragged it back to my ear.

"Hello?"

"Radic, it's Quinn." Why the fuck would one of

Wilkie's Betas be calling me? And why was he whispering?

"What's wrong?"

"It's Susannah," he whispered, and I could hear the fearful tremble in his voice. "She won't wake up. And she smells wrong, and Wilkie is being weirder than normal, and the guys are acting fucking crazy and I don't know what to do."

Fuck. Fuck, fuck, fuck. "Are you safe?"

"Yeah, I barricaded myself in her room and I'll hold them back, but I don't know what's wrong."

Shit, I didn't know what was wrong either. "I'll send someone up to get you guys out right now, okay? Someone will sort out Wilkie, and we'll bring Susannah down to the infirmary to get her checked out. Hold on."

I hung up again, and called Murphy and Merrick. Murphy answered his phone on the first ring with a grunt. "Murphy, it's Radic." I lowered my voice so no one could hear. "Something is wrong with Susannah. I need you to go and extract her from Wilkie's Pack. Quinn too."

"What?" Murphy asked, but he was already relaying my message to Merrick.

"Look, I don't know what the hell is going on, and I'll know more when I talk to Doc. Just get Susannah to the infirmary as soon as you can—I don't give a fuck what Wilkie says. Got it? I'll pass it by the Alpha

General, but Courtland isn't going to give a fuck if you steal Susannah from her abusive Alpha, I can tell you that. He's not like the old Alpha General."

Yeah, that old bastard had believed Pack business was between an Alpha and his Pack, and it didn't matter if there was proof of abuse, no one was allowed to interfere. I could hear Merrick growl down the line.

"I've wanted to punch that asshole in the face for a while now. We'll get her to the infirmary." He cut the call, and I quickly punched the speed dial for Courtland.

"Yes?"

"It's Radic. We have a fucking huge problem. More Betas are getting sick."

"What? You sure it's just the Betas?"

"Yeah, I'm sure. Only the females too, if we use Bonnie as case zero. You need to get Doc and head up to John Fairweather's place. Merrick and Murphy are grabbing Susannah and bringing her to the infirmary."

"Okay, I'll be right there. I'll bring Doc." Then he hung up.

And my phone rang once more.

By the time the sun set, fifteen female Betas were unconscious, most at home, though Susannah was in the infirmary with Bonnie. Elizabeth Fairweather had been patched up and was resting at home.

With the exception of Susannah, they were all young and unmated. What the hell was happening?

The fact there were two extra doctors in town had never been more appreciated, though everyone was acting defensive considering they were outsiders. But eventually, all the women presented the same. Fever, loss of consciousness, pain. Doc had learned with Bonnie, and quickly made them all comfortable. The Legion Generals had been conferring all day, trying to work out if this was a virus or some kind of poison. They locked down the borders, though I don't know what they thought that would achieve.

The whole town was starting to panic though; women were whisked away indoors just in case it got them too, and the commissary was picked clean, as well as the bakery. I'd had a million phone calls, and it got to the stage where I had to stop answering, instead leaving a voice recording of important information.

On top of that, Wilkie and Merrick had gotten into a brawl, and Merrick had bitten Wilkie's ear clean off. Doc had been too busy stabilizing the female Betas to sew it back on, so one of Wilkie's Betas had done it. Somehow, I didn't think it would stick.

Finally, the calls had slowed down, and there were no more cases coming forward. I forwarded the phone to my cell, and got the hell out of the office. I needed to find Bonnie and Pryce, make sure everyone was okay.

The streets were eerily quiet when I left, and I

shook off the chill that stole down my spine. I drove the ATV a little too fast to the infirmary, barely bringing it to a stop before I was out of it and up the back steps. Murphy was standing guard at the back step, his face a hard mask.

I slowed my pace. "You okay?"

Murphy slid his eyes toward me, grinding his back teeth. "I just really hate that fuck, Radic. I hate him." I didn't even need to ask who 'him' was, because I hated Wilkie too.

"I know, man. I kind of wish Merrick had eaten his ear."

Murphy gagged a little. "I kiss that mouth."

A surprised laugh burst out from between my lips. "Yeah, fair call." I went to step past him, but paused, thumping him on the arm. "She'll be okay, you know. She's tough, Susannah; she always has been. Wilkie..." Yeah, Wilkie was a fuck. We didn't need to expand on that. And Merrick and Murphy had been 100% in love with Susannah growing up. They'd been heartbroken when Susannah had chosen Wilkie, and then had to sit back and watch him treat her little better than a fucking glory hole in a cheap gas station bathroom wall.

Murphy nodded, and I stepped into the back of Doc's house. There were a lot of people in the infirmary. Susannah and Bonnie were in the same room, pushed to separate sides of the space. In the center was a blond kid who smelled like a shifter. He was playing with our cubs, blowing raspberries and playing peek-a-boo, and the cubs were smiling in a way that made my chest feel too full.

But he was still a stranger. A low growl slipped from my mouth, and everyone looked at me. Pryce stood, slipping toward me quickly. "That's Bohdie. He's with the doctors from out of town. He's, uh, bored, I guess." He lowered his voice. "My Beast doesn't think he's a threat. He's a nice kid. It's allowed me to focus on Bonnie, because something is wrong, Rad, and I *can't* pull myself away."

The desperation in his voice made me pause, and even as I searched his face for answers, he was moving back toward Bonnie. I looked over at Merrick, who still had Wilkie's blood on his shirt, and he rested against the wall beside Susannah's bed.

"What the hell is going on?" he demanded, the Alpha power from his Beast all up in his tone.

The sound of a growl at my back had me spinning around and coming face to face with Courtland. He looked stressed as fuck, still letting out a low grumbling sound as he stared down Merrick.

The Alpha in question dropped his eyes. "Sorry, Alpha General." He looked up at me through long eyelashes. Too long for a man. "Sorry, Rad. I didn't mean to Alpha you. It's been a hell of a day."

I gave him a tight smile. I knew he was stressed;

we'd been friends for long enough that I recognized it in the lines of his body, the tightness of his face. "It's all good. We're all stressed about the unknown."

Another voice interrupted. "Well, I can fix that."

I looked over to see a girl, who was definitely still a teenager, flounce into the room, her curly hair bouncing with each step. She looked pretty happy with herself, and honestly I was confused as hell until Doc appeared. He was side by side with a man who looked about thirty but had the eyes of someone much older. Definitely the Lycanthrope. I tried not to let the scary stories of my childhood color my perception of the man.

"This is Stacey. She is a doctor," Courtland explained.

"And genius," the kid on the floor added proudly.

Courtland raised an eyebrow. "That's her Alpha."

Well, I guess that was cute.

"I noticed that she had an imbalance of proteins in her gamma-aminobutyric acid receptor A—"

"In English, Stace. We aren't all doctors," Bohdie said softly.

"Or geniuses," I added, smiling so she knew I wasn't being an asshole.

"Uh, okay," the girl—Stacey, I guess—started. "So the brain chemicals that increase during anaesthesia, or like, when you get blackout drunk, were elevated in Bonnie, which is what is causing her to sleep. This can be reversed fairly easily with a cocktail of drugs, in the same way you'd reverse a medically induced coma."

My heart skipped and I stepped toward her. "Then do it?"

She frowned at me like I was an idiot. "The body just doesn't shut itself down like that for no reason. Prematurely waking her up could cause her indescribable pain or damage. So I searched for a reason why the body would take such a drastic measure."

She handed me a clipboard. On it were three columns of abbreviations and numbers I didn't understand. I handed it to Courtland, who frowned down at it too.

"You're going to have to spell this out like we're idiots."

Stacey huffed and got a pen. She pointed to the first column. "So this column here is the hormone levels and other bloodwork that Doc did on Naja. I believe that's your sister?" she said to Courtland, who nodded. Then she pointed to the third column. "This is the bloodwork I did on a mated female Beta, for a baseline, while we were treating her daughter who'd collapsed." She flicked her pen with a flourish, like she'd just delivered a smoking gun.

"Still confused, kid," I grumbled, and she frowned at me.

"The middle column is obviously Bonnie, which I drew yesterday. Which other column does her bloodwork most resemble?" she asked slowly, like we were first graders.

I looked between the numbers, matching them up, and then sucked in a breath. Courtland went totally stiff beside me.

Pryce made a whining noise beside Bonnie's bed. "What is it?"

I looked at Courtland, my eyes so wide they would pop out of my head if I so much as sneezed.

"Bonnie is turning into an Omega."

The girl—this smart, amazing doctor—was shaking her head. "No, not turning into an Omega. She *is* an Omega."

Holy fuck.

My brain kept banging up against the idea that Bonnie, my Bonnie, was now an Omega. It made sense, I guess. The change in her scent, the change in how Pryce responded to her—hell, how we all responded to her.

My Beast howled with happiness, but I wasn't quite so quick to celebrate. The man knew there had to be more to it than this.

"How is that even possible?"

Stacey shrugged. "The Manix are a bit of a biological anomaly in general. There are certain species in nature that can change their gender due to social or environmental factors, and given that the projection for the complete extinction of your race was sitting at"—she paused like she was doing the math in her head, which apparently she was—"fifty-six years until functional extinction of your species as it is now, then I'd say the environmental factors were quite compelling."

"We aren't talking fish and frogs here, Stacey," Doc protested, though he looked just as shocked as the rest of us. And tired. The old Manix looked exhausted.

"It was just a small alteration of equipment already possessed by the female Betas. This is not such a huge scientific leap. Has there been a change in the general makeup of the Pack?"

I nodded. "I came into power and the old Alpha General was executed."

Radic nodded. "Plus we found the first Omega female in over a century." He paused. "And she just went into heat again."

Stacey grinned, like we were small children finally working out that one plus one equals two. "Hormones are a crazy business. They can change things in the space of a moment, or over the course of a week. Things such as altering the body of unmated Betas into the thing that the species desperately needs for survival—unmated Omega females."

Fuck... I didn't know what to say. Actually, yes I did. "If she's now an Omega female, why isn't she awake?" I didn't mean for it to sound like an accusation, but suddenly the Alpha lion kid was there, sliding his body between mine and the human's, a low growl being pulled from his chest.

I bowed my head. "Apologies, Doctor. I didn't mean to be so forceful." I was in shock, that much was for sure. I needed to plan. So many unmated Omega females, but at least I had a few days to plan the best course of action.

"I don't know, but I think her body was waiting for the pheromonal indicators that synced her heat to the original Omega female."

My brain was whirling, as I turned that over. "So you're telling me she could awaken any moment now and be in *heat*?"

The doctor nodded happily. "The others too. Their transformation seemed to be a lot quicker than Bonnie's for that very reason. Susannah has almost progressed to the same stage already."

I swallowed hard, sweat breaking out across my brow. "Just to reiterate, you are saying that I will have fifteen unmated Omega females, all in heat, at any moment?"

Stacey frowned. "Well, when you put it like that, it sounds like a bad thing."

Fuck.

What did I do? It was very hard for a Manix male to resist the call of a female Omega in heat, almost impossible for male Omegas. Even my Beast was already roaring to make them both mine, to breed Bonnie and Pryce until they were begging for my knot.

Radic looked pale too. Shit. "How many non-Manix personnel do we have in town?"

"Four, if we count Dominic, Loren and these two shifters here." He winced. "The old regime didn't like outsiders."

Shit. Shit, fuck. The Manix were known for the insanity they fell into—when female Omegas went into heat, male Omegas went into rut, and we were just crazed fucking machines, who would fight to the death to either protect our mates or keep back prospective suitors from a potential mate. The word 'mania' had been coined from an ancient scholar's account of the breeding season of the Manix, at the height of our species' existence.

I pulled my phone from my pocket and dialled Dominic. "Hey man, I'm just on my way to the infirmary."

"Don't come," I growled.

"What?"

"I've got great news and bad news. Good news is we know what's wrong with Bonnie and she'll wake up any moment now."

I heard his rapid inhale. "Really?"

I let myself smile, because I truly was so fucking happy about that. "Yes. Now for the bad news—which is also good news, I guess. Turns out she has metamorphosed into a female Omega. However, the fifteen other female Betas that went down? They did too. And they'll all come out of their comas and into heat at once. You remember those stories Abuela used to tell us of the frenzy?"

Abuela had told a story that she said her husband—my grandfather—had told her. She said that an unmated female Manix had gone into heat during a Pack gathering and six Manix males had died in their manic need to get to her. She said it was worse than the rut. It had been dubbed 'the frenzy.'

Now we were about to have fifteen unmated females in heat.

"Oh, fuck." Yep, that was the general consensus.

I gritted my teeth. "I don't think I am going to be above the insanity, especially not with both Bonnie and Pryce in the same room. It's gotta be you, man. I'm giving you entire authority to protect the female Omegas and anyone else. Kick whoever's ass you want. We'll deal with the fallout later."

I heard him swallow hard. "Okay, I'll get Loren and see if we can't figure out some kind of plan." He paused. "You'll kiss her for me, right? Tell her that I missed her?"

I smiled, despite the stress of the moment. "You know I will."

When I hung up, I looked at everyone in the room, who were all staring at me like I had a solution to this situation, but I did not. Not really.

I looked back at the doctors. "Is it safe to move her?"

Doc nodded. "Yes."

I looked at the other group. "If you need to leave, now would be the time. If you choose to stay, the Manix would be grateful and would owe you a favor."

The girl was looking between Alistair the Lycanthrope, and Bohdie. "I don't think anyone in the last century has witnessed a frenzy. It would be an interesting research opportunity."

Bohdie scoffed. "This guy is preparing for Armageddon, Stace. It's too dangerous just to appease your scientific curiosity."

"Lucky I have you then, isn't it?" she said, raising a single challenging eyebrow. Bohdie looked at Alistair.

"We'll stay. I believe you'll need the help before the worst is over."

I bowed low. "Thank you." I turned to Merrick and Murphy, who were hovering over one of the fallen Betas. "Do you trust yourselves?"

They both seemed to pause, looking between the unconscious female and her Beta packmate. Merrick straightened his spine. "They'll be safe with us."

I nodded. "If I hear otherwise, I will flay the skin from your body while alive." They both grunted, but I was glad I got the point across. "Go, stash her somewhere safe. Do not touch her without her express permission and do not mate her. Am I clear?"

"Crystal, man. She's already mated, remember?" They scooped her up and ushered the male, Quinn, out the door.

It was time to go. "Rad, help Pryce with the cubs." I stepped toward my Omega, who was watching us all with wide, anxious eyes. "It will be okay, Omega. I promise. Let's go home, okay?"

He nodded, going to scoop up the second cub from the middle of the room. I pulled back the blankets of Bonnie's hospital bed, scooping her into my arms. She squirmed, letting out a low sound in her throat.

My dick went hard as a rock. Shit, we had to hurry.

Doc frowned at me. "She's coming out of it already, Courtland. I would hurry."

He didn't have to tell me twice. I sprinted to the van I had parked at the rear of the property when I'd dropped Pryce off this morning. Pryce and Radic strapped the cubs into their carseats as I slid Bonnie into the back, then climbed into the driver's seat. "Radic, call the families of all the sleeping Betas, uh, Omegas? Explain. Warn them what's coming."

Radic nodded, pulling out his phone. I drove the short distance back to the house we now occupied. When I stepped out, I wasn't surprised to see one of the Alphas of Bonnie's Omega friend striding toward me.

"Alpha General," he said, dipping his head respectfully, even as he eyed me lifting the unconscious body of Bonnie from the back of the van. "What the fuck is going on?"

Bonnie stirred in my arms again, and my Beast was rapidly roaring to the surface. "Short version. Bonnie has changed into a female Omega. So have fifteen other unmated female Betas. They are all about to go into heat."

Corvin stumbled back like I'd hit him. "What? How?"

I shrugged. "Only mother nature and the Goddess herself know. And an extremely smart human girl." I paused. "Will you be okay caring for the Sanctum?" Shit, why hadn't I thought of that? They were a Pack of Alphas with a sole Omega; they would feel the full effects of the frenzy.

Corvin tightened his jaw. "We'll be fine, Alpha. I'll go lock down the Sanctum now."

Then he was gone and I was striding into the house. Rosa was standing at the door, her mouth wide open. "Is it true? Is everyone going to go into rut?" She'd heard the same stories from Abuela as Dominic and I had.

I nodded. "I need to put Bonnie down, and then I'll come back and speak to you, Rosa."

I took the stairs two at a time until I was on the very top floor. I found a smaller size spare room, and laid Bonnie down on the bed. I didn't want to destroy her room, and I knew she'd appreciate the more enclosed space.

When I turned, Radic was behind me, looking desperately hopeful. I grabbed him and hugged him tight to my chest. "It's going to be okay, Beta. Go and gather all the pillows and blankets from our rooms—she'll want a familiar, comfortable space when she wakes." He moved away, and I called out. "Rad? I'm going to... It's going to be crazy. I'm going to need you, Beta. Need you to protect our cubs, our Pack, and our mate. I promise, next time? Next time, when we make a decision, it will be all of us. But this time? I need you to be the strong one."

He chewed his lower lip but nodded, taking off down the hall to gather things for our female Omega. Our Bonnie.

I breathed out the word "Fuck" as I sprinted back down the stairs. I had to explain everything to Rosa and give her a damn gun. She would be the last line of defence for the kids if things got... insane.

Then I had to have the birds and the bees talk with my male Omega.

This should be interesting.

## 32

BONNIE

You know when you have a really long nap, and rising to consciousness feels like wading through soup? Well, waking from a coma didn't feel like that. It felt like a shot of adrenaline right to the heart.

I gasped as I ratcheted upright, my body feeling shaky and weak. Someone was there, their hands smoothing over my shoulders. "Shush, Bonnie. It's okay," came whispered words, and it took me too long to recognize Pryce's voice, though his Omega essence flowed over my skin like cool water.

It was dark, and I wasn't in my room. I didn't remember anything. Well, anything except Courtland asking me to be his Beta.

"What happened?" I said, but my throat felt rough.

"You've… uh, you've been in a coma. Or unconscious, at least."

I ran my hands over my body, looking for injuries or something that would explain Pryce's words. I felt wrong, that much was obvious. My skin was on fire, and my body felt like it had been wound up like a spinning top. Also, I could feel my hip bones a little more prominently than usual. "For how long?"

"The longest five days of my life. And I lived in a damn white-walled cell for sixteen years."

I frowned at him, but he really did look a bit crazed. "Are you okay? Am I okay?"

He hesitated. "I should get Courtland or Radic or someone," he choked out, and then he was out of the bed and gone.

Shit, was I dying? Is that why I felt like this?

The door slammed open, and within a blink, the familiar weight of Radic was on top of me. He kissed every inch of skin he could reach: my face, cheeks, my neck. He didn't stop kissing until I groaned under the weight of his body. He rolled off, but didn't let me go. "Baby, I've never been so fucking scared in my whole life. Thank the Goddess you're awake." He squeezed me tightly to his body.

"Radic, Bonnie needs to breathe," came Courtland's dark voice, and something shuddered over my body like a caress. I whined low in my throat, an embarrassingly sensual sound, and Radic sprang away.

I curled my fingers in bedsheets that smelled clean, but all the blankets around me smelled of the guys. "What's wrong with me?" I asked again, and it was Courtland who came over, sitting beside me on the bed like he was made of stone.

"Bonnie, you were unconscious because your body was changing."

I cringed. "This sounds like the speech Doc gave me when I hit puberty, though there were more diagrams then." I shuddered. That had been awkward for us both. Radic snorted a laugh, because he remembered my horror.

Courtland huffed, shaking his head, and I swore I could feel his scent brush across my face like a stroke of his hand. "It's not much different. Bonnie, by some quirk of nature, you have changed designations. You're now an Omega female."

The whole room was silent. I didn't even breathe, waiting for the punchline to the joke he was obviously telling, but no one was laughing.

"Come on, that's not possible," I argued, because it was legitimately the insanest thing I'd ever heard. And I was from a race of beings where the men gave birth.

Radic grabbed my hand. "It's true, Bonnie. Happened to you and every other unmated female Beta in town. And Susannah," he said, frowning. That made no sense at all.

I just blinked at them slowly as my brain tried to process. "Are you sure?"

Courtland nodded. "The smartest person I have ever met proved it, and Doc agreed." He paused. "Plus, your scent," he groaned.

I sniffed my armpit, but that was a bit gross. Ew. I didn't smell any different to me though. I looked over at Pryce and my body clenched, which made him make a pained noise.

Radic swallowed. "Also, you're about to go into heat, and smell like..." He trailed off like there wasn't a word, but judging by the look of absolute lust on his face, it was good.

My eyes whipped to Pryce. "You need to get him out of here!"

His face fell like I'd kicked him straight in the gut, and I felt like shit. I crawled over the comforters toward him. "No no, not like that. I would love to, uh, make love to you. Actually, it's the only thing I want to do right now," I moaned, leaning forward to nip his chin with my teeth. "But this isn't how you should experience your first time, with this out of control feeling pushing you into it. You should choose, with a clear head."

The smile he gave me made both my heart and my lady parts clench simultaneously. "I could be sober as a judge, and I'd still choose you, Bonnie. Omega. My

Omega," he purred, and I let the word roll over me. Me. An Omega.

Oh shit. I swung my head to Courtland. "You aren't going to try and impregnate him, are you?" Ice traveled down my spine, cooling the fire in my belly. "Oh shit, the other Beta, I mean Omega females. You're protecting them, right? Shit, how? How can you protect them? The whole Legion Force is unmated males. Oh, shit, Courtland, you have to do something... Where's Dominic?"

The panic was beginning to spiral out of control inside of me, like everything was heightened to eleven. Courtland gently pulled me to my feet and into his arms. He thrummed low in his chest, and my whole body went lax. "It's okay, Bonnie. Dominic is acting in my stead, and between himself and Loren, we got word out to the families of the new Omegas. It doesn't seem to affect males who already have a female Omega either, so I've had to beg Gatlin, Finlo and Seven to drag themselves away from their own mate to make sure everyone is safe. They have an impressive cell system down in the Legion basement, and anyone who messes up will go straight to the brig. Doc will shoot the ones who are too wild with a tranq strong enough to bring down a bull elephant. Loren isn't exactly a weakling, and this will be good for his abilities. To incapacitate and not kill."

I swallowed hard when I realized I'd been stroking

my face across his chest as he spoke. He ran his hand down my hair soothingly. "To answer your other question, no, I don't intend to get Pryce with cub. I can control myself, Bonnie, so you guys do what you need to. *If* you choose to let us help you with the heat, that is entirely up to you, Omega. Your choice is the most important. But to assuage any lingering fears, no matter your decision, I do not intend on knotting the Omega tonight." His voice was confident, but there was a tight strain around his eyes that said that might not be as easy as he made it sound. "Radic will be here, guarding us all, so if you feel uncomfortable at any point, you can call for him. Either of you."

My eyes swung to Radic, and I tried to read his face. It was a face that I knew as well as my own, and he'd never been able to keep a secret from me.

"You're okay with this?"

He frowned. "With you being an Omega female? It's scary, Bonnie. I've never been more scared." He stepped closer until he was bracketing my body between his chest and Courtland's. "With you making sweaty crazy love with our Alpha and our Omega? No. I'm cool with that. Next time it'll be my turn." I felt his low chuckle against the side of my neck, where he nipped at the sensitive skin. "No mating marks until we can all be together though," he warned me, or maybe Courtland.

Courtland grabbed his chin. "I promise, Beta. Not

until we are all together, all ready to be a Pack." His eyes drifted over to Pryce. "There is no rush, despite the new circumstances."

This was fucking nuts. "I need… a shower."

Despite the fact my uterus had decided to declare war, my temperature was rising and my vagina was about to pull a triple combo move and scream "FINISH HIM!", I needed space to think, to breathe, to process. Plus, I smelled like a three-day-old corn chip left down the side of the couch cushion, and as much as they were looking at me like I was a freshly baked cookie, I wasn't comfortable letting anyone go to town until I'd scrubbed away four days of lying in a flipping coma.

They all jumped up, moving out of the way so I could get to the hall bathroom. Leaving my nest—and there was no doubt in my mind that's what they'd created me—was like physically ripping off a band-aid. I didn't want to leave, even hesitated at the door, and if I had any doubt about their claims that I was an Omega, they disappeared then and there.

I gritted my teeth, and by pure stubbornness I made it to the bathroom, locking the door. I threw on the shower as my body cramped and my emotions went insane. I hated that they weren't in the room with me, hated that Pryce wasn't on his knees in front of me, or fucking me, and it shook me to my core. Like I'd become possessed or something.

I stepped into the shower before it was even warm, hissing at the cold water that poured over my skin. Slowly, I made the water warmer, scrubbing myself on weak limbs. I was just out of a damn coma. I shouldn't be thinking about sex. I should be thinking about getting my strength back or something. But my Beast, my new Omega Beast, felt like She-Hulk. She was raging to get to Pryce, with his long, lean physique, and those big blue eyes. I'd seen him shirtless more times than I can count, and every single time I'd wanted to run my tongue from his navel, up through his six pack. And Courtland…

My abdomen clenched, and the deep ache was almost like period pain, if my period was like an anvil to the gut. I'd need to put up with a whole week of this?

Yeah, no, that wasn't going to happen. As another wave hit me like a punch, I slumped to the shower floor with a yell. Courtland was there, bursting through the locked door before my screech had even stopped. "Bonnie? Are you okay? Omega?" he growled, like I was supposed to answer in the breaths between words.

From my knees, curled in a ball, I looked up at this man who I wanted to consume me. "Fuck me, Alpha. Make this go away."

He bent down and scooped me out of the shower. "I've got you, Bonnie."

## 33

DOMINIC

Radic's phone call had been like a weight off my chest. "She's awake and she's fine. Freaked all the way out, but she's okay."

I wanted to race home, to bury myself against the soft curves of her body and make love to her until she was begging for mercy, because she'd scared the shit out of me.

Instead, I was stuck patrolling the streets in wolf form, making sure these fuckers kept their shit together. Every one of the families had been notified, and had closed ranks around the still waking new Omega females. A super pissed off Gatlin was patrolling with me, and I could legitimately smell his disgruntlement like an acrid smell in my snout.

"Get the fuck in your house, Emmitt, or I swear I will make you. I don't care if you're lonely, or if your dick gets so hard it falls off. You know where my dick should be right now? *Do you, Emmitt?*" he growled at one of the Manix who'd been trying to sneak out his window like a horny Doberman. Gatlin was not playing around, and I let out a wolfy laugh.

I lifted my head as I caught a smell on the breeze. It was sweet, even to my shifted senses, and Gatlin went ramrod straight. And Emmitt? Well, he went nuts. Like livin' la vida loca cray cray. He launched himself at Gatlin with snapping jaws, and I pounced toward them, snapping my teeth and growling.

But this guy wasn't scared of my teeth or Gatlin's serious fuck off vibes. He'd lost it. Oh shit, we were in trouble. I shifted back to a man as Emmitt grabbed Gatlin, flailing like a crackhead on a binge.

I grabbed the gun from Gatlin's waist and shot Emmitt. The guy went down like a heap of shit, and Gatlin whirled on me.

I grinned. "Don't stress, Alpha. Tranqs. It'll keep him out for a bit, anyway."

"Fucking Goddess. Does Finlo have one of those?"

I shook my head. "Nah, he has Loren. He's worth a hundred tranq guns." We dragged Emmitt back into his house, shutting the door. "Doc says that will knock them out for twelve hours or so without many side effects. I'll stop back and check on him later anyway." I chuckled. "This could be fun."

Gatlin nodded, but then slid me the side eye. "Are

you going to cover your dick, or are we kicking ass with your balls swinging in the breeze?"

I shifted back to the wolf and gave him a toothy grin, my tongue lolling slightly. I trotted into the darkness, but barely made it a hundred feet when another Manix was raging out of his house, his face lifted to the air and a wild look in his eyes.

Fuck, this wasn't going to work. I growled at the giant Manix who stood in front of me, and while his power wasn't anything close to Courtland's, or even Gatlin's behind me, he was more than a match for me and that burned. My growl turned vicious, but the guy kept squaring off with me, his own lips pulled back over sharp teeth. Then a dart came from nowhere and the big Manix went down, his head hitting the pavement with a thud. He'd have a headache, but no permanent damage.

Good. Asshole.

I changed back. "This isn't going to work. There's not enough of us."

Gatlin nodded. He was distracted by the perfume of unmated Omegas in the air, I could tell that, but he wasn't consumed with mindless need. "We need to move the Omegas to a central point and defend that."

"Safest place is the cells below the Legion building."

I frowned. I hated the idea of locking the Omegas in. What if we got overwhelmed? They'd be sitting ducks there. We needed non-Manix help, and that grated even more. "Let's get them all together, get some of the mated female Betas in there to care for them."

Gatlin grimaced. "That's all well and good, but moving them is going to be its own problem."

Fuck me, I couldn't believe there was going to be a whole week of this. I knew what needed to be done, and I just hoped Courtland wouldn't kick my ass for it. "Pass me my phone?" I'd given it to Gatlin to hold because let's face it, it wasn't like I could stuff it up my ass in wolf form and carry it around.

Gatlin dragged it out of his jeans, which were kinda tight, and I took a moment to appreciate that he was a fine-looking man. Not as hot as my Pack, but still attractive. He handed me my phone, giving me a sour look. "Stop undressing me with your eyes."

I snorted. "You'd be so lucky, asshole," I said with a grin, and then searched through my contacts. Eesh, I was definitely going to get my ass kicked for this, but Courtland was probably balls deep in my girl so he could suck my dick.

I hit dial, and the person at the other end answered on the second ring.

"Hello?" She sounded surprised.

"Ma'am, we need help."

· · ·

I t turned out that when vamps said, "We'll be there soon," they fucking meant *soon.*

After the longest hour of my life, where we must have tranqed sixteen Manix Alphas between us, I felt a cool breath fan over the back of my neck. I whirled, snapping, but all I found was the smiling face of X.

"Hello, Wolfie," he said, grinning widely and showing some impressive fangs. "You're looking awfully sweaty there. Busy night?"

"Man, you have no fucking idea. Never been so happy to see a bloodsucker."

Gatlin groaned, but X just grinned. "Obviously, you've never met Judge." Another vampire lifted his head from where he was walking up with Raine, the Convocation member. And he was hot as fuck. Holy shit. X threw back his head and laughed, and I scowled at him again. "He has that effect on anything with a heartbeat, Wolfie. Don't take it personally."

Raine was shaking her head. "We got here as fast as we could. It's been awhile since we've had a good run. Didn't think I'd have to come back here so soon. For a race that was previously thought extinct, you're a lot of drama."

I winced. "Sorry, Ma'am. But the Moon Goddess had other ideas."

"And where's your Alpha General?"

I tensed my jaw. "He's taking care of our Pack, as he

should be. I'm more than capable of taking care of this situation in his stead. That's why we are a Pack, why I'm his Beta."

Raine laughed, throwing her hands in the air. It was insane to think someone who looked twenty could be one of the most powerful supernaturals in the world. Not physically, but her words could save or sacrifice any one of us.

She reached over, patting my arm like I was a wayward child. "Easy there. I don't mean to be offensive. Family first, always. Okay, catch me up on what I've missed, because the last time I was here, you were almost extinct and your Alpha was still a bachelor." She raised an eyebrow. "I do enjoy some good gossip."

I told her about Bonnie's coma, and her waking up as an Omega female, and the whole town going into rut. As if to punctuate my point, a small group of Alphas sprinted around the corner toward the big house behind the main street. There was a new Omega female named Tia up there. X grinned and sprinted after them.

"Incapacitate, X! I mean it," Raine yelled after him, shaking her head. "This is why I brought these two and not Lucius." Uh, yeah. Good move. "So, you were saying?"

"Yeah, so Doc got in two other doctors. I swear, the youngest one is like fifteen but she's brilliant, and her father I guess is a Lycanthrope, and they said—"

"Stacey's here?!" Raine screeched, and I jumped away. But she seemed happy about it. "She's my daughter's girlfriend. Is Bohdie here too? I can't imagine Enit letting her come up here without him; she's very protective of Stacey."

I guess there wouldn't be many child geniuses with a Lycan as a father, so I just nodded. Honestly, the supernatural world was like a small town sometimes.

Before I knew it, we were over at Doc's house, and Raine was hugging Bohdie and Stacey, who didn't seem like she was a huge fan of hugging but withstood it anyway. While they caught up, the hottie vampire—I mean, Judge—came to speak to me, his face serious.

Hot as fuck but still, he had nothing on Courtland.

"What is your plan?"

I cleared my throat. "We move all the Omegas to a central location. The heat... Well, they tell me it's rough, and the Manix are literally genetically predisposed to ease their suffering with the added benefit of propagating their race. With so many new Omegas, the males have gone..."

"Manic?"

"They call it the frenzy. Doesn't happen very often, but often enough that it has a special name. It's basically when the whole town goes nuts. So I think we put the Omegas in the cells down below, make them comfortable, and guard a single point rather than spreading ourselves around. None of the Omegas were in relationships from what I can work out, so now is not the time for them to be making crazy decisions anyway. They are all drugged on their hormones."

Judge was nodding slowly. "Makes sense. You don't think they'll try to burn them out or anything like that? Smoke them out of their foxhole?"

I shook my head. "It would literally go against their biology to harm the Omegas, or even potentially harm them. More likely is that they'll try to get through the guards. Or they'll congregate outside and fight amongst themselves."

With a plan of action decided, we set about moving all the Omegas to the one spot. Loren looked exhausted, and Finlo looked absolutely gleeful as he shot his fellow Manix full of elephant tranquilizers.

Moving them one at a time was hell. Mainly, getting their families to hand them over was a pain in the ass every single time. It wasn't that they were opposed to the idea—if anything, they all looked exhausted too. No, it was giving them over to a six foot five vampire covered in tattoos, who quite frankly oozed deviancy, that was the problem. Raine had to step in quite a few times, and it ended up being Raine doing most of the ferrying back and forth. I guess looking like a college student had its perks, because in the face of danger, they could forget she was just as capable of killing a person as easily as the big bastards who were her bodyguards.

Speaking of guards, Raine had also called in her personal contingent of protective security personnel, who looked super pissed that she'd super speeded her way to a different country in the middle of the night, but took the direction to guard the Legion building with little grumbling.

Finally, all fifteen Omegas were secured in the holding cells—holding cells that were *constructed* to withstand the force of a Manix, and were giant to boot. I'd seen smaller apartments holding entire three generational families. There were mattresses lining the floor and so many blankets and cushions that it looked like Bed, Bath & Beyond had thrown up in there. I breathed a relieved sigh.

The keys were in the cells with the Omegas, with the females that we had in there anyway. Finlo's mom and sister had volunteered—or been commandeered, depending on how you looked at it—plus Doctor Stacey, despite Bohdie's protests. The vampires and the Convocation guards were keeping everyone at bay, though they were beginning to amass out the front of the doors.

I followed Gatlin outside, and he lifted his nose to the air. I did the same, even though my senses were weaker in this form.

"There's still another one out there," he grumbled. I frowned, because how was that possible? Radic had accounted for every female Beta in town; there weren't that many.

"Bonnie?"

Gatlin shook his head. "Wrong direction."

"I'm going to assume you'd know if it were Naja."

Gatlin gave me a droll look, and I shrugged. Couldn't hurt to ask, right?

I shook my head. Whoever it was, they were on their own. "I need to sleep." I looked over at the supernaturals who were holding back the Manix with ease, and Gatlin slapped my back hard.

"Yeah, sleep. I'm sure. Go home to your mates, Dominic. I'll watch over this clusterfuck for a while." He gave me a stern look. "But be back by lunch tomorrow because I've got my own mate that needs my attention, and Ellar and Seven will be dehydrated husks if I don't hurry back."

He didn't have to tell me twice. I shed my clothes, picked up my cell phone in my mouth, and sprinted home.

## 34

PRYCE

My body was out of my control, and normally that would freak me out, but right now? I was happy to let the Beast take the wheel and run off pure instinct. You'd think that the Beast's first desire would be to fuck the Omega in heat, but it wasn't. I mean, I definitely wanted to do that, but it wasn't the first instinct I had. No, the first thing I did was race down to the kitchen, grab all the snacks and water I could find, and race back up the stairs.

Now, I was feeding her grapes one by one, bathing in her scent like it was the oxygen I needed to live, while she sat naked under the blankets, the sheet tucked under her arms.

Courtland watched from the end of the bed, his hand wrapped around her ankle but not pushing for anything more. Just comforting her. She seemed calmer when we were both touching her.

"Are you feeling better, Omega?" Even my voice had dropped low. She nodded, her gaze catching mine before falling to the huge hard-on that was tenting my sweats. "Ignore that," I mumbled, my cheeks growing hot.

She gave me a sweet smile, raising a single eyebrow. "Hard to ignore," she teased, and I felt myself grinning back, and just like that, the intensity of the moment was broken. I fed her a little more, my Beast seeming to alternate between wanting to feed her and wanting to eat her, and it probably had something to do with the fact that I'd thought she was dying for nearly a week.

I had two warring urges, but given the ache in my balls, one of them was definitely winning.

"Pryce? Will you kiss me?" she asked softly, and I launched myself across her body. I was aiming for her lips, but my hand got caught in the blankets and I ended up face-planting in her boobs.

The silence in the room was so fucking loud. Honestly, even crickets would have been gobsmacked. I buried my face further in her breasts to hide my shame. Then they started shaking. Actually, her whole body started shaking. Was she having a seizure or something?

I lifted my head to see she was red in the face. But I

realized it was because she was trying to hold in a laugh.

I dropped my head back down on her chest and sighed. "Just let it out."

The laugh that burst from her chest echoed around the room, filling me with so much damn love that I couldn't help but tilt my head back to watch her happiness. Her hands came up to brush through my hair as she laughed, and I was pretty sure in that moment that I loved her. How could I not love her? She made it so easy.

"Come here, Pryce. I still want my kiss," she chuckled. I lifted myself up on my arms, slowly this time, until my body was pressed along hers, my lips only an inch away.

"I'm glad it's you," I whispered, and her eyes went soft. It was true too. Even though my Omega panted after Courtland like he was a prime rib and I was starving, Pryce the man wanted Bonnie to be the first. The man loved Bonnie.

"Me too, Pryce," she whispered before raising up on her elbows and brushing her lips across mine.

That was the only prompting I needed as I lowered myself down, pressing tightly against her as her lips and tongue caressed mine. I tasted her lips, memorized their touch, because I didn't want to forget a moment of this night. Not a single sensation.

She spread her thighs so I could press even closer,

and feeling the warmth of her core through my sweats made me groan and get impossibly harder. I ignored it for a moment, instead concentrating on the way she nibbled my lips and stroked her tongue across mine like she was making love to my mouth. It was heady and I swear the longer we kissed, the more drunk I felt.

Then her warmth on my dick turned to moisture, and the smell of her slick hit my nose like a freight train. "Oh, Goddess," I breathed, dragging my lips away from hers. "I want to taste." I paused, because I didn't know what the fuck I was doing, so I hoped this was one of those instinctual things again.

There was a low, rumbling noise, and I looked over my shoulder at Courtland, whose pupils had blown out wide in his darkened gaze.

Bonnie's hand in my hair tugged my face back to hers. "Yes, Omega. Please," she begged, and I couldn't have resisted her if I tried.

I moved down her body, dragging the sheet with me. As soon as she was bare to me, the sweet scent of her arousal hit me like a lead pipe, and I moaned deeply. She smelled like perfection. I pushed her thighs wider, gazing at her core in wonder. She had a small tuft of hair the same color as her hair on her head, and her core was glistening with her slick.

"Do you want to taste her, Omega? That wetness between her thighs is all for you," Courtland purred in my ear. As if he could sense my hesitation—because seriously, what if I fucked it up and like, mauled her clit or something?—he stroked a hand down my back. "I'll talk you through it."

It sounded like the dirtiest of suggestions, but honestly, I was happy for the help.

"Start by taking a taste, Omega. Maybe lick all those precious juices from her thighs. She'll taste like the best thing you've ever had on your tongue."

I scooted back a bit more and did what I was told, licking from her knee, up her inner thigh, my tongue flat so I didn't miss a single spot. I moaned deeply, because Courtland was right. She tasted like everything good in the world. I quickly moved to the other side, and her thighs fell open wider as I lapped and nipped at the soft skin. When I reached the apex of her thighs, I paused.

"There's nothing like lapping those juices straight from the source, Omega. Easy now, be gentle until she asks you not to be." Courtland's words were like a caress, and I leaned forward, burying my face in her pussy until her juices coated my cheeks. I flattened my tongue and lapped at her like she was an ice cream cone, hard and sharp, making sure to hit that little bundle of nerves that made her legs twitch around my head. She made a keening noise, and I pulled back with a gasp. Did I do it wrong?

"Was I too rough?" I looked up at Bonnie's face, which was scrunched in a frown.

She shook her head wildly. "No, it's perfect. Please, Pryce. Don't stop." She buried her hand in my hair, pulling me back with gentle hands, and I loved it.

"Can I die here?" I whispered, and she let out a choked sound somewhere between a moan and a laugh.

"I'd prefer you didn't die at all, Omega. I still have plans for you," she mumbled back, and this time I swirled my tongue around her clit but watched her face as I did it. Watched her lips part in a pink O, her head falling back with pleasure.

This was going to become an addiction, I could see it now.

"Mmm, good job, Omega. Look how well you're pleasing our girl. Let's take it up a notch, don't you think?" I hummed my agreement around Bonnie's clit, and she slammed her thighs around my head, making my ears ring.

"Fuck, sorry, oh god, do that again," she moaned breathlessly, and I decided I didn't mind having my head crushed at all. So I made a purring noise on her clit again and her thighs started shaking. Yeah, she liked that. I couldn't resist smiling around her clit. I didn't suck at this at all.

Courtland grabbed my hand, lacing our fingers together. "Next step, Omega, now she's close. Can you scent how she's perfuming the air with her slick? That's all because of you. But now we're gonna make her come all over those pretty lips." He moved my hand, his fingers still laced with mine, until our fingers slid through the wet folds of her pussy. He notched my fingers at her entrance and stilled.

"Yes?" I looked up to see Bonnie's eyes locked with our Alpha's.

"Yes!"

Courtland laid his hand over mine, and together we pressed a finger inside Bonnie. Well, two fingers, I guess? My skin felt tight all over my body, but especially my dick. I was going to blow on these sheets before I'd even gotten inside her.

"Feel that?" He curled my fingers upward, and I guess I did feel a different texture or something. "That's where her G-spot is. You curl your fingers, like you're telling her to come here, and she'll definitely come for you, won't you, beautiful Bonnie?"

"Yes," she breathed again, completely transfixed by his words. He was fucking magic in that moment. He moved his hand away, withdrawing from the warmth of her body, and she rolled her hips against my hand. "More, Omega," she begged, and I slid another finger inside, doing the motion that Courtland told me.

She moaned something incomprehensible, so I picked up the pace, leaning in to flick my tongue over the tight button of her clit once more, and that was it. Her slick coated my hand, as her pussy clenched around my fingers in a pulsing motion and she screamed my name. I wanted to keep going, wanted to make her do it again, and again, but Courtland's hand came out to grip my chin.

"She'll be sensitive now, but she's ready. She's so fucking ready for you, Omega. Go and make her yours." He lifted my hand, still coated with her cum, and sucked my fingers into his mouth.

A moan bounced off the walls, and I realized it was both mine and Bonnie's.

I pushed off my sweats and climbed back between her thighs. Fuck, I was beginning to freak out. What if I sucked at this? What if I came in three seconds? I leaned over her, holding her gaze until she pulled me close, kissing me softly. My dick notched against her entrance, like it knew its damn job and I just needed to get the hell out of its way.

I sucked in a deep breath, kissed her hard, and thrust inside.

I found heaven, and then the Beast went wild. Pressing deeper, I slammed inside of her with probably little to no finesse, but I felt urgent. My Beast needed something, and it was going about getting it with single-minded focus. Bonnie was wrapped around me, pulling me into her harder with the heels of her feet pressed into my ass.

"Omega," she panted on every breath, making me even wilder. Because that's what we were right now.

Two Omegas doing what nature intended us to do: fuck and fuck and fuck until we procreated.

As if triggered by the thought, I shuddered as hot pleasure washed over my body and then my dick... well, it started to suck. It felt like I was coming, but it went on and on, until I collapsed on top of her, barely coherent enough to remember to hold some of my weight off her chest.

She didn't seem to care, gasping as she clenched around me over and over again, chanting the word "Fuck" in my ear.

I sucked on her neck, every part of me wanting to bite her, to make her mine. Make her my mate.

There were firm fingers on my chin, tilting my head to the left. I looked up into Courtland's burning eyes as he shook his head. "Not today, Omega. But soon. Soon she'll be ours."

I dropped my head back to her neck and breathed in. For the first time in my life, I felt like I was home.

Well, this was hell. The sounds coming from the top floor were making my dick so hard that I was about to pass out from blood loss. The house was quiet, all the kids asleep, and even Rosa had drifted off on the couch.

Pulling the gun gently from her hand, I covered her with the blanket from the back of the couch and stuck the gun in the waistband of my pants. Shutting the door to the living room softly, I moved down the hall toward the front of the house. Opening the front door, I caught the insane pheromones of the collective heat, and my Beast banged against my waning control. He didn't want to rush out there though, didn't want to go chase down any of those other scents.

No, his mate was upstairs, getting dicked by his Omega. The thought made me smile.

Movement in the shadows had me drawing my gun again, and I quickly searched the trees. When Corvin stepped into the moonlight, I breathed a small, relieved sigh.

Then I saw the girl in his arms.

"Stop!" I shouted, and Corvin froze. I was moving before I thought through the consequences. What if Corvin was frenzied? The girl in his arms was still unconscious, but there was no doubt she was an Omega. Her hair was a mess of knots, and there was a smudge of dirt on her cheek. Her clothes were old and by the look of them, frequently mended.

Worse than that, I had no fucking idea who she was.

"What the fuck, Corvin?" I hissed, making the girl stir in his arms.

"Fuck off, Radic. This has nothing to do with you."

I lifted my gun and pointed it at his head. "I like you, man, but if you think I'm going to let you take a fucking girl who's unconscious into a house full of Alphas while she's in heat, you're fucking nuts. You don't even know her."

He pulled back his lips into a snarl. "I know her, Beta. She is mine. Has always been mine. Now back the fuck away before I make you."

The weight of his Alpha command sat heavy on my chest, but my gun didn't waver. Yay for me. "Who is she?"

His jaw flexed, and then Beckett appeared from the darkness too. Neither of them seemed crazed, but how the hell did I know? "Her name is Kitten. She's... wild. Feral. We've been taking care of her for a decade."

I shook my head because none of that made sense. "You've been keeping an Omega prisoner for a decade?"

Corvin's warning rumble sent chills down my spine and I wanted to drop to my belly and supplicate myself, but I resisted. Beckett stepped between me and Corvin.

"No, Rad, you've got it all wrong. We didn't find her until she was about thirteen. We were kids. I can explain, but right now Kitten isn't safe, and if she wakes up here..."

I chewed my lip, uncertain what to do. "She knows you?"

Beckett nodded. "We've been giving her supplies for years. Teaching her language. I promise, she's safe with us."

I narrowed my eyes, my gun hand steadying. "And you won't touch her? Swear it, Beckett. Even if she begs for it, you won't touch her."

Beckett growled. "She's safe," he reiterated. "We won't touch her. She might be feral, but she isn't an idiot, Radic. She can make her own decisions."

"She's stubborn as fuck," Corvin muttered.

"What about Darius?" This shit was insane.

Beckett shook his head. "Darius didn't know about her. Neither did Cooper. This is… a surprise. I promise none of us will touch her. And when this shit is all over, she's free to do what she wants."

I grunted in frustration. "Fine. I'll come and check on her though, and if she doesn't wake, call for Doc. Or the visiting doctor, Stacey, if you think she'd respond better to a female." I'd known these guys my entire life; I trusted them with Bonnie and with the Sanctum. They were good Alphas, good men.

I was betting with this girl's future that they were good under pressure. That they had control of their Beasts.

Beckett slapped my shoulder. "I swear it, Rad."

Then they were gone.

I turned back toward the house, and moved inside. It was still silent except for the faint sounds of the rut upstairs, and I rested my head against the cool glass of the front door. Well, I did, until it flew open.

A giant wolf stood in the hall, and my nose twitched as I breathed in the scent of Dominic. God, he was so beautiful in this form. Standing at five feet tall, he was bigger than any natural wolf. His coat was thick, and I couldn't help but bury my fingers in it. The wolf crowded closer to me as he inhaled my arousal, and literally nuzzled at my dick with his snout.

I laughed and pushed his head away. "You're pretty

in this form, but I'm not fucking a wolf, Dominic." He let out a wolfy huff, and then shifted back to the Dominic I knew and loved. A very naked Dominic.

Fuck, he really was sexy—all rough edges and darkness. He made me want to drop to my knees every time he gave me that knowing grin, the one that said he'd busted me checking him out and he would gladly give me a ticket to ride... all that.

He stepped closer, pushing me back against the front door. "What about now?" he growled softly, and my dick jumped at his words. I gripped his hips, pressing the length of his cock against mine, and kissed him. I tongue-fucked him with every ounce of pent-up lust I had, and after listening to Pryce make love to Bonnie for the last hour, that was a lot of lust.

He shoved his hands down my sweatpants and grabbed my cock, making me moan into his mouth. He dragged his hand over the head of my cock, and I broke the kiss as I let my head fall back. He sucked at my neck, nipping his way down to my collarbone. He tugged at the neck of my shirt until it tore right down the middle, making me grip his hair. I'd be pissed about my shirt later but man, that was hot. He moved down until he could take one of my nipples between his teeth and bit down, making me hiss.

"Quiet, Beta. Don't want to wake the house up," Dominic said with a shit-eating grin before moving to my other nipple and doing the same thing. Asshole. Delicious, sexy asshole.

He spun me around until my hands were pressed against the glass of the door, his chest to my back, but managed it somehow without taking his hand from my dick. It was kind of impressive.

Stroking my cock faster, he held his other hand to my mouth.

"Spit."

I did what I was told, and he moved his hand away, but soon enough I felt the push of his cock on my ass. "This is gonna be a bit hard and fast, Rad. Say no now, and I'll give you the best blow job of your life and we'll call it happy days."

I was shaking my head, pushing myself back against his body. "Fuck me, Dominic."

He growled and thrust into me hard and fast, the tight, burning stretch making me grunt a little. But he had his face buried in my neck, and his body was moving in and out of mine in time with his hand on my cock. The scent of Bonnie's heat was in the air like an aerosol Viagra and if I couldn't be buried in her, this was the next best thing.

"Goddess, I want to bite you right now. I want to make you my mate, body and soul. The things I feel for you..." he moaned out, and my whole body prickled with pleasure and something more. Something like love. Because this Pack—that had stormed into my life like a hurricane—had its hooks in my heart like no one had ever done before, except Bonnie.

I wanted to tell him to do it, to make me his, but deep down, I knew we should wait. We should cement our Pack together, and not when we were riding high on pheromones and dick.

But a good dicking would make you do some crazy things. I dropped my head forward to the wall again, and Dom curled his body over mine, finding new leverage and making me moan louder until his hand came up to cover my mouth.

"Shh, Beta," he groaned into my ear. "Fuck, you feel perfect." I could have told him it didn't matter if we were loud, because the sound of his hips snapping against my ass would have woken the dead.

My balls pulled up tight, and I panted, "I'm going to come. Harder, Dom."

My words sent him crazy, his body moving in jagged thrusts until I was spilling myself into his hand. And on the wall. Oops. Dominic pushed me tighter to the wall and then tried to fuck me through it, until he was growling my name as he came inside me. He collapsed against the wall, his body tight up against mine as we both caught our breath.

He pushed off the wall, planting small, gentle kisses across my shoulders. "Come on, Beta. Let's get this mess cleaned up and then I'll stand guard while you go make love to our girl." He gathered up my torn shirt, using it to wipe the cum off the glass, before smirking at me. "Sorry about the shirt though."

His grin said he wasn't sorry at all, but then again, neither was I. I'd happily sacrifice my whole wardrobe if we could do that again and again and again.

I dragged my attention from the two Omegas in front of me to listen to a noise from downstairs. Concentrating on the rhythmic slapping noise, I grinned wide when I realized it was Radic and Dominic fucking.

I briefly wondered what Dominic was doing at home, but I trusted him more than I trusted any other person in the world. If he was sure things were under control enough that he could come home and fuck the ever-loving hell out of our Beta, then so be it. I turned back to the two Omegas who were collapsed together on the bed like two parts to a whole. My heart thudded heavily in my chest as I watched them, their connection to each other in this moment so fucking beautiful.

I gently tilted Pryce's face away from Bonnie's neck because I could almost feel his urge to mate her, to tie them together for life. I wanted that as well, but not right now. Tonight was not the right moment.

"Not today, Omega. But soon. Soon she'll be ours," I murmured, and stood as he nuzzled his face into her hair. I was barely holding back the Beast, because they needed their moment, but I needed to be inside one of them now.

I soothed the Alpha inside of me, reminding myself that Pryce was new to this whole thing, and we needed to go gently. But he just wanted to fuck, and fuck some more until our cubs were buried in Pryce's womb, and he'd grow big with them. Some days being half-Beast was harder than others.

I stroked a hand down his spine, relishing in the way goosebumps rose in the wake of my touch. He looked like that lab had created him just for me, with his perfect olive skin and the long line of his muscles that flexed down his back. So perfect. "Shift out of the way, Omega, so I can show Bonnie how much I missed her too," I said softly, and like a good Omega, he rolled to the side. I held out my hand and pulled Bonnie to her feet, clutching her to my chest like I might lose her again.

I'd been so fucking worried. "I'm never letting you go again," I murmured, leaning in to catch her lips in soft nibbling kisses. She smiled that fucking beautiful smile that got me in the gut every time, which I couldn't help but echo back.

"Lucky there's nowhere I'd rather be, Alpha," she teased, and I grinned. She was all softness against the hard edges of my body, and I deepened my kiss until she was curling into me. I lifted her into my arms, and she wrapped her legs around my hips.

"Are you feeling better?"

She laughed this time, leaning forward to bite her way up my jaw. "If I felt any better, I'd be a puddle on the floor at your feet."

I thrummed low in my chest. "Mmm, you at my feet is an enticing prospect, Omega, but I'm dying to be inside you." I pushed her back against the wall, balancing her there as I reached down to line up my cock with her slick center.

I groaned as I lowered her right down my dick, her body already prepped and ready, and I resisted the urge to pound into her until I buried my seed deep in her womb. The fucking heat was making me crazy, and holding back was torture.

Bonnie dug her nails into my shoulder as I drove her up and down my cock, and the feeling of rightness was an aphrodisiac in itself.

"Touch yourself, Bonnie. I want to feel you come around my cock, and when I am soaked with your slick, I am going to fuck our Omega. Would you like that?"

She nodded, panting as she held on with her thighs

and sliding one hand between us. "Fuck, you have the dirtiest mouth, Alpha."

She grinned at me as she touched herself, moaning as she threw her head back, and I ground her hand between our bodies so I was in control of the pace. I slowed right down, grinding into her deep and slow, and her panting turned into mewls.

"Yes, yes, yes," she whispered over and over, her cheeks flushed, her hair sticking to her face. She was a fucking work of art in that moment. I wanted to take a photo so I could put it in my wallet and look at it every time I missed her.

Finally, she clenched around me hard, and I gritted my teeth to stop myself from blowing inside her. It took every ounce of my control I had, to still myself inside her and let her ride out her orgasm around me.

"Pryce, come here." My voice was rumbly, more Beast than man at that moment. But my Omega male followed direction well, and appeared beside me. "Isn't she the most fucking beautiful sight you've ever witnessed?"

"Yes," he breathed, and I knew he meant it with every fiber of his being.

"Do you want to make love to her again?"

"Yes."

I smiled at them both, admiring the way they both gazed at me with pupils that were huge with need. I stepped toward the bed, and lifted Bonnie off my cock.

She let out a moan of protest, but she needn't have worried. She wasn't going to be empty for long. I turned and kissed Pryce hard, pouring all the things I wanted to say, all the promises I wanted to make, into that embrace. I let my hand drift down his body, the touch possessive. These were my Omegas, my Pack, and fuck yeah I was possessive.

I needed Radic and Dominic here too, and they would be, soon. But right now, I needed to be inside Pryce before my balls exploded. I pulled my mouth away, looking over at Bonnie. "On your stomach, Omega," I commanded, and she did what I asked without hesitation. I let out a purr of satisfaction. She was exactly what I'd always dreamed about.

I looked at Pryce, staring into those aqua blue eyes that sparkled even in this dim light. "If you permit it, I am going to fuck your ass while you are inside our Omega; I am going to make you both mine. Do you want that?"

He nodded, though I could still sense the wariness in his eyes.

I tried to keep the frown from my face. "It is okay to say no, Omega. This has been a crazy kind of night. It can wait."

My Beast was rebelling like crazy, but he wasn't in control right now. I was. And I didn't like the hesitation in Pryce's eyes. "Are you sure?"

I hated the flush of shame on his cheeks, or the fact

he wouldn't look me in the eye. I grabbed his chin so he'd be forced to meet my gaze. "You are in control. I am Alpha, but I am yours to command. Today, tomorrow, ten years from now—we will wait until you are ready."

Pryce nodded, and I smiled. "Now, if you feel like it, I'm pretty sure our beautiful Bonnie would like to show you the absolute joy of watching her breasts bounce as she rides you. "

The woman in question laughed. "Pretty sure my vagina is broken, because I've already had like four orgasms and she's ready for another four."

She crawled onto all fours and grabbed at Pryce's hand, dragging him to her body, and he went willingly. Happily. As he kissed her neck, she looked at me, her eyes soft.

"Thank you," she mouthed, and I smiled back. She didn't need to thank me. I would live and die for them. Not getting my dick inside wasn't a big deal.

The door opened, and I noticed the mussed hair of Radic in the hall light. "I think I arrived at the right time?"

I grinned, and the expression was feral. Oh yes. He'd arrived at the perfect time.

·　·　·

A full twenty-four hours after Bonnie woke up, we finally emerged from her temporary nest. Having satiated the heat, the duration of the craziness had been cut significantly. At least for Bonnie. The rest of the new Omegas would have to suffer through the next week, miserable, which meant the whole town would remain frenzied. Still, my Beast was appeased that our Omega didn't scent of need anymore, and should be reasonably safe from the Alphas in the town.

Now I could go back to being the Alpha General. First stop was to see the freaking Convocation member for Endangered Supernaturals.

I dressed in my usual armor of a three-piece suit and headed down to see them where they were camped out in the Legion building. Dominic was at home, curled around Bonnie like a second skin, and Radic was by my side, his hair perfectly arranged and completely unlike the man who had been fucked like it was our last day on earth last night.

As I stepped into the center of town, I could tell that Dominic hadn't been exaggerating about the level of mania the town had descended into. Even now, they were circling the building, and there was blood—and shit, was that a tooth?—littering the streets.

I growled low, flexing my Alpha for every person in

the vicinity. They didn't scurry away, but they did pause their fighting.

"We can't do a whole week of this, otherwise I'll be Alpha General of a town of mangled beings."

Radic hummed his agreement as he stepped over a fallen Manix Beta, a tranq sticking out of his neck. I leaned down and checked he was still breathing, and was happy to see that he was just out cold.

Walking through the doors of the Legion building, I was greeted immediately by the smiling vampire assassin himself. Fuck, I'd forgotten how huge he was.

"Ah, Alpha. Nice to see you. You've missed all the fun though." He licked his lips and grinned.

I frowned. "You haven't been feeding off my people, have you?" I growled.

He shrugged. "Not much? And only the ones who offered themselves to me. Which is a surprisingly large amount. Who am I to turn down a snack?"

I growled, and the vamp just shrugged. "Calm down. I don't often get to eat from the source, and there's a 'no eating from humans' rule back home, so it's nice to get a bit of warmth in my food. Call it payment for rushing down here to save your ass." He rolled his eyes. "I'll stop though if it squidges you out."

Someone cleared their throat, and Raine appeared. "There's no payment for doing our job, X," she chastised softly. "Hello, Alpha. I assume your Omegas are feeling better."

I bowed my head respectfully. "Yes, Ma'am. We are thankful that you made the trip to help us out."

She shrugged. "It's my job, but I gotta say, I've been tempted to eat a few too because they literally have no sense of self-preservation. You know how many we've had to tranq in the last twenty-four hours?"

Loren appeared, and he looked tired as hell. "One hundred and fifty-eight, and counting. At this rate, we'll run out of tranquilizers before we run out of days."

I gritted my teeth because that was not good. I didn't want to do any more harm to my people than necessary, but even I was not completely immune to the pheromones swirling from this building.

"Can't you do anything to dampen the scent?" I asked Loren, and he shook his head.

"It's not a spell I've ever needed."

"What about knocking them out?" Radic asked, and again Loren shook his head.

"All fifteen hundred of them? I don't have the juice for that."

Raine and X shared a look, and the vampire sighed. "I know someone who might be able to walk you through a dampening spell." She pulled out her phone, mumbling to herself. Hitting a single button, she raised the phone to her ear. "Hello, it's Raine." Rolling her eyes, she huffed. "Don't be dramatic. I'm looking for Miranda." She was silent for a long time, her foot tapping. "Stop fucking around, Alexander. I know she's there."

Shit, she was calling Miranda? Loren blanched but it was too fucking late. Raine pushed the phone at Loren, and he took it with a gulp.

"'Lo?" Silence. "Yes, Ma'am. What? No. I don't have one." Pause. "I don't know why." Pause again. "I'd rather... Okay, fine." The look Loren cut me was pure pissed off witch. "Yes, Ma'am. I need a dampening spell to stop the fucking Manix from turning into horny mutts and trying to fuck everything that moves."

I cleared my throat, and Loren sent me a panicked look. Then he frowned, all seriousness once more. He mimed writing, and Radic rushed away, appearing in seconds with a notepad and pen.

"Okay, yes. Uh-huh. Yep." Loren's eyebrows lifted in surprise. "Really? I've never thought of it that way. Oh, um, I'm self-taught." Whatever Miranda said at the other end of the line made Loren gulp. "I mean, it's fine. I was a drug runner, ma'am—exploding people was the point." He dropped his head, and whatever the Witch Miranda was saying on the other end, it was obviously a tongue lashing. She was scary as fuck; scarier than even Alexander, the motherfucking Dragon Lord. I'd met them both rescuing Naja and I honestly hoped I never had to meet them again.

Loren nodded once more. "Thank you. Yes, ma'am. Bye." He handed the phone back to Raine and strode past me with a huff. "You owe me so fucking big, Alpha. So. Fucking. Big."

Within twenty minutes, the scent of Omegas in heat dissipated, and the world went back to normal.

Well, normalish.

---

BONNIE

**B**eing a newly minted female Omega was a weird freaking experience. Before, I'd been dismissed, disregarded by most people except Radic and a select handful that I'd known my whole life. When I became close to Courtland, the new Alpha General, people started to see me.

Now? I may as well be a giant fucking pimple on the ass cheek of a Victoria's Secret model. I was stared at no matter where I was, and it was always followed by whispers.

Most of them, especially mated Beta females, were just curious about what it would be like to win the genetic lottery. Some weren't as nice, and there was a lot of talk that I had trapped Courtland during my heat. They didn't know he'd asked me to be Pack before this whole damn thing happened.

Nope, they thought I'd snared their Alpha General, and the pretty new Omega to boot, with the power of my magical vagina. I didn't care. Not even a little. Let those fuckers think what they wanted. I didn't know how the other Beta-Now-Omega girls were coping—we didn't have a support group or anything—but most of them had squirreled themselves away to come to terms with shit, I guess. This madness that was now their life.

Susannah had gone back to Wilkie as the Omega he always wanted, which made no fucking sense, but Susannah had always been a bit of an enigma. The only one of the new Omega females who seemed to be just lapping up the attention was Electra. She was the daughter of one of the Legion Generals, and was already used to being fawned over. Now, as an Omega female, she'd been exalted to nearly goddess-like levels of adulation. She was young and beautiful, and all the bachelor Alphas were panting around her still, despite not being in heat.

But an Omega always chooses, and it didn't matter that a week ago, we'd been Betas.

I rolled my eyes as Electra fluttered her eyelashes and pretended to be a demure Omega, despite the fact I knew for certain she'd thrown coffee in the face of one of the Sanctum kids who worked here after school last week because she didn't like how it was made. Our designations had changed, not our personalities. And Electra had always been a spoiled child.

"Why are we glaring daggers at that girl?" Dominic whispered into my ear.

I looked over my shoulder at him, lifting my chin for a kiss. "Because she's an asshole. Now kiss me."

He chuckled low in his throat, before taking my lips with his. Dominic didn't believe in demure, I was beginning to learn. Dominic kissed you like you were his to devour every damn time. By the time I pulled away, the whole cafe was staring at me.

Purposefully ignoring them, I walked up to Taylor at the counter, who had his nose screwed up. "What?"

"No offense, Bonnie, but that's kind of like watching my mom kiss someone. Ew."

I didn't know whether to laugh or cry—laugh because his face was hilarious, or cry because he saw me as some kind of parental figure who he didn't want to see making out. It meant I was getting somewhere with him, getting him to open up, and that made me happy as hell.

"I'll have you know that I'm not that old and I still like kissing."

I laughed as Taylor pretended to gag. "Just, no more PDA's okay?"

Dominic nuzzled my neck and took a big step away. "Sure thing, kid. Just for you."

Someone made a choking noise, and I realized

Electra had come to stand in line behind us. She looked me up and down, then looked at Dominic. She pursed pretty pink lips like she'd just sucked something sour. "You could do better."

Dominic turned toward her, his smile upping in wattage until Electra looked like she'd forgotten how to breathe. He loomed over her a little, his eyes hooded in a classic bedroom expression.

"Are you offering, baby girl?" he purred.

I knew her parents were fundamentalists who'd have a coronorary if their child fucked a shifter, but little did they know, she'd blown every Manix in town under forty with a dick still attached.

"Anytime," she whispered back, her eyelashes fluttering.

Dominic grabbed her chin and tilted her head back, making her lips part in a pant. "What if I said right now? What if I asked you to drop to those knees, in those pretty five hundred dollar jeans, and suck my cock? You'd do it, wouldn't you?" He moved his hand away and wiped it on his pants. "You'd do it because you are the kind of person who has no substance. You're an empty vessel for someone to put their dick in, and eventually their kid." He pointed at me. "She is worth three of you on her worst day."

Electra spluttered. "She's about the size of three of me, that's it."

Dominic threw back his head and laughed.

"Maybe? But wrapped between those thighs, while she's screaming my name? That's fucking heaven, Manix Barbie. The kind of nirvana you'll never find because you're a taker. A drain on society." He dropped his voice. "Ugly, inside and out." Then he stepped back toward me and gave me one more kiss, before looking over at Taylor. "Broke my promise already. Sorry, kid."

Taylor grinned. "No worries."

With that, Dominic grabbed our coffees and left, his eyes sliding over Electra like she wasn't even there, his grin so wide that the whole world could tell he didn't give a shit about anyone but me. And it was heady.

When we were finally outside, nearing my van, he let the smile drop and he gave me a concerned look. "Are you okay?"

I raised my eyebrows. "Me? Other than being ridiculously turned on by you right now, I'm fine." Dominic continued to frown, and I reached out and grabbed his hands. "Honestly. I got kind of used to that through school. Electra is like, what, twenty? She probably learned that shit from her cousin who was in my class in high school. It's not like she's ever had an independent thought in her life." I sighed, because it was true. It had been a few years since anyone had been so openly hostile about my differences, which honestly weren't that significant. A little curvier. A little shorter. My parents had abandoned me. All of those things were normal occurrences in most societies. But Maxton wasn't most societies.

"You wanna burn the whole place to the ground and start again?" Dominic asked as we climbed into the van, and I laughed like he was joking. But when I looked at his face, he was dead serious.

I punched him in the shoulder. "No, I don't want to commit mass arson, Dominic. Electra is a kid with a big mouth and a bad attitude. The Goddess will kick her in the ass one day, probably because eventually her parents will find out shes been fucking half the Legion Force bachelors in late night gangbangs, then they'll overreact and sell her off to one of their cronies and she'll become a miserable, gin-for-breakfast housewife who hates her life because she's bitter and ugly on the inside."

Dominic blinked, then blinked again, before bursting out laughing. "Can't argue with that." He leaned forward, kissing me hard. "I meant what I said in there. I love you, Bonnie."

My mouth dropped open. "You didn't say you loved me in the cafe," was all that came out.

"I didn't? I called your pussy nirvana. If that isn't a declaration of love, what is?"

This utterly ridiculous, violently beautiful man. "Love you too, Dom."

He kissed me again, sucking my bottom lip into his mouth, before pulling away. "Normally I would suggest climbing into the back seat and fucking you so I could hear you say those words to me on a moan, but I have a meeting with Courtland and he's still a little pissed at me for calling in the vampires."

I stroked my fingers through his mussed hair. "I have to get back to the Sanctum anyway. Darius deserves the week off."

Kissing me once more, and again skirting the edge of public decency, Dominic slid from my van and jogged toward the Legion building. I shook my head and watched him go. He was so fucking fine.

Finally, I shifted the car into drive and headed back to the Sanctum. I tried to imagine telling myself six weeks ago that I'd be in this position—I would have voluntarily committed myself. Realizing that Dominic had left his coffee in the car, I picked it up to give to Darius. Wasting good coffee was just a little above kicking puppies, in my opinion.

Hip-checking the door open, Darius appeared. He looked... stressed.

I raised my eyebrows. "You okay?"

Darius nodded, giving me a smile that didn't quite reach his eyes. When I snorted incredulously, he threw his hands in the air. "I'm fine, Bon, I mean it. Did my Alphas have a secret Beta on the side for nearly a decade? Yes. Are we coping with that?" He paused. "Yeah, I guess so. But they aren't off my shit list yet."

I shook my head. Radic had mentioned the strange

girl Corvin and Beckett had brought here unconscious, but when Radic had come to check on her, she was awake and actually hissed at him. She didn't seem to be in any distress, was the general consensus, and she wasn't a prisoner. Rad had said that if anyone looked distressed, it was Corvin and Beckett.

"Give them hell, Darius," I said, slapping his arm. "Now get out of here and go have angry make-up sex."

Darius shook his head. "They should be so fucking lucky. Okay, so dinner is in the crockpot and the little ones are all down for their nap. I had the birds and the bees talk with the older kids during the frenzy, so you're welcome for that." Picking up his duffle from beside the door, he gave me a soft smile. "I'm glad you're back, Bonnie. I missed you."

I hugged him tight. "I missed you too. Thank you for taking good care of our kids." He kissed my head and then left, sighing as the morning sun hit his skin.

I moved further into the house, and was secretly glad that Darius was so damn organized. In the fridge were six meals, and I could kiss that man again.

A knock at the door made me turn on my heel. Pulling it open, I grinned. "Miss me alread— Oh, hey."

It wasn't Darius at the door, but rather, one of the Legion Force soldiers. One of the younger ones whose name started with C, that I could never remember. He looked as solemn as if he were attending a funeral. Shit, that was never a good sign.

"Is everything alright?"

His face didn't move from its downcast mask, and panic set in. He looked up at me with regret in his eyes. "Sorry, Bonnie. Collateral is needed in every war."

What the fuck did that mean?

His meaning became clear when he pulled out a gun and shot me twice in the chest. Flying backwards, I fell onto the tiles and gasped. A scream from the back of the house made me turn, but not fast enough to miss the burn of a lead bullet against my skull.

The last thing that crossed my mind was thankfulness that Pryce and I hadn't mated during the heat—at least they'd all survive my death.

Then nothingness.

## 38

RADIC

Apparently, the entire town shutting down for a week while we were all horny as hell had actually led to a backup of paperwork that I now had to work through every day. Honestly, I was going to talk to Courtland about digitizing the system.

The doors to the office opened, and I smiled at the Legion General who was here for his appointment. "Sorry, Sir. He hasn't arrived yet."

"That's fine, Radic."

On the inhalation of a single breath, the man in front of me pulled a gun and aimed it at my chest, loosing three bullets into my body before I was even able to gasp. The force of the hits tipped my office chair backwards, and I collapsed onto the ground.

Hot blood bloomed on my business shirt, and I choked on the viscous liquid pooling in my throat.

Bonnie.

## 39

PRYCE

While the babies slept, I headed into the backyard to soak up the sun. It would be winter soon, and these beautiful days would give way to snow. I wasn't ready to give up fresh air and blue skies yet, but there was something to be said for staying holed up inside with my new Pack. Well, they would be my Pack by first snow. I was determined.

Three cracks echoed through the air, and I shot to my feet. The fuck was that? Sounded like gunshots, but that made no sense. I ran toward the back door, but a huge, shifted Manix appeared from nowhere, swinging a baseball bat at my head before I could dodge.

No. No. This couldn't be happening.

The world spun as I fell to my ass, but I quickly

crawled to my feet. Had to get inside. Had to protect the babies...

"We need you, so consider yourself lucky," the huge Manix grumbled.

The baseball bat hit the back of my head, and the sky disappeared behind the edges of darkness.

"Listen, Washington. If you're going to shoot at something, you're gonna want to be able to at least clip it. Keep practicing because you couldn't hit the broad side of a barn right now," I chastised because, fuck me, these guys sucked. Most of them hadn't kept up with their shooting practice and it showed. Claws and fangs were only good in one type of situation and being a giant fucker wasn't always going to be helpful either.

You'd think with enhanced senses, the guy would be set. But no. He missed seven times out of ten.

Loren chuckled beneath his breath beside me. "I think Rosa might have been better when you taught her." I snorted, because there was very little that kid wasn't good at, and if she was bad at something, she practiced until she was perfect. She was a good kid; she'd go far in life because she was as stubborn as she was kind.

"She gave more lip though, and I'm not going to lie, what she lacked in raw talent she made up for in pure brass balls."

Rosa had been eight when Loren had joined Courtland's crew, so he'd only known her as the precocious, mouthy little shit we all knew and loved. But I remembered when she'd looked up at me as a tiny baby, like I was the only thing that would keep her safe in the world.

I hoped she never wanted to date because I would probably make a eunuch out of the guy first, just as a precaution. Hell, Courtland just might eat them out of principle.

I sighed as Washington turned to ask more questions. How much instruction did I need to give him? Point. Shoot. Get the target. Not fucking rocket science. I swear this kid was dumber than a box of nails. "Washington, the target is that way, man. Just gotta fire until you hit something."

I didn't expect him to raise his gun. Didn't expect him to point it at me. I definitely didn't expect him to fire.

A force thumped into my chest, the world went bright, and then I was lying in the dirt. Except I wasn't in the dirt in Maxton. I jumped to my feet, looking for an enemy, but there was no one. No scents of anything but open air and trees. But the trees were wrong, not the kind that I'd marked the hell out of in wolf form in Maxton. The sun was at a different place in the sky. We weren't in Kansas anymore, that was for sure.

A choking noise made me drop my gaze. Loren lay at my feet, gasping. Blood stained his chest, and my heart stopped. Oh shit. He'd been hit by fucking Washington's bullet. I was going to kill that inept fuck when I got ahold of him.

"Fuck. Fuck, it's okay, man." I dropped to my knees, tearing at his shirt. I winced at the mangled hole in his chest. "Just a scratch." I bundled up the torn shirt and pressed it to the wound to stem the flow. We needed a doctor or a hospital or a goddamn miracle right now.

Loren continued to gasp air. "Li...ar."

"Don't be a fucking pussy, it's fine," I lied. "And no offense, man, because I love pussy." I looked around but couldn't work out where we were. The scents weren't any I recognized, the terrain neither Montana or Mexico. "Loren, where are we?"

He was beginning to let out wet gargles instead of breaths, and I didn't know what the fuck to do. His eyes were closed, so I shook him.

"Loren, stay awake, where are we? I gotta get you help and then I have to rip Washington's head off for being an inept asshole. Stay with me, buddy."

"Home."

Uh, no we weren't. We weren't anywhere near Maxton, or the compound in Mexico which had been our home for a decade.

"Meant to... shoot you."

I stopped, pressing down on his chest to step the bleeding. "I told you he was a shit damn shot. Why'd you do it, brother? Why'd you jump in front?" I knew I'd answered my own question though—we were brothers. I would have done the same thing for him in a heartbeat. Hell, I *had* done the same thing for him once.

"Go... Prince." I knew what he meant. If someone was trying to kill me, then Courtland would be next. Or Radic. Surely not Bonnie or Pryce, unless they wanted to extort Courtland. My blood went ice-cold as the words I'd heard a few weeks ago came back to body slam me into reality. It was a motherfucking coup. Washington was a pawn in a fucking hostile takeover. This was bad. So, so bad.

"Fuck, okay, come on asshole. Let's get you up and then we can get back to Courtland and kick some ass."

Loren shook his head, coughing as blood bubbled over his lips. "Dying."

"Fuck off, let's go. We'll get Doc to patch you up in no time. Open up a shiny portal or some shit."

"Can't... Dying. Only one."

He lifted his hand and waved it, and a portal

opened. Fuck. I tried to grab him up but he slapped my hands away. "Go!" he yelled. "Can't hold. Go!" His voice was a roar now, somehow amplified by magic as it echoed off the trees around us.

I scrambled back, looking between my dying friend and the portal back to Maxton and my possibly dying Pack.

"GO!" he screamed, but this time it was like a compulsion, my legs walking haltingly toward the portal and throwing me through it.

"LOREN!"

It was like one of those dreams where you're falling and you know the bottom means death; your body starts to freak out even though you're safely tucked up in bed. However, I wasn't safely tucked up in bed and perhaps my body was right on this one. Maybe we were about to die.

When the portal opened and deposited me in the woods outside of Maxton, my heart was beating so fast I thought I was having a heart attack.

Loren.

I wanted to scream and yell, but I didn't dare. "Goddess, if you can hear me, take him into your loving arms until I can return for him," I whispered the prayer to the trees, trying to push down the image of Loren's skin turning gray, his gasping lips, his teeth coated in blood.

I shifted to wolf and ran back to Maxton as fast as I could. Had to get to the Pack house, had to find Courtland. Had to protect my Pack, the people who held my heart. I stayed in the shadows because I didn't know who I could trust right now.

I circled around town so I could come up to the house from the woods at the rear, freezing as I smelled blood. So much fucking blood. No. This couldn't happen. Couldn't happen to us after we'd finally found what we needed, what we desperately wanted. Now that I'd finally found my Pack.

I prowled out of the woods, but I couldn't sense anyone else around me. Didn't mean much because the Manix had a camouflage that made them stealthy as fuck. But I'd grown up around Courtland, so I knew a few tricks of my own. I stopped close to a pool of blood, and my wolf whined when it recognized Pryce's scent.

I tried to console myself that it wasn't a big pool of blood, so he could be okay. I transformed back, grabbing a gun from where I had it stashed behind a pot plant. Stepping into the house, I stilled, but I couldn't detect any scents that shouldn't be here, except a really strong scent of the cheap ass perfume Rosa used. Patchouli or something. How she could be a shifter and wear it was a miracle to me.

It was fucking with my nose, so I whispered. "Rosa? Bonnie?" I kept creeping through the house but there was no movement. I walked up the stairs slowly, keeping one eye on the front door and one eye on the landing in case of an ambush. When I reached the top, I still heard nothing, so I called out again. "Pryce? Bonnie?"

The smell of perfume up here was insane, and I couldn't smell anything but patchouli.

"Rosa?" I yelled a little louder.

The manhole above my head opened, and I swung my gun up. But there was a gun looking down at me, as well as the face of Rosa. She was in the fucking roof cavity.

"Dominic?"

I huffed out a relieved breath. "Are you okay? Are all the kids up there with you? Pryce and Bonnie?"

Rosa's face crumpled as she swung down from the ceiling like a spider monkey. She fell into my arms, sobbing. "They took Pryce. I saw them surround the house while I was studying for my chem quiz and I gathered the kids up and stuck them in the roof cavity, but I was too late to get Pryce. They hit him in the head and dragged him away." She choked around another sob. "I broke my perfume to throw them off and hid like a coward."

Fuck. I squeezed her tighter to my chest. "No, Rosa, you did the right thing. God, you're so fucking smart. Now I need you to be brave again, alright? Let's get the kids down. We need to get you out of here."

I grabbed a chair and Winston handed down the babies first, then the smaller kids until he jumped down himself. "Okay, you have two minutes. I need you to get your cell phones and charging cables, diapers, bottles and formula. That's it," I told the two oldest kids. I handed the babies to the two younger ones. "Hold them properly and follow me, okay?"

I walked down the hall to my bedroom, going to the gun safe and pulling out a gun, a box of ammo and a spare clip. Then I grabbed a stack of cash. I stuffed all that into a backpack in my closet. By the time I got back to my door, Rosa and Winston had the other stuff. I threw it all into the backpack and zipped it up.

"Let's go."

I jogged back down the stairs, my gun at my side, but still I didn't see anyone. I needed to get the kids to Bonnie's car, and then I was going to make Bonnie leave, take all the kids, including hers from the Sanctum, and run. But where?

Naja's? You couldn't get there by van, only by ATV, and they needed the vehicle.

When I got to the van, I was happy to see the keys in it. But then I smelled the blood. So much of it.

Rosa threw me a panicked look, and she looked a second away from freaking the fuck out. I gave her the second gun and pointed to the van. "Get the kids in." She blinked toward the door, her face growing more and more pale as her brain caught up to what that tangy metallic scent meant. "Now, Rosa!"

My tone snapped her into action and she threw open the sliding door, ushering the kids inside. I slowly crept to the front door of the Sanctum, which was partially ajar. Blood had pooled underneath.

Blood that smelled like Bonnie.

I pushed it open slowly, and came face to face with a Manix. I lifted my gun, pointing it at his face. "Get the fuck away!"

"Dominic?" he rumbled. "It's me. Taylor." He transformed back into a boy I'd seen at the cafe only hours earlier, looking terrified. "I came home for my lunch break and—"

He pulled back the door, and Bonnie was there, lying on the floor, blood pooled around her body.

"NO!" I slid along the floor, no longer keeping watch, no longer caring if someone snuck up behind me and shot me. I checked her pulse and huffed a small, relieved breath that it was still there, but thready. If I didn't get her help soon, she wouldn't make it.

Taylor looked like he was trying hard to keep it together, but he was just a fucking kid. "One of the other kids said it was Legion Force, that they just walked up and shot her. They're keeping the little ones away so they don't see Bonnie, but I didn't know what the hell to do? Who do I call?"

I needed to get her to Doc. But I needed to get all these kids safe first or Bonnie would have my balls when she got better. I assessed her wounds quickly, realizing that one of these kids had been keeping pressure on them and I could have hugged Taylor.

"Rosa and her siblings are out by the van. I need you to gather up whoever is in the house right now and get in the van too." Taylor disappeared to do what I asked without question.

I scooped up Bonnie, trying to ignore the tacky sensation of her blood on my fingers. I carried her to one of our blacked out SUVs and laid her on the back seat, before racing back over to Bonnie's van. It felt like everything was going too fast but yet not fast enough.

Rosa was in the passenger seat, and all the kids were belted in, including some of the Sanctum kids, with Taylor in the driver's seat. I grabbed Rosa's phone from her lap, quickly typing something in. "Drive as far as you can without stopping. Not for gas. Not for food until you are out of the state. When you reach the border to Canada, call this number. This is the doctor who worked on Bonnie—he owns some kind of refuge for supernaturals. He'll get you somewhere safe. Tell him what's happening, okay?"

I grabbed Rosa's chin so she was forced to look at me. "*Do not come back* until one of us comes to get you okay. Me, Courtland, Pryce, Radic or Bonnie. Or Naja herself, okay? That's it." My voice cracked on Bonnie's name but I kept it together. "They're your mission, kid. I need you to get them to safety, got it?" Rosa nodded and I scruffed her hair. "I love you guys. Now go."

I ignored Rosa's tears as Taylor hit the gas. I would get them back soon enough. First, I had to save one of the pieces of my heart.

I woke up chained to a wall and struggling to remember how I got here. I'd been getting out of my ATV, and something bit me on the neck, and then nothing. I didn't have to be a smart man to realize I'd been tranqed. My body ached, so I guess they hadn't stopped there after I was out.

"Fucking cowards."

Someone laughed from the shadows. "Maybe, but that's not how we'll spin it if anyone comes asking around about your death. We'll say you started pedaling Omegas for cash or something. I mean, you do have a history of criminal activity."

Eldridge, the smarmy fucking Legion General who I really should have killed before today, stepped closer to the bars in front of me. I was obviously in the cells beneath the Legion building.

"Why don't you challenge me like a worthy Manix?" I growled, and he had the audacity to laugh.

"Because I'd lose. I'm not an idiot, Courtland. I know I can't win in a fight with a younger, stronger Alpha. I am not like the old Alpha General, who was too bullheaded to remember that every leader is usurped eventually. Your time is just coming a little earlier than expected."

I tugged on the manacles holding my wrists, and they groaned ominously. Eldridge frowned. "Easy now. Wouldn't want you escaping."

I just glared, not giving him the satisfaction of asking why. But his next words were like a lead weight in my gut.

"Wouldn't want to have to kill the Omega. I mean, we need him for breeding purposes, but I'm pretty sure we can break him in other ways, don't you think?"

The chill that went down my spine simultaneously froze my blood and set it on fire. I was going to kill this fucker. I was going to tear his intestines out through his mouth. I was going to eat his fucking heart like a Wendigo.

A noise at the top of the stairs was quickly followed by something tumbling down. When Eldridge picked it up, I realized it was Pryce. He looked banged up, his head crusted in blood and bruises littering his body.

"Pryce," I breathed, drawing his swollen eyes to me. He looked... furious. Not scared, though I could smell the fear on his scent, underneath the coppery smell of blood. No, Pryce had never been weak; a weak person wouldn't have survived as long as he did in conditions that were made to break even the strongest of supernaturals.

Pryce looked at the Legion General before him and then spat on his shoes. Eldridge backhanded him hard, sending him flying into the bars.

My Beast simmered beneath the surface, the rumbling growl echoing around the stone walls. "I wouldn't put your hands on him again."

Eldridge cackled. "Or what?" With more balls than common sense, he opened the doors to the cell, stepping in like these chains attached to a wall could really stop me. "You're worthless, Alpha. Can't protect your Pack or this town."

I yanked on the chains again, and while they groaned, they didn't snap. Yet.

Eldridge pulled out a gun, waving it lazily in my direction. I sneered at him. "You can't kill me. Overthrowing me will only bring the Convocation down on your head. We are on their radar now—there's no going back to hiding in the shadows like a coward."

I'd hit a nerve, given the tensing of his jaw and the furious burning in his gaze. "This is true. You did undo centuries of work building a virtual fortress to keep our people safe. Destroyed it all when you invited fucking vampires onto Packlands." His voice began to rise, but I could see him sucking in calming breaths like it made him more authoritative. Delusional maybe. "You're right. I can't take the Alpha General position from you with your murder." He dropped the barrel of the gun, then pulled the trigger, blowing out one knee and then the other.

I screamed as white hot pain seared through my body, my body falling hard and yanking my arms against the chains.The agony was unimaginable, making darkness spread through my vision, and only the sound of Pryce yelling my name kept me conscious. I wrapped my hands around the chains above me, pulling myself up to relieve the pressure on my now obliterated joints.

Eldridge's grinning face appeared in my vision. "Alpha General? I challenge you for control of the Manix. But don't say I didn't bring you anything to lay your head on. Here, I'm sure these scents will comfort you."

He stuffed a sweater behind my head, and I was assailed with the smell of blood. Two different scents, both achingly familiar. Bonnie and Radic. I roared my pain as Eldridge laughed. He swung the butt of the gun at my head and I lost my fight with consciousness.

. . .

I woke up with sand caked in my mouth like I'd been thrown face first onto a beach. No. Not a beach.

An arena.

I pried my eyes open, and rolled onto my back. My body ached like I'd been kicked around, and my knees were on fire. I realized it was because there was sand in the wounds, each grain feeling like knives in my brutalized flesh. I shifted to Manix, praying that the change would heal some of the broken cartilage, but it was fucking torture. I gritted my teeth because I refused to give an audience a glimpse at my pain.

The shift had healed some of the muscle aches, and rearranged my knees so they weren't gaping holes, so I guess I should be glad for that. But they were still useless. I couldn't bend them, or stretch them in any way.

I sat up and looked around. Contrary to when I'd fought for control of the Manix, the stands were empty right now. Only the Legion Generals were here, and by the looks of it, a portion of the Legion Force.

I searched for familiar faces, people I thought of as allies. But I couldn't see Murphy or Merrick, nor any of the other members I'd promoted to leader positions. Interesting. The fact that I hadn't been stabbed in the back by people I thought of as friends was subconsciously reassuring. My eyes did stall on Joshua and

Doc, but neither of them looked happy. And there seemed to be a disproportionate number of armed men around them, so I was mentally giving them a pass. I had to believe that not everyone in this arena right now wanted me dead.

Eldridge stepped in like he was king fucking shit rather than a cowardly little worm, and strolled over to me. "Are you ready, Alpha General?" he asked mockingly.

"I could use an extra sixty years, thanks."

No one laughed, and at that moment, I missed Dom. His scent wasn't on the sweater, and I didn't smell his blood anywhere. But if he was alive, he'd be here at my back. My brain shied away from the thought of him being dead.

I looked at Doc, seeing the strain around his eyes. Did he know his daughter was dead? That these bastards had killed her?

"Get to your feet," Eldridge commanded with a smirk, like I was down here supplicating myself rather than the fact he'd blown out my fucking knees.

"Eldridge, I can defeat you from the ground," I said with complete confidence. "You should have gone for the hands."

He gave an enraged snarl, leaping toward me, and I rolled out of the way. It was a lie, of course. I could put up a damn good fight, but this guy was still a strong Alpha and I would probably still die in this dirt. He stalked toward me, and I ducked his claws again, swiping out with my own. I managed to get his thigh, but fate wasn't kind enough to let me puncture a femoral artery and end this quickly.

He spun again with a roar, not learning anything from his wide open attacks, and I thought maybe I could kill him slowly, with a thousand slices. My knees burned like someone had shoved hot pokers into my flesh, but I compartmentalized the pain.

Fighting with rage instead of his head, Eldridge swiped hard and fast, getting my claws as often as he got me. But he was still getting me, and my body was fatiguing fast. I was fighting through pain, as well as physically having to shuffle my body through sand, and it just wasn't going to work.

But quitting had never been in my DNA. That was evidenced by the fact my father pursued his wife and Naja until his dying day. The fact I was in this position to start with. The fact that I had a Pack of beautifully stubborn people.

I got a good slice across Eldridge's calf, making the fucker drop to one knee. I took the opportunity to launch myself at him, because this was it. Do or die. And I didn't want to die, not really. I still had a family to protect, and Pryce needed me. He'd need me most now that Bonnie and Radic... No. Until I saw their fucking bodies with my own two eyes, they were alive. I refused to believe otherwise.

I screamed as I slashed at Eldridge's face and body, and he scrambled away as quickly as he could, dragging himself to his good leg and hopping away faster than I could commando crawl.

Spinning on his good leg, he switched directions, diving until he was on top of me, his claws buried in my gut.

All the air left my body. This is how I died then, against an unworthy opponent.

Eldridge was saying something, but I couldn't hear over the sound of nothingness rushing through my head. Maybe it wasn't nothing.

Noise suddenly roared in my ears and I realized it was someone screaming, turning my head to see Dominic sprinting toward me. He'd be too late, I knew this, as Eldridge clenched his fist, pulverizing my insides and making me scream.

Fuck. I was going to die screaming in the dirt. Not how I thought it would happen.

I watched Dominic get closer, pulling his gun, but he was too slow. Like he was running through quicksand. There was a boom, and then it was raining gore. Eldridge's head exploded, and his hand released as his body slid to the side. The momentum tore his claws out of me slowly and torturously, and I thought it might have pulled out some of my intestines too. I looked into his now unrecognizable face.

Yeah, now I could die happy.

I turned to look back at Dominic, who slid onto his knees beside me. The sand around us was so red that the color was visible to my eyes even in this darkness.

Beyond Dominic was a head staring sightlessly at me from the sand. I hissed when I realized it was Doc's head. Blood loss made my brain confused, because how the fuck did that happen? Didn't matter. I had no strength left to wonder.

I looked up at Dominic, who was crying. I didn't think I'd ever seen Dominic cry, ever. Not even when he was a kid and his Pack sold him to us for a few bricks of cocaine and a blow job.

I tried to lift my hand but I was no longer in control.

"Love you."

Goddess, keep them safe.

*Thirty minutes earlier*

When I got to the infirmary, no one was around. No Doc. No one. Radic wasn't answering his phone, and neither was Courtland. Fuck, fuck, fuck.

Laying Bonnie down on a hospital bed, I checked her wounds. I didnt know what the fuck to do. I wasn't a surgeon. Where the fuck was Doc?

"Stay with me, baby. I'll find him, okay?"

There was a bang on the front door, and then Murphy was in my face, his gun pointing at me. I bared my teeth, pulling my own gun, but he raised his hands.

"Hey, we're cool, we're cool. Merrick!" There was blood all down his shirt. "We heard the gunshot and found him like this—I swear it, Dom." Merrick walked in, and my heart dropped to my stomach. In his arms was a bleeding Radic. Murphy looked around me at Bonnie and gasped. "What the fuck is going on?"

I couldn't help the snarl that climbed up my throat. "A coup. A motherfucking coup. They have Pryce," I choked out. "I can't find Doc, and Courtland isn't answering his phone. Is anyone else medically trained?"

Merrick was shaking his head, lying Radic down on the metal examination table in the corner. "Not really. Bonnie was Doc's backup, and even she can't do anything more technical than field medicine. Can Loren do any kind of magic to heal it?"

A lump so big I thought I'd suffocate on it lodged itself in my throat. "Loren is dead. He took the bullet meant for me."

Merrick's face morphed from shock to pity. "I'm sorry, man."

I didn't have time to think about Loren's death right now. I dragged my cell from my pocket and dialled.

It answered on the third ring. "Hello?"

"There's been a coup. They've shot everyone." My voice broke, but I pushed it down. "We need help. I know—" My voice broke. "I know that you aren't meant to interfere but they're innocents and I can't find the surgeon and they're dying." I sucked in a deep breath. "Please."

"Can you keep them stable for forty-five minutes?

Pack the wounds, give them blood transfusions?" I looked at Merrick and Murphy, and they nodded.

"Yeah, we can do that."

"I'm sending Nico. X and I will be right behind him. Nico isn't a surgeon, but he's very old and very fast, and he'll be able to get things under control. X is a doctor; he'll fix them." She covered the phone and there seemed to be a brief argument. "I'm sending Lucius too, in case you, uh, need backup of a less life-saving variety."

I'd never been happier that someone was sending me a psychopath.

Raine's soothing voice came down the line. "It's going to be okay, wolf." And I believed her. I wasn't sure what kind of voodoo sorcery she had, but that panic that had felt like lead in my gut and ants crawling under my skin all but disappeared. The anger remained though.

"Nico and Lucius are twins, so they'll be there before you know it, since they won't be able to help themselves but make it a competition. Hold tight. We're coming."

She hung up, and I looked between Merrick and Murphy. "I have to find Courtland."

Murphy nodded. "Merrick will stay and keep them stable until help arrives. I'll go with you and call in reinforcements."

I was shaking my head before he'd even finished.

"No Legion Force. The kid from the Sanctum said it was a guy in Legion Force uniform who shot Bonnie. I don't know who to trust."

Murphy nodded. "Only people I would trust with my life, or Merrick's, I swear." He pulled out his phone and started talking to someone in a low tone as we jogged toward the Legion building.

Only one place was strong enough to hold Courtland, and that was the cells underneath. We crept along in the shadows, but it seemed eerily quiet in the streets.

"Hear anything?" I asked Murphy, and he shook his head. We moved closer, climbing the stairs to go through the side entrance. I pushed the door open with my foot, ready to kill anyone who appeared, but the inside of the building was oddly dark.

"We found Radic behind his desk," murmured Murphy. "His computer was still booted up so someone had obviously surprised him. We killed the lights in case anyone else appeared to finish the job."

I nodded, hoping I wasn't walking into a trap. My gut said that Merrick and Murphy were good guys, but my gut had been wrong before. At the top of the stairs that led to the cells was motherfucking Washington, guarding the door in his human form. Piece of shit dumbass.

I choked down a growl. You couldn't sneak up on a Manix. I'd learned that early on in life. You had to be crazy and erratic and pounce out of nowhere. Fuck it. I sprinted down the hallway faster than I'd ever made my human form move, jumped up and wrapped my thighs around Washington's neck in a move that was usually only seen in action movies with female badasses in spandex. Didn't fucking care because that big bastard went down, and by the time I had him on the ground, blinking up with wide-eyed confusion at me, I had his throat in my palm. Literally tore it out.

"For Loren, you fuck." Then I spit in the gaping hole where his larynx had once been.

He gasped for air for a moment, and I held his eyes the whole time, so he knew exactly why he was dying. Knew he'd fucked up, failed, and now I would be the last thing he saw before he burned in hell.

When the life left his body, I pulled off his head so the fucker didn't respawn somehow. Murphy had raced down the stairs ahead of me, because if there were reinforcements down there, I'd totally just fucked the element of surprise, so I ran down the stairs after him.

There was no one down here though, except the strong smell of Courtland's blood and... Pryce.

"Pryce!" I yelled hoarsely, and a lump in the corner unrolled.

"Dominic?" His voice was a whisper, but it was the most beautiful thing I'd ever heard. I tugged on the door of the cell he was locked in, but it didn't budge.

Racing back up stairs, I rifled through Washington's pockets, finding an honest to god skeleton key. I took the stairs back down four at a time, and it was only good luck that I didn't fall and break my neck. Unlocking the cell, I across the room in a single step, dragging Pryce up and into my arms. "Thank fuck you're okay."

He wrapped himself around me like he'd never let me go. "They shot his knees and challenged him to an Alpha fight."

No. Fuck.

My whole body went rigid, and I squeezed Pryce a little too tightly until he gasped. I instantly relaxed my hold. I had to get out there, had to help him. It couldn't be too fucking late. I refused.

I passed Pryce gently to Murphy. "Take him and keep him safe."

Murphy shook his head. He knew I didn't mean just for now. That if Courtland and I both died, an unmated Omega would be a target in this town, especially with all the new Omega females. "Murphy, please," I gritted out, and the Manix tensed his jaw.

He huffed out a breath. "You know I will. They'll have taken the Alpha General to the arena. I'll drop Pryce off with Merrick and meet you there." He paused. "We should wait for the vamps."

I nodded. "You should wait for the vampires." I leaned forward and kissed Pryce once more. "The babies, plus all the kids, are with Rosa on their way to the Eden Academy in Canada. When it's safe, bring them home. If it isn't safe, go to them. They're your responsibility now. You are their family, their Pack."

Then I raced up the stairs as quickly as I could. I wanted to shift to wolf and race there, but I didn't want to lose my weapons or my cell. I might need both. So I ran as fast as my human body would carry me.

Turns out that was too fucking slow. I skidded into the arena in time to see fucking Eldridge bury his fist inside Courtland's body, a fucking gleeful grin on his face.

What happened next seemed to happen in slow motion. I pulled my weapon and aimed at Eldridge, but Doc was doing the same. We both fired. Both got the Legion General in the head, essentially blowing his brains out from both directions.

A big fucker, his face distorted by my horror, stepped up behind Doc and decapitated the older Manix with a sword. As I got closer though, I recognized him. A Beta from the Pack of that fuckhead Wilkie. Didn't know his name but like his Alpha, he was a fucking prick. Doc's head went rolling, and then there was chaos.

Or maybe there was chaos because a fucking vampire appeared from thin air and tore out the Beta's heart.

I slid to my knees beside Courtland. Eldridge still had his fucking intestines wrapped in his claws, even though that bastard was dead. I untangled them and stuffed them back in as best I could. Were there rules about returning someone's insides back to where they belonged?

Tears cooled on my face and that's how I realized I was crying. Fuck.

Courtland stared up at me with those dark eyes, and he looked like he was trying to smile. Trying to console *me.*

"Love. You."

His eyes closed, and I let out a pained sound. "No, you fuck. Come back here. I love you too. *You do not just get to die!*"

I was screaming at him now, shaking his shoulders, until someone touched my arm. I looked up into the cool face of Lucius, who seemed completely unperturbed by the fact my heart was shattering in my goddamn chest.

"He's still alive, barely. Move, and I will get him to your clinic."

I scrambled away so fast I fell on my ass, and this psycho vampire just lifted Courtland into his arms like he weighed nothing. Then he was gone, moving so fast even my supernatural eyesight couldn't follow.

I looked around the arena and noticed that Gatlin was standing in front of the Legion Generals, all except Joshua, who was squatting in the sand near Doc's body, tears running down his face.

Fuck. Doc. Bonnie would be devastated.

I stood, walking stiffly toward Gatlin. He looked at me, his eyes filled with rage and just a tinge of pity. "Is he alive?"

I winced, but nodded. "For now."

Murphy came up to me then, resting his hand on my shoulder. "We've got this. The vampires have arrived, and they'll get everything squared away and eat anyone who was a traitor to their species." He said it loudly, and I was pretty sure I heard someone whimper. I didn't care. I hoped Lucius gorged himself on their blood. Murphy pushed my shoulder a little. "Go, Dom. Your Pack needs you."

Not as much as I needed them.

When I'd imagined what having a Pack would be like, I didn't think it would be sitting in the center of a room, surrounded by hospital beds containing the people I loved. That wasn't in the brochure, and if I'd had known, I would never have been brave enough to even try. I would have kept myself in my self-imposed isolation forever.

Dominic was asleep, propped against the wall beside the door, his body too exhausted from everything that had happened to stay awake and process this. It meant it was my turn to be the strong one, a role I'd been conditioned to play for a long time but never had the opportunity to use.

Radic had woken first, flinging himself around

until he saw me. The first word past his lips was "Bonnie?"

I'd pushed his bed closer to hers, and when he could touch fingers, he went back to sleep. He'd only had a single gunshot wound, but it had nicked his heart and it was a miracle he'd survived long enough for X to arrive and fix it. How that giant, tattooed vampire knew how to do heart surgery was a mystery, but I was eternally grateful.

Bonnie had stirred, but still hadn't woken. She had a collapsed lung and a gunshot wound to the chest, though luckily the bullet had missed anything vital. She also had a gunshot wound to the head, but it was just a graze. I had no idea who was watching over her, but she was so damn lucky. She'd take a little longer to heal apparently, but X had been happy with her progress.

My eyes kept drifting to the third bed, to Courtland's washed-out complexion. X had sworn a lot as he performed surgery on my Alpha, muttering about them not being called outsides—whatever that meant —and growling at the ancient vampire helping him.

Nico. He was so old he made fear skitter down my spine, despite his pleasant smile and his Hawaiian shirt with cats in party hats.

But after three hours, they'd emerged, with Courtland's legs in traction and his gut bandaged heavily. As soon as they'd said that he should be okay, that his body would begin to heal itself, Dominic had slumped against the wall and fallen asleep.

I should sleep too, but I didn't want to be out of it if one of them woke up. I laid my head on Courtland's bed, watching him breathe. Today had been the worst day of my life, and I couldn't even begin to process it. I didn't know where we even went from here. How could we live in this town, always expecting someone to jump out of the bushes and kill us to get to Courtland?

What about the kids? Would they need bodyguards in their own home? For their trips to school?

Dominic had called Rosa while Courtland was in surgery, to let her know what was going on. He'd also called ahead to the school, Eden Academy, and they were sending down Lycanthropes to collect them and escort them back to the safety of their compound.

But what if the babies suffered while they weren't with us?

The bed shifted and my head snapped up, and I looked straight into the glorious abyss that was Court- land's gaze. "Omega."

I stood, the chair scraping back, and I wrapped my arms around his shoulders and kissed him. "You're okay. You're okay," I chanted over and over, because despite my bravado, I hadn't been sure he'd wake up. "Thank fuck you're awake. Goddess, I love you. Don't fucking do that to me again, okay?" I swore a few more times, and Courtland laughed, then groaned.

"Harder than that... to kill."

"You can say that a-fucking-gain, you giant asshole." I looked over my shoulder at a furious Dominic. "Do you have any idea?" he gasped, like he was in physical pain.

"Come here, Dom."

Dominic stood his ground, like he was going to refuse, but Courtland quirked an eyebrow and he crumbled. Squeezing in beside me, he kissed our Alpha hard. It was a kiss filled with fear, like he didn't think he'd get another so it was laced with desperation.

"You guys... having an orgy... without us?" A sweet gasping voice had me whirling around, and tears flowed from my eyes and down my cheeks.

"Bonnie!" Courtland tried to sit up, then groaned with pain.

Dominic slapped him back down. "Are you fucking insane? You had a double knee reconstruction. The goddamn Executioner played with the cartilage of your knees like it was a puzzle."

He was still muttering about stupid Alphas as he pushed Courtland's bed over to Bonnie's, so she was sandwiched between him and a still sleeping Radic. Where she should be. I wanted her home in my bed so I could kiss her and stroke her and love her until I was sure she'd never leave me again. But she needed to be here a little longer. In Doc's house, but without Doc.

My face fell, but I quickly covered it. Bonnie

needed to recover, and this? This would be a huge blow. Bonnie loved Doc, and Doc had loved Bonnie. He'd loved Bonnie so much that when Eldridge had apparently gloated about murdering her to everyone who would listen at the arena, Doc seized the opportunity and avenged his child the best way he knew how.

He was a fucking martyr. The gold standard of Manix. He'd be irreplaceable in this town, and in Bonnie's heart. But none of that would help Bonnie with the pain in the coming days.

Dominic gave me a worried look, like he wasn't sure if he should console me or remind me to keep my mouth shut, but I gave him a tight smile. I could keep my shit together for her. At least for a few more hours, until she noticed that her attending doctor wasn't the person she expected.

Courtland reached out, hooking his fingers around hers. She was attached to oxygen and had a tube in her chest. She'd been too close to dying too, and I wasn't sure I could have survived without her. Without any of them.

"As soon as you are all better, we are bonding as a Pack. No arguments."

They all stared at me. Hell, even Radic woke for long enough to stare. I smiled gently at him, walking around to kiss him softly too. "Hey. I was worried about you. You nearly died on me."

He lifted his arm toward me, cupping my cheek softly. "Seems like a trend." He was groggy, having nearly exsanguinated by the time Merrick and Murphy had found him. He still didn't look quite the right color.

"Will you be my Beta, once you're recovered?"

He smiled, his eyes drifting closed again. "Yes. Always yes," he said drowsily, until he was asleep. I sat beside him, my fingers twined in his. They were okay. I was okay. That was all that mattered.

It felt a little less okay the following day when Bonnie finally realized that vampires were here taking care of her, and not Doc.

When Dominic told her what had happened, how he'd saved Courtland, the sound that came from her mouth was so tragic I never wanted to hear it again. She wailed endlessly, gasping for breath, and it was the worst thing I'd ever heard. The pain that came out on every sob shattered my heart, even as I held her close to my body and murmured how sorry I was.

On the other side of the coin though was Courtland, when Dominic told him what had happened to Loren. He shut down, his face once again a scary, impenetrable mask that blocked the world out as he hid behind his stone-walled fortress. He was silent for a long while, then asked Dominic for his phone. I wasn't sure who he called or why, but he seemed more at ease when the call was over.

"They'll find him and bring him back to us," was all he said, and that seemed to appease Dominic too.

The day of the coup had been brutal and violent, but this slow aftermath was a different sort of torture. After a few days, when it was time to go home, it was a relief, but also filled me with a fear so strong it made me weak in the knees. What if it wasn't over?

It was the same reason we'd hesitated on bringing the kids home, even though I missed my cubs furiously. Rosa called every day, sometimes three times a day, to make sure we knew they were okay. Eden Academy, the sanctuary, gave them a house, and Stacey—the doctor who'd helped discover what was wrong with Bonnie—had moved in with her Pack to help take care of the smaller kids. Apparently, her Omega wolf girlfriend had instantly become den mother, and she had an incredibly calming effect on the shifter kids, including the cubs. So they were fine, happy even, and while I was stressed at being separated, I could acknowledge that it was the safest place for them right now.

Unsurprisingly, Radic was moving about the best, now that he'd rested for a good couple of days. Supernatural healing had sped up Bonnie's injuries too, though she still got easily tired. Courtland was healing slowest, because the shit they'd done to his knees would have crippled a human. The vampire X had some serious skill under that sociopathic exterior, which meant that Courtland could now walk several steps, but not much further without great pain. Still, it was something, and it would get better as time went on.

I could see he hated it though, and that was understandable. He was our Alpha, our protector. Being laid up made him feel like a failure. Sometimes I caught him watching Radic and Bonnie, completely consumed by guilt, especially if they were having a tough day.

They were all resting at the moment, with me playing nursemaid and Dominic playing prison guard. Sounded rough, but honestly, if you didn't make them rest, they kept getting up and reinjuring themselves. Especially Courtland. Radic was allowed to move around, and I was pretty sure that pissed off Courtland and Bonnie even more. The only way we could get them to stay in bed was to put them in there together.

A knock at the door made me sigh. There'd been an endless rotation of people swearing black and blue they had no idea that Eldridge was arranging a coup. It was such a surprise. Blah, blah, fucking liars. Half the damn Legion Force had been at the challenge—the boyfriends and brothers and sons of these oh so contrite people, and I didn't believe for a moment that none of these bastards knew. I was glad that Radic handled most of those visits, even though I forced him to take it easy.

I walked to the door, and saw Rad creeping down the stairs. "You're meant to be resting, now go. I'll tell them to come back if they need to!" Radic grumbled about bossy Omegas as he climbed back up the stairs, but that just made me smile harder.

I opened the door and squeaked in surprise. On the other side were Raine and her consorts. And a vampire I didn't know.

"Oh shit, I mean, hello. Hi, Ma'am. It's nice to see you."

"Stop stressing, Omega," she said, waving a hand. "And my proper title is THE. Oh, here comes Raine, she's The Shit." The Convocation member on my doorstep actually laughed at her own lame joke, and I couldn't help but smile.

X groaned. "Honestly, Love. That was bad even for you."

"Do you want to come in?"

Raine shook her head. "No thank you. We were just leaving, but wanted to drop by and give you a present." She reached behind her and grabbed the unknown vampire. "This is Tanner. Tanner is a doctor. He is also an excellent fighter and can act as your Alpha's champion if anyone tries anything stupid, like challenging an injured Alpha in the coming days. Also, I hear he makes a mean pasta alfredo. He's basically a Swiss army knife, but also a vampire."

The vampire, Tanner, looked at Raine. "But I'm not Swiss. I'm Australian."

Raine pinched the bridge of her nose. "Tanner, I'm trying to convince the nice Omega that you are smart enough to be a doctor, and that's what you choose to say?" She turned to me, minutely widening her eyes as if to say *see what I put up with?*

"Well, I am a doctor. I went to university. Worked in a hospital."

"Got bitten by a shark then turned into a vampire, we got it, mate," X said, not even trying to hide his eye roll. "He's new, but he's strong and he's a good kid. Doesn't mind a bit of a fight and has some pretty good skills. He'll be a good backup plan in case shit goes pear-shaped and you need immediate backup. Just until Courtland is back on his feet."

Um, how did I say thanks for the gift of a living being without letting on how fucking weird it was? So I just went with an awkward "Thank you?"

Raine surprised the hell out of me by stepping close and pulling me into a hug. "It's gonna be all okay now, Pryce. I can feel it."

Then they were all gone, except Tanner, who was smiling at me happily.

"Uh, wanna come in for coffee?"

His face lit up. "Sure thing. Then I'd like to check out the chop-shop, if I could?"

I stared at him for a bit, until I realized he meant he wanted to look at the Doctor's offices. "Sounds like a good idea."

Now I had to go and tell Courtland that we had a permanent guest. Maybe I'd butter him up with a blow job first.

# EPILOGUE
## BONNIE

I skipped backward across the carpet, my smile wide enough to crack my face. Courtland walked slowly toward me, looking simultaneously annoyed and predatory. "Come here, Omega."

I shook my head, grinning. "No way, Alpha. If you want me, you have to catch me."

Courtland hated walking with the crutches, hated having a limp. Hated everything about not being fighting fit, but I found that he did well with sexual motivation. Right now, if he caught me, he got to kiss me.

He swiped out at my ankles with his crutches, making me laugh. "That's cheating!" But I bumped to a stop when I stepped back against the wall. I inhaled deeply, a familiar scent wrapping around me, and I leaned back into Radic. Oh, definitely not a wall then.

"No, *this* is cheating," he said, grinning as Court-land caught up and was now pressed against my front.

"Got you," Courtland growled before kissing the ever-loving hell out of me. His tongue stroked mine as he threw aside his crutches and grabbed my hips. Radic nuzzled his face in my neck, kissing me softly.

"We should bond," I whispered, and they both froze.

"Now?" Radic asked.

"Mmm, why not? The kids don't get home until tomorrow. The house will never be this free of tiny ears again." I looked up at Courtland. "I'm ready and I'm done with waiting."

Courtland looked down at me, his face covered in two days' worth of growth, making him look wilder and more devilish. Finally, he nodded. "Call Dominic. Tell him to get his tail home," he told Radic over my shoulder. "Let's go find our Omega, shall we?"

Yes!

I resisted the urge to run up the stairs, instead waiting for Courtland to make his way up one at a time. I kept my face impassive, but he didn't look fooled. "Go and get him, Bonnie. I'll meet you in the nest."

I stopped on the stair above him, leaning forward to kiss him hard. Then I spun and raced to the room we'd turned into the theatre room. Pryce was binge-watching a show about Lucifer, and he was completely immersed.

Hmm, I could change that. I walked over and sat in his lap, meaning his face was about boob height. Never one to miss an opportunity, he buried his face in my cleavage, making a happy humming noise.

"Oh, hello."

I laughed, twining my fingers in his hair. "Are you saying hello to me or my boobs?"

He grinned up at me, the expression heart-stoppingly beautiful. "Both?"

I leaned down and kissed him, because who could resist? "Want to be my mate?"

He kissed along my jaw. "You know I do. We're just waiting for the right time."

"Now is the right time."

He pulled back, his blue eyes shiny with hope and excitement. "Like now now?"

"Yep."

"Yes!" he hissed, picking me up and carrying me. He seemed to just know we should head to the nest. "I've been waiting for this, but I didn't want to rush your injuries."

We arrived in the nest just behind Courtland, and Radic was racing up the stairs behind us, already getting naked before he made it through the door. I laughed from Pryce's arms. "Hold on, we have to wait for Dominic."

Radic laughed and shook his head. "He hung up before I even finished the sentence. I think he'll be here before I finish—"

On cue, the front door slammed and there was the heavy thud of footfalls up the stairs. A wolf stuck its head through the door, then it changed into a very naked Dominic.

"What did I miss?"

Courtland huffed. "We are all still fully dressed, Dominic. I'm not talented enough to make love to anyone through sweats."

We all kinda stood around, looking awkward for a moment. "So, how do we do this?" Pryce asked, and then everyone looked at me, like I was some kind of expert on Manix matings.

"It's not like they gave us how-to manuals. It's all… instinct, I guess."

Dominic grinned widely. "So we fuck until we feel like taking a nibble?" he said incredulously. "Fuck yeah. Stand aside, guys, I'm going to practice on our pretty little Omega female here." He stole me from Pryce's arms and dropped me into a pile of pillows, nuzzling my neck and making nom-nom noises.

But when it came time, when we were sweaty and breathy, we didn't have to think. We just had to feel. The first bite, the first kiss, the first orgasm of mated life were things that I would never, ever forget.

I had a Pack, and I loved them more than anything.

. . .

"I don't know why you're complaining, Court. You look gangster as fuck with a pimp cane."

I smothered my smile at Rosa's words, and at Courtland's huffing response. Goddess, it was good to have them home. I'd missed the kids like a physical ache, and no amount of healing, or healing sex, could make up for that.

The bond felt amazing, to feel the love that shone from Courtland for his sister, despite the fact she was being a brat. Or to know that Dominic was watching one of us and feeling horny. Actually, that was the standard response for Dominic. I cuddled Duncan to my side, and kissed the top of Georgia's head.

Everything was back to being okay. As long as I didn't think about Doc. Didn't think about putting him in the ground, or how the whole town had turned out for it. Or about how Wilkie got off scot-free by insisting that he'd had no idea what his Beta had been up to in his spare time.

That was bullshit. We all knew it. But the Legion Generals had voted, and Wilkie got a reprieve, but he was being watched. And by watched, I mean Dominic stalked him day and night, watching him from the shadows, making him uncomfortable as fuck. The guy wouldn't brush his teeth without Courtland and Dominic knowing about it.

Actually, Courtland had locked down everyone he even suspected of being involved in the coup. Half the Legion Force was stood down, the remainder given promotions. Courtland had decided that it was better to have a small, elite, loyal force than a big army out for power. While he couldn't stand down the Legion Generals he suspected of being involved, they were all under suspicion except Joshua. I thought that perhaps there may be a complete overhaul of positions soon, and some new blood leading the Manix into the future. But not yet. Not while Courtland was still recovering.

Most of the town had expressed shock and anger, but then, most of them were sheeple. Who knew how many of them would have gone to see that asshole and given him the same platitudes?

I wasn't ready to write off the whole town yet. Today, everyone had turned out to welcome the kids home, and to celebrate our bonding. We were now the De Léon Pack, and it felt like all the pain and heartache was worth it somehow.

Naja came over and hugged me close to her side. "I'm glad you stayed, though I wouldn't have blamed you for leaving."

It had been tough, especially for Pryce, who'd had all his hard-won confidence ripped away in an instant. Watching him being cautious walking out our front door had been more painful than my recovery.

But I'd grown up here, so had Radic. Courtland

was bringing the change the town needed. Our families were here. We weren't running.

Still, it had been hard.

Courtland lifted his chin at me, and I wandered over. He wrapped an arm around my shoulders, and the rest of the Pack closed ranks around me.

Courtland cleared his throat, but the voice that came out was deeper, rougher than usual, and laden with Alpha power.

"Friends, family. It's my pleasure to present"—he looked down at me, and then over at the guys—"the De Léon Pack."

# NOTES FROM THE AUTHOR

Well, that was a bit of a crazy ride, right? Don't worry, we'll revisit the Manix again soon. If you missed the MPREG and all the knotting, don't worry, it will be back in the third book.

Preorder FERAL (Shadow Bred Book 3) HERE

Want to see what's happening next? Check out my upcoming contemporary RH:

INSIDE THE MAELSTROM (Preorder here)

# INSIDE THE
## *Maelstrom*

USA TODAY BESTSELLING AUTHOR

## GRACE MCGINTY

# INSIDE THE MAELSTROM
PROLOGUE



There was an elephant on my chest and it was doing the samba.

I turned up the music, ignoring the harsh way my breaths were falling from my lips. I ignored the clank of empty bottles from the passenger footwell. Ignored the check engine light on my dash that had been on for twelve months. Ignored the flashing of my phone, my mother's face glaring at me from the screen.

Instead, I drove down the quiet back street of my middle class neighborhood. I chewed my lip incessantly, but I enjoyed the way it puffed up. I enjoyed the way it stung and the slight metallic taste of blood. I told my parents that I was going to my friend Alison's house, but we hadn't been friends in two years. They didn't know that, how could they. I was an adult. I went to college. The need to police my friends ended when I became an adult. Alison had gotten a boyfriend in freshman year. She had a life, or maybe I'd stopped talking to her. I can't remember. Everything blurred together.

I watched the people stroll down the sidewalk, their dogs on long leads, frowning as they jogged, or glared at their phone. Were they happy? Is that what it looked like? Did they wake up in the morning and want to shower, want to go to school or work, want to talk to other people and eat breakfast, and make plans?

I dragged my eyes back to the road. The Petersons lived right at the end of this block. I knew it was their house because I dated their son in Senior year. Lost my virginity to him in a truly uninspiring way. He got accepted into Harvard. He was a good guy. Beige. Safe. The Peterson's as a whole were unremarkable. The only exceptional thing about them was the magnolia tree in their front yard. It was huge, bigger than it had any right to be in this climate. It must have been thirty feet high. It was in full bloom, and it was something bright and magnificent in a world where it didn't have any fucking right to be so exceptional.

It was in the front of a freaking box house, architec- turally designed to be devoid of personality. I could relate to the house, but that fucking tree taunted me. It had no right. None.

Suddenly, my chest felt looser, but my blood had turned hot. Scalding. It chased away the bone deep chill. No, a chill would insinuate I felt something underneath this cloak of numbness.

I felt nothing. Nothing except this rage now.

I pressed my foot further to the floor, my shitty middle of the range card revving loudly but it was a high, tinny sound. I unclipped my belt, letting it whip back up to where it belonged, safe and secure.

I pointed my car at that magnolia tree, and I grinned. It felt wrong on my face, foreign, as if my face had somehow morphed, my cheeks pressing up toward my eyes. I reached down to turn the music up as loud as it would go, and slammed my foot until the pedal hit the floorboards.

I mounted the curb, my car flying high as it hit the outer branches of the magnolia tree before slamming into the trunk.

My head slammed into the steering wheel, bouncing off to hit the side window, as the front of my car crumpled in slow motion.

The last thing I saw before everything went black was a downpour of perfectly waxy magnolia blooms.

Good. Now we were both ugly and dead.

The neck brace ruined the lines of my responsible white blouse. My head wound ached. The Judge's eyes saw too much. My mother sobbed softly into her linen handkerchief behind me.

"Aviva. It's the opinion of the doctors who admitted you that you require treatment in an inpatient setting. That you pose a significant danger, not only to yourself, but to the wider community." He looked at the paperwork in front of him. "Looking at the police reports, I have to agree. Your blood alcohol level was twice what it should be. You had amphetamines and prescription drugs in your system. If anyone else was involved, if you'd hit a pedestrian, you'd be going to jail right now. Do you understand?"

I nod. I never wanted to hurt anyone else.

The Judge gives me a look that is part jaded, part desperately sad. I knew the look. "The Peterson's are generously not seeking any remuneration or pressing any charges for the property damage you caused. But I don't believe you'll be so lucky next time. And Aviva, there will be a next time. Until you get the help you need, there will always be a next time. I am committing you to a mental health facility for ninety days. At your parents request, I am happy for you to undertake this involuntary treatment at a private facility." The judge took a deep breath, her eyes filled to the brim with a compassion I couldn't comprehend her still feeling after sitting in this courtroom for days on end. "I know this feels all-encompassing. That you're drowning every time you take a breath. But believe me, you just have to wake up every morning, put one foot in front of the other, until one day you look back at this moment right now and realize it was the life-buoy you needed. I'm throwing you a life preserver, Aviva, and I need you to grab it with both hands."

The rest was a blur as the case wrapped up, and my parents stood beside me, my father's hand on my shoulder and my mother gripping my fingers so tightly like she could feel me slipping away. It wasn't their fault, but I knew they wouldn't believe me if I told them that. They'd still blame themselves. That's just what parents do.

But something was broken inside me.

People buzzed around me like flies in the wide halls of the Court building, and a nice looking police officer with a soft face was murmuring reassurances to my parents that I would be fine. That was audacious of him, if not an outright lie. But I was glad he could give them something that I couldn't right now. Assurances that I was going to be okay.

I was put in the back of a police car, and I let my eyes drift to my parents as they cried on the sidewalk. I watched them get smaller and smaller, and saw the moment my mom collapsed into my father's arms.

Guilt washed over me. I was a failure, really. I couldn't even die right. It was all cry for help bullshit, at least that's what they told me. They were wrong, but I'd fucked it up too. The policeman thankfully didn't try to talk to me, didn't give me any reassuring words. He just drove quietly out of the city and I stared blankly out the window. The houses became more sparse, the trees thicker, until we rolled through a set of heavy wrought iron gates.

The sign on the gate said the 'Heath Buckley Center'. It had manicured gardens, and artificially planted woods at the edges that carefully obscured the fences. The illusion of freedom. The policeman drove down the long, gravelled driveaway, and I was kind of glad that this was an unmarked police car. And the cop was in plain clothes. Felt less like the first time I was delivered to a mental health ward.

The cop climbs out and opens the rear door for me. He gives me another one of those smiles that doesn't quite reach his eyes, and tilts his head for me to get out. I'm probably the most docile person he's had in the back of the police car because I do what I'm told, pulling my backpack out after me. Everything is supplied, apparently, but my parents packed me a few things they thought I'd need.

I didn't need anything, especially not the stuffed toy cat I've had on my bed since I was five, and three battered paperbacks. But it made them feel better, and I was enough of an emotional blackhole that I could let them have this comfort. The cop held opened the front door for me, and I stepped into the foyer. A plain woman bustled over, smiling politely at me and beaming at the cop.

I looked over my shoulder at him, and I guess he was kind of handsome in a plain, moon face kind of way. So was she. They'd have plain, round-face, average looking kids. The cop grinned back.

"Hey, Peaches. Got another Invol for you. This is Aviva. She's a good kid."

I tilted my head at the smiling woman. She had orange blond hair that kind of resembled the fruit. "Peaches? Is that a nickname?"

The woman shook her head, gently taking my bag from me. "Nope, just my parents being optimistic that I'd keep my blindingly red hair, I guess." She points to a little door. "Come on, we'll get the initial paperwork done, and then I'll take you to your room. Dave, there's cupcakes in the break room if you want to have a coffee before you leave?"

There was a desperate hopefulness in her voice and I let it wash over me. But I felt nothing for their budding romance. Not giddy excitement or embarrassment for Peaches or jealousy. Nothing.

I signed my name on a bunch of paper, I was officially an adult and just because I was here involuntarily, it didn't make me medically incompetant, go figure. After signing and initialling six hundred pieces of paper, Peaches went through my backpack, searching for contraband or anything I could finish myself off with I guess.

Giving it a tick of approval, she led me from the office with a calm efficiency. Peaches was a little bit like a balm. Her nonchalance was refreshing. She didn't look at me like I was a waste of potential, or like I was broken, or like I was some tragic statistic. She just shooed me along like she'd seen a million girls just like me. There was something reassuring in that.

She used her ID Card to go through a locked set of doors. It opened into a short hallway, and then another set of doors opened into a bright, sunny room filled with recliners and bookcases, a huge TV, and dozens of round tables.

"This is the common room. You're welcome to come here and relax at any time."

I looked around at the other inhabitants of the room. They ranged in ages, from a gray haired old man to a few middle aged women, to a guy who had to be my age, or maybe a year or two older. His eyes watched me closely, the look in his eyes predatory.

A shiver ran down my spine. I dragged my eyes away, but watched him out of the corner of my eye. He was cruelly beautiful, his lips full and twisted in a cruel expression. It was like he was appraising my weaknesses in that fifteen second stroll across the Common Room, and he'd pinpointed every single one.

When I looked back over my shoulder, his cruel

pout had formed into a grin, and if it was possible, that scared me more. When the double doors slid shut behind us, I almost sagged with relief.

My heart thudded, and I realized it was out of fear. I frowned, unsure if I should be happy I felt something, or if I should run away screaming.

GET IT HERE

# ABOUT THE AUTHOR

Grace McGinty is eclectic. She has worked as a chocolatier, a librarian, a forensic accountant and finally a writer. Like her professional career, the genres she writes are also eclectic. She writes romance, reverse harem romance, fantasy, contemporary young adult and new adult books.

She lives in rural Australia with her crazy family, an entire menagerie of pets, and will one day be crushed by her giant piles of books that litter every room.

**Head over to www.gracemcginty.com and join my mailing list for sneak previews into what I am working on and to stay up-to-date with new releases and giveaways!**